Re:ZeRo
-Starting Life in Another World-

"I hate to weigh you down, but thanks. I want to be useful as soon as possible."

"First, we'll begin with basic I-script, since Ro-script and Ha-script are perfect forms of I-script."

Ram&Rem

Characters

Re:ZERO -Starting Life in Another World-

The only ability Subaru Natsuki gets when he's summoned to another world is
time travel via his own death. But to save her, he'll die as many times as it takes.

Ram

Older twin maid at
Roswaal Manor.
Flat.

Ram

Younger twin maid at
Roswaal Manor. Master
of all domestic chores.

Roswaal L. Mathers

A nobleman known for his eccentric taste in clothes and clown-like makeup.

Roswaal

Beatrice

Librarian for the archive of forbidden books. Calls Puck "Puckie." Violent.

Beatrice

Re:ZERO -Starting Life in Another World-

The only ability Subaru Natsuki gets when he's summoned to another world is
time travel via his own death. But to save her, he'll die as many times as it takes.

CONTENTS

Re:ZeRo

-Starting Life in Another World-

VOLUME 2

TAPPEI NAGATSUKI
ILLUSTRATION: SHINICHIROU OTSUKA

YEN ON

NEW YORK

RE:ZERO Vol. 2
TAPPEI NAGATSUKI

Translation by ZephyrRz
Cover art by Shinichirou Otsuka

This book is a work of fiction. Names, characters, places, and incidents are the product of
the author's imagination or are used fictitiously. Any resemblance to actual events, locales,
or persons, living or dead, is coincidental.

RE:ZERO KARA HAJIMERU ISEKAI SEIKATSU
© TAPPEI NAGATSUKI / Shinichirou Otsuka 2014
First published in Japan in 2014 by KADOKAWA CORPORATION, Tokyo.
English translation rights reserved by YEN PRESS, LLC under the license from
KADOKAWA CORPORATION, Tokyo, through Tuttle-Mori Agency, Inc., Tokyo.

English translation © 2016 by Yen Press, LLC

Yen Press, LLC supports the right to free expression and the value of copyright. The purpose of copyright is to encourage writers and artists to produce the creative works that
enrich our culture.

The scanning, uploading, and distribution of this book without permission is a theft of
the author's intellectual property. If you would like permission to use material from the
book (other than for review purposes), please contact the publisher. Thank you for your
support of the author's rights.

Yen On
1290 Avenue of the Americas
New York, NY 10104

Visit us at yenpress.com
facebook.com/yenpress
twitter.com/yenpress
yenpress.tumblr.com
instagram.com/yenpress

First Yen On Edition: November 2016

Yen On is an imprint of Yen Press, LLC.
The Yen On name and logo are trademarks of Yen Press, LLC.

The publisher is not responsible for websites (or their content) that are not owned by
the publisher.

Library of Congress Cataloging-in-Publication Data
Names: Nagatsuki, Tappei, 1987– author. | Otsuka, Shinichirou, illustrator. | ZephyrRz,
translator.
Title: Re:ZERO starting life in another world / Tappei Nagatsuki ; illustration by Shinichirou
Otsuka ; translation by ZephyrRz.
Other titles: Re:ZERO kara hajimeru isekai seikatsu. English
Description: First Yen On edition. | New York, NY : Yen On, 2016– | Audience: Ages
13 & up.
Identifiers: LCCN 2016031562| ISBN 9780316315302 (v. 1 : pbk.) | ISBN 9780316398374
(v. 2 : pbk.)
Subjects: | CYAC: Science fiction.
Classification: LCC PZ7.1.N34 Re 2016 | DDC [Fic]—dc23
LC record available at https://lccn.loc.gov/2016031562

ISBNs: 978-0-316-39837-4 (paperback)
978-0-316-39838-1 (ebook)

10 9 8 7 6 5 4 3 2 1

LSC-C

Printed in the United States of America

PRoLoGUÆ
THE ROAD TO REDEMPTION BEGINS

—Even now, she deeply recalled the feelings she had at the time.

Familiar sights had flames all around them; people she knew had turned into silent corpses.

A world coming to an end. A closed world. A thankless world.

A world that was harsh, senseless, and brought nothing but pain.

Even so, she reached out with her hand, moved her fingers, quivered her lips, and pleaded.

After all, while it was a world beyond saving, it was still the only one she had.

It was a world that always had its back turned to her, locked away before her eyes, a world she could gaze into only from afar.

She wanted to abruptly tear down that wall; squint at the broad, dazzling world before her; and carve into her unopened eyes the color of sunbaked skin, the color and smell of burned meat, the color of the beautiful "horns" that danced in the sky—

Here was the world about to end, and what was she thinking about?

For even then, she could still remember the feelings she had at the time—

Thereafter, she devoted each and every day to expunging her guilt over those feelings above all else.

CHAPTER 1
SELF-CONSCIOUS FEELINGS

1

The first thing that flew into his eyes as they blinked open was an artificial sense of dazzling white. Beyond the light, a broad ceiling spread before him, with crystals attached to it providing flickering light that illuminated the room's interior.

Confirming in his head that he was waking up, Subaru's mind immediately grasped how good his wake-up felt.

"…The pillow feels different, huh. Smells better, too… Definitely higher class than usual."

Subaru savored the feel of the blanket and the other fine scents as he sat up in bed.

At a glance, he knew it was a room for the upper class. Subaru had slept in a king-size bed that could fit five people to spare; the room was about ninety square feet, oddly spacious with only a bed in it.

"The quality of the painting on the wall is so high it makes the room feel lonelier, huh. A guest room, then?"

Subaru, now completely awake, gently swung his legs over the side of the bed and checked his physical condition. He made sure he could rotate his legs and shoulders, finally pulling up his clothes and gingerly touching his belly.

"Abdominal wound…totally gone. No bruises, of course no scar, either… This world's medical tech is pretty awesome to not leave sewing marks. Assuming my big scene wasn't all just in my imagination, anyway."

He recalled the string of events leading up to his abdomen being deeply slashed.

Subaru, a completely ordinary Japanese schoolboy, was abruptly summoned to another world in a painfully cliché manner, coming face-to-face with death, literally, on multiple occasions.

That he was still alive was thanks to a string of coincidences that one could only call miraculous.

"But how much time's passed since then… No way to tell the time, huh?"

He glanced all around the room, unable to find any sign of calendars, clocks, or anything similar. The gold-glowing crystal above the door stood out; the darkness outside the window told him it was night, which was news to him.

Subaru slumped his shoulders and took a deep breath. Then, he voiced the inescapable conclusion on his lips and finally resigned himself to face reality.

"Any way you slice it…this time I managed to avoid Return by Death, huh?"

2

"First time, it was a pathetic death; second time, it was a bold death; third time, I died like a dog; fourth time, I got involved in mortal combat and died from a stray blow—is what I would be saying if I hadn't overcome that development. Man, if I died then, I'd be on a one-way ticket to mob-ville."

Flopping back into the bed, Subaru counted the causes of his deaths on his fingers.

Looking back on it, armed robbery included, he'd been slashed to death every time. He didn't want to see a blade again anytime soon.

At any rate, he'd somehow managed to avoid Return by Death and had finally been able to move time forward. The fact that he was all right after sustaining a plainly lethal wound meant...

"Considering the situation, it was that girl's...Emilia's healing magic, huh?"

An image arose in the back of his mind of a beautiful lilac-eyed girl with silver hair—Emilia.

He thought it was safe to assume she'd healed his abdominal wound. Having had a wound healed by Emilia once before, it was a natural assumption for Subaru to make. Subaru reasoned that, as a result, the guest room he was resting in was part of a mansion owned by Emilia. *Then again...*

"It's entirely possible this mansion's connected to Reinhard's family... But, well."

Glancing toward the door, Subaru let out a dissatisfied sigh at the lack of information on his current situation.

"Normally, there'd be a pretty girl at your bedside when you open your eyes, saying, 'Are you awake?' And there weren't any pretty girls when I was summoned, either. For a summons, this one sure has some glaring inadequacies..."

This summons was definitely third-rate. He couldn't slice through armies, and he'd barely had any meaningful encounters.

"Besides, nothing's happening so far... So it's up to me to do recon and make myself comfortable."

Subaru practically leapt to his feet and put his hand on the door. The refreshingly cool air blew in through the open doorway and the floor transferred the cold directly to his bare feet.

When he left the room, the walls and floor of a corridor, all in warm colors, unfolded before him. The passageway continued on and on to both the left and right.

Frighteningly, he couldn't see either end of the corridor.

"It's so much like a palace that all I can say is whoa. It's insanely huge... Can't even tell if anyone's here."

Delicately walking down the corridor on bare feet, Subaru scowled at the silence. It was as if he couldn't hear any signs of life that should normally be there.

"It's too quiet, even for the night… Makes me not wanna raise my voice…"

Personality-wise, Subaru was geared toward asking, *Is anybody here?!* in a loud voice, but the present circumstances made that too dangerous.

After all, Subaru had not yet determined whether this was a safe place for him or not.

Subaru had accepted as a matter of course that the host was friendly, but in the worst case, it was possible the assassin with a love of slitting bellies might have returned and abducted him.

All the same, he wouldn't be able to lift a finger if he assumed everything was doomed.

"Kenichi once said, *life must be lived.* That's what I think, too."

Incidentally, Kenichi was Subaru's father. It was very fitting that a person like him was his father.

Subaru's steps forward did not falter. But after walking awhile, Subaru twisted his neck a bit.

"I've walked this much, but I haven't hit a bend. Is that even possible?"

Unsurprisingly, he could not contain his misgivings. Subaru turned around, thinking about going back the other way.

Then he raised an eyebrow and remarked, "Huh…? That painting… I think it was right in front of me when I came out of the room…"

Subaru crossed his arms as he stood in front of the oil painting decorating the corridor.

The painting was of a forest scene at night. He felt like it was the same as the one he'd seen when he stepped out of the room.

Unless Subaru had moved at the literal pace of a snail, he jumped at the only possibility he could think of.

"Maybe the floor has some trick that makes it move around on its own or…could it be that the corridor loops around…?"

He'd probably turned in the opposite map direction after going a certain way. It was a field trap like you'd see in an RPG.

"If the corridor's looping, maybe it's got something to do with Return by Death."

Subaru, hoping someone out there agreed with him, grasped the doorknob of the closest room and opened it. When he did, a no-frills room that had nothing within greeted him. Of course, no one was in it, either.

"A looping corridor with any number of rooms... So if I don't find the right one, I can't get out?"

Though he hadn't yet truly accepted he'd been summoned to another world, here he was facing a new fantasy element right after waking.

"So if this goes according to cliché, it could take me *hours* to find the right one. I'll go hungry; my mind'll give out, then my body will, too. If that's the case..." The situation made Subaru want to hold his head.

Taking a deep breath, Subaru wiped the sweat off his brow and took the first decisive step forward.

He twisted the doorknob of the door facing the oil painting—in other words, the door that looked like the one Subaru had exited.

"I'll sleep in my room till someone comes. Maybe that first room was the goal anyway."

Speaking his characteristically flippant thoughts, Subaru entered the room—

"...How do you look like such a *deeply* irritating person, I wonder?"

Within the book-filled archive that Subaru had no recollection of seeing earlier, a girl with curly hair glared right at him.

3

—It was a room that truly screamed *book archive* at you.

The breadth of the room was about twice that of the first one, chock-full of bookshelves that rose to the ceiling. Each shelf was lined with books; it hurt to even try to guesstimate.

"Man, here in a place full of books and I can't read a single one... What a bummer."

His breath caught when he looked all around the bookshelves, unable to find a single one with the title on its spine in Japanese.

It wasn't some sort of alphabet, either; rather, these were characters like those he saw in the royal capital—the characters in common use in that world.

Subaru let out a sigh as he looked over the characters he couldn't read no matter how hard he tried.

"Looking all over someone else's bookshelves, and sighing on top of that.... Are you *trying* to offend, I wonder? Perhaps I should respond in kind?"

"Your pretty face'll go all to waste if you're that prickly. C'mon, smile, smile!"

"I am simply pretty by nature. I suppose my contemptuous sneer should be enough for the likes of you."

Putting the tips of her fingers to her cheeks, the girl formed a cruel smile.

Betty was a sweet, lovely girl—a sight he'd seen several times in this world already.

She looked younger than Felt in the slums, no more than eleven or twelve years old. Her frilly hairstyle matched her ornate dress, both framing her lovely face.

Her pale, cream-colored hair was worn long, distinctive for its swirling rolls. If she'd only smile properly, there was no one's heart she'd fail to melt.

She held a large book in her hands as she sat on a wooden footstool, from which she looked up at Subaru.

"You know big words like *contemptuous sneer*, huh…and you're in a bad mood because I got it right in one go? My bad! I've been doing stuff like this since *way* back."

Subaru Natsuki had a knack for picking the right answer to difficult questions with many options, without hints, on the first try. In the past, Subaru had unwittingly ruined many a scheme like that. The corridor from before made one more on the list.

"All my hard work constructing the domain, all for naught, just like that… It is quite horrid."

"I suppose GMs would want me to trigger all their events instead of skipping to the end, so I get it. My bad, my bad."

Subaru made a light wave of his hand in apology while the girl glared at him with half-lidded eyes. Apparently, it was this girl's scheme that Subaru's thoughtless act had foiled.

"Well, let's make that water under the bridge. Could you tell me where this is?"

"Hmph. It is my archive, my sleeping quarters...my private chambers, perhaps?"

"Shouldn't that make me feel kind of sad for you? I mean, you don't have your own bedroom to sleep in? That's horrible. Or about you using a library as your private chambers...maybe I should just laugh?"

"Are those remarks intended with a touch of teasing, I wonder?!"

The annoyed girl replying with blunt sarcasm, who called herself Betty, puffed out her cheeks and advanced upon Subaru.

"I am finally reaching the limit of my patience. You should be put in your place a little, I suppose."

"Hey, whatever you're planning, let's not? I'm just an ordinary guy, no combat ability at all here?"

His eyes became smaller and damper as his body made tiny quivers in a showy pose. But the speed of the girl's soft footsteps increased.

"—Stay right there."

Suddenly, Subaru was assailed by a feeling like a chill up his spine.

The girl, already before his eyes, stretched out her hand all the way to Subaru. Subaru froze as the girl, her height not reaching near his upper chest, stared at him with pale blue eyes.

His skin broke out in goose bumps as a quiet, high-pitched ringing echoed inside his skull.

"Is there something you wish to say...?"

As the girl posed her question, he unfroze for a moment. Subaru searched for the best thing to say during the instant he had been permitted. Subaru's gaze wandered as his lips quivered.

"I-it's not gonna hurt, is it?"

"Should I applaud your devotion to your flippant tongue, I wonder?"

Speaking with a tone of genuine admiration, the girl reached her hand to Subaru's chest. Her palm pushed against his breast, her fingertips pressing softly against the surface. It felt ticklish. And—

"Bwah…!"

—the next moment, Subaru felt like his entire body was on fire.

Something was running wild inside him, making him feel like he was on fire from the tips of his fingers to the very ends of his hair. The eerie pain was as if a finger of flame were tracing his internal organs.

His vision darkened. When Subaru came to, he had fallen onto his knees, a large amount of tears flowing from him.

"It seems you did not faint. Perhaps you are as sturdy as I heard?"

"Wh-what did you do, drill loli…"

"I simply interfered with the mana inside your body. Does the circulation feel slightly off, I wonder?"

The girl calmly murmured as she knelt down and jabbed a finger into Subaru's body.

"Well, it would be good to confirm whether you had hostile intent or not. And, for your rudeness toward my hard work, your mana should be confiscated before letting you go, I suppose."

Subaru, having reached his limit, was unable to remain upright from the jab, his head falling to the floor. Despite this, he was able to slowly use his neck, looking up as the girl glared down at him with a sadistic smile.

"You're not…human, are you? And I don't mean your personality…."

"You are quite slow to grasp that for someone who has met Puckie already."

The girl looked down with amusement as Subaru crawled. She looked younger than her choice of words hinted at, feeling like the sort of little girl who'd rip the wings off an insect in a cruel game.

"Correction… Your personality's…inhuman, too…"

"Surely a sublime being far beyond your ability to measure, *human*."

It was an overly glacial statement coming from the lips of a little girl. Subaru felt the inside of his chest smolder. But he had no strength left to describe the heat with words. Subaru's consciousness sank into darkness against his will.

—*Geez, I just woke up and I'm getting knocked out again?!*

"If you died here, your husk would be troublesome to remove. I shall speak to the others."

—*Don't say husk, it makes me sound like an insect, you little brat—*

Subaru returned to sleep once more, unable to move even his frivolous tongue.

4

"My, it seems he has awakened, Sister."

"Yes, Rem. He is awake."

When he next awoke, two girls spoke, their voices sharing the same timbre.

He was in the same soft, comfortable bed as before. The slight opening of the curtains let in the dazzling rays of the sun, burning sleepy Subaru's eyelids. He instinctively assumed it was morning.

"Ugh, I'm not so much nocturnal as I am a denizen of the night. Waking up in the morning makes my chest burn…"

Wide awake, Subaru sat up as he remembered that his day and night cycles were inverted while school was out. He looked around, rotated his shoulders, and shifted his hips toward the window as he looked in that direction.

"Dear Guest, it is now Seven Solartime."

"Dear Guest, it is about Seven Solartime."

Their friendly voices conveyed the time of day. Seven Solartime—he didn't know what that meant, but he guessed it meant something similar to seven AM.

"That being the case, if you don't count the wake-up earlier, I've slept for about a whole day, huh? Well, my record is two and a half days, so this is no big deal, really."

"Sister, did you hear? Quite a lazy thing to say."

"Yes, Rem, I heard. Quite a good-for-nothing thing to say."

"So who're these ladies who've been chewing me out in stereo here?!"

Subaru sat up quickly, taken by surprise at the girls, sandwiching the bed from both sides. The girls rushed a short distance to a corner of the room, joining hands and drawing their faces close as they looked at him.

Standing side by side, their faces were two peas in a pod; the girls were obviously twins.

Both stood about a hundred and fifty centimeters tall. Their big eyes, pink lips, and the soft, youthful loveliness of their faces made them outright adorable. Both wore their hair in short bobs, with their hair parted to fall across one eye—the right eye on one and the left eye on the other.

The way their hair was parted and the fact that one had pink hair and the other blue were the only visual clues to tell them apart.

The twins watched Subaru carefully. His mind quivered, as though it were all scratched up, as he suddenly realized.

"No way… There are maid outfits in this world, too?!"

They wore black apron dresses with white accents and white lace headpieces on their heads. These outfits were specially modified to expose their narrow shoulders, which, combined with the short skirts, flaunted their body lines in scandalous ways. Subaru didn't know a whole lot about maid outfits, but he was certain the level of skin exposure represented the designer's personal taste…though the twins who wore them were beautiful regardless.

"I thought maids were supposed to dress modestly…but I think I'm a fan!"

"This is terrible, Sister. Right now, in Dear Guest's head, you are the subject of obscene, degrading thoughts."

"This is dreadful, Rem. Right now, Dear Guest's head has become filled with completely disgusting thoughts about you."

"Don't take my mental capacity for granted, ladies. You're *both* going to star in my fantasies!"

Subaru crossed his forearms and made suggestive motions with his fingers. The gesture made the two maids' faces tremble; the girls wrapped around each other, releasing their hands and pointing at each other.

"Please forgive me, Dear Guest. Let me go and defile Sister instead."

"Please stop this, Dear Guest. Let me go and humiliate Rem instead."

"Where's the sisterly love here?! I mean, selling each other out and making me some archvillain?!"

The two maids pushed the role of scapegoat onto the other, looking at Subaru as if wondering which one he'd sink his evil fangs into first. That was when he suddenly noticed…

Knock, knock. The girl stood inside the open door, tapping it softly while looking at the three of them.

"…Couldn't you wake up with less drama?"

Today, she was letting her long silver hair hang naturally all the way to her hips. Her outfit was not the robe he'd seen at the capital but rather, an outfit that accentuated her light skin and slender physique with its design.

The skirt was unexpectedly short; Subaru, marveling at how it showed off her long legs, pumped a fist.

"I get it! Whoever chose this, I get what they were thinking!"

The silver-haired girl—Emilia—gawked at Subaru's praise.

"…I'm not quite sure what you're referring to, but I'm veeery disappointed that I know it's something meaningless."

In one move, Emilia's sudden visit had greatly improved Subaru's mental state.

In a place full of unknowns—his incident with the first little girl he had met was especially poignant—seeing Emilia, a friendly face he'd known since just after his summoning to another world, made it all the more special in his mind.

"To think I was worried a bit when I heard Beatrice was rough on you when you were low on blood… I *really* shouldn't have bothered."

"I'm in a super good mood from waking up to your face, though. And I'm a little afraid to ask this, but…"

With Emilia giving him a suspicious look, Subaru put both his hands together and timidly looked at her with upturned eyes.

"You, ah…remember all about me, right?"

"That gesture, for some reason I don't like it. Also, that's an odd question. I don't think I'd forget someone who stands out as much as you do, Subaru."

With Emilia smiling charmingly at him and calling his name, Subaru slumped his shoulders in relief. Then, realizing that for once a girl was calling him by name, he was rather flushed.

"Please listen, Lady Emilia. This person was terribly humiliating. For Sister, that is."

"Hear this, Lady Emilia. This man has trapped and violated girls. Rem, that is."

The twins left Subaru behind, who was now red to the tips of his ears, as they rushed to Emilia's side to make their baseless charges. Emilia made a strained smile at their slander and glanced sideways at Subaru.

"I…don't know Subaru enough to say I know he *wouldn't* do that, but I trust that he probably did not. Don't tease him *too* much, okay?"

"Yes, Lady Emilia. Ram shall reflect on this."

"Yes, Lady Emilia. Rem will reflect on this."

Despite their statements, the twins didn't appear to mean it even a tiny bit. Emilia showed no signs of objecting to their attitude; perhaps she was simply used to it.

"Anyway, Subaru, are you doing all right? Nothing feels wrong anywhere?"

"Mm, oh, yeah, before I slept I felt like my whole body was on fire and I was going to die, but I don't feel one bit of that now. I actually feel like I slept a bit too much."

"If you're no worse than that, good. Can you handle a little stroll?"

"Stroll?"

Emilia was making a small smile as Subaru tilted his head.

"Yes, a stroll. I try to go into the garden once a day, and this seems like a good time for it, no?"

"Once a day…doing what? Watering the flower bed?"

"Not exactly. One of the conditions of my pact with the various spirits is that I make contact and speak with them every morning."

When Emilia said *spirit*, Subaru thought back to the cat spirit he'd seen with Emilia.

A stroll and a chat with the spirits. It was a nice idea that provided fodder for his curiosity—and his ulterior motives. "Sounds like great rehab to me, Emilia-tan. How about I stroll around the garden and exercise while you're talking to the spirits?"

"Well, if you don't talk loudly or make a big fuss, sure... Eh? What did you say just now?"

"Okay, it's a deal. Let's go to the garden!"

"Hey, what did you say? What is *tan*? Where'd that come from?"

The pet name seemed to throw off Emilia. Subaru was hiding his blush at having her call his name so openly when he turned toward the faces of the two maids standing side by side. "Hey, maid sisters. Where are my old clothes? Feels like I got in a hospital gown while I was out. I figure the mansion here lent this to me, but..."

"Do you understand, Sister? Perhaps he means that drab gray rag?"

"I understand, Rem. He means that bloodstained mouse-colored piece of filth."

"Some guts there, calling it filthy and looking like a dirty rat. If it's in one piece, could you hand it over?"

Faced with Subaru's request, the twins turned to Emilia. Their looks said they wanted permission. When Emilia responded with a nod, the twins politely bowed and left the room.

"You don't need to hear this from me, but you mustn't strain yourself. You were terribly injured."

"You closed the wound perfectly, though. Oh yeah..."

As if remembering something, Subaru straightened his posture and slowly bowed his head to Emilia.

"Thank you for healing my wounds, Emilia-tan. You saved me. I really am scared of dying. I'd like to do it only once."

"Normally once is all you get...? But, mm-hm, never mind that..."

After the spontaneous verbal jab, Emilia's purple eyes wavered as she looked at Subaru.

"I should be the one thanking you. You risked your life for mine when you barely knew me. Healing your wounds was the least I could do."

Subaru's breath caught at her sincerely apologetic look.

He hated himself for being unable to give her the reply he wanted to.

—Emilia had said *never mind that* at her saving him. Yet it had been Emilia who'd saved him first.

But the only record of that was inside Subaru's memories.

Subaru smiled, holding in the gratitude he could never properly convey.

"—Well, since we saved each other, I think we're all square here."

"Square...?"

"It means that neither of us owes the other a thing, so let's get along, brotha!"

If he were talking to a resident of the Poor District, this would be the time for him to kindly clap them on the shoulder. But at that moment, it was all Subaru could do to cover up his embarrassment and blushing face as best he could. Emilia made a small smile at Subaru.

"Do I really need a younger brother this weird?"

"That's a pretty harsh comment?!"

He slumped his shoulders at the casual put-down.

Both laughed at the exchange as the door opened and the twin maids returned. Subaru straightened as he saw them carrying the top and bottom of his tracksuit, one part each.

"Guess it's time to restart the day."

His first day since surpassing Return by Death was truly beginning.

5

Subaru shook his head when the maids offered to dress him, changing clothes by his own power before heading to the manor's garden with Emilia.

Subaru let out a sigh of admiration as he looked over the broad garden.

"This is really big, too. The mansion's huge, but this is more a grassland than a garden."

He'd seen gardens of the manors of the well-off in manga and anime from time to time. They were the sorts of places where you held dinner parties. There, in the middle of the huge garden, Subaru began stretching exercises to begin his rehabilitation posthaste.

Emilia looked on curiously as she watched Subaru's movements.

"Those are odd moves. What are you doing?"

"Oh, don't you do warm-ups here? You do them before starting strenuous exercise."

"Hmm, I haven't really seen much of that. But I do understand it's dangerous to make sudden, hard movements."

"So people don't do stretching in this world? Oh well, it can't be helped—how about I teach you? Genuine warm-up exercises from my homeland, passed down through the generations!"

Emilia seemed to yield in the face of Subaru's confident proclamation. "R-right. Just a bit, then," she said, copying Subaru. Subaru stood beside Emilia and gave out instructions.

"Morning Warm-Up Part Twooo! Reach high with your hands and stretch that back~~!"

"Eh, what, no way?!"

"Just do what I do. I'll pound the essence of radio calisthenics into you yet!"

With Emilia lost, Subaru scolded her and followed the beat of a routine famous around the nation.

Emilia was still bewildered at first but proved a quick study. When both finished making their final deep breaths, Subaru spread both hands into the sky.

"And last, raise your hands. Victory!"

"V-victory!"

"Okay, there you go, Emilia-tan, you are now a Radio Calisthenics Novice!"

Having finished doing calisthenics with all her might, Emilia's face showed the new title had made a deep impression. But she made a face like she'd just remembered her original purpose.

"Right. Things *really* got off the beaten path, but if I forget this, they'll be upset."

Emilia, making a thin, pleasant smile as she spoke, brought out a green crystal from her pocket and showed it to Subaru.

"Ah, that's…"

"A crystal for spirits to inhabit. You know, like Puck."

"The kitty cat that slept through all the big stuff? Bet he doesn't know about my heroic scene, then?"

The crystal glowed as if to rebuke Subaru's taking him lightly. The indifferent voice came from the crystal at first.

"Oh, not at all, Subaru, Lia told me *all* about it after things got wrapped up."

Finally, light poured out of the crystal and condensed into an outline forming atop Emilia's palm.

"Heya. Morning, Subaru. Nice weather."

"It's been an up-and-down night and morning for me, though. First the looping corridor, then that menacing little girl. Now I'm past that and working up a sweat with Emilia-tan…"

Emilia's lips tapered into a pout.

"People will get the wrong impression if you say that."

Emilia then looked at Puck, sitting atop her palm.

"Good morning, Puck. Sorry for pushing you so hard yesterday."

"Good morning, Lia. I'm the one sorry for yesterday, though. I almost lost you. I can't thank Subaru enough, really."

Puck looked up at Subaru with his round black eyes as he stroked his pink nose with his paw.

"Well, I owe you something. I wonder if there's anything you want? Something I can do, I mean."

Subaru's reply to Puck's grandiose statement was immediate.

"All right, let me touch that fur of yours to my heart's content."

Puck's and Emilia's eyes went wide. Apparently, the speed of the reply had surprised them as much as the content.

"Sh-shouldn't you take a little longer to decide? Puck might look small and unreliable, but his power level really is quite something."

"Hey, to me, being able to feel fur like from the finest fabrics is a really huge thing. I wouldn't take any amount of money over it. No, seriously."

As Subaru spoke, he indulged his right and stuck his finger toward Puck: first belly, then chin, and the ears to finish him off.

"Oh, these ears are addictive! I'm totally into your fluffiness here!"

"I know from reading the surface of your thoughts, but to hear you actually say it, wow."

Subaru liberally toyed around as Puck made pleasant noises from his throat.

Emilia let out a sigh of resignation as she watched Subaru and Puck play.

"Well, I'm going to talk to the lesser spirits, then… It's fine if you two play, but don't interfere, okay?"

"So, she dumped us."

"Yep, she dumped us."

As both slumped their shoulders, Emilia made a point of ignoring them as she softly went to a corner of the garden. She gave the ground a light brush before sitting down. Emilia closed her eyes as pale lights began to surround her.

—He'd seen that sight before.

"Lesser spirits, huh?"

"That's right. Most are classified as lesser or greater spirits… though a lot are outside of those categories."

"Not that it doesn't help…but I don't know how to classify them."

Subaru knew that the lights frolicking around Emilia were lesser spirits because Emilia had said as much during the loop in the royal capital.

As Emilia sat, she spoke softly to the minor spirits, smiling from time to time; the minor spirits seemed to brighten or fade accordingly.

"You said 'a pact with minor spirits,' but, like, what is that?"

"A ceremonial pact with a spirit—forging a covenant."

Subaru frowned at the term he hadn't heard before.

"Err, you see, a Spirit Master can't use spirit spells unless she makes a pact with spirits first. The details of the pacts differ according to the spirits. Still with me?"

"So it's not like interest and collateral for a bank loan, then. Gotcha."

"My name's not Gotcha, but let's move on. So individual spirits want different things…but minor spirits like that just want pacts with simple conditions like contact with the caster."

"So it's like easy stuff for beginners. I take it that doesn't work for other spirits?"

"It helps that you're quick on the uptake. This won't get far if you keep going off on tangents, though?"

Oops, said Subaru with a blushy smile. For his part, Puck gave him a warm look as he toyed with his own whiskers.

"Right, it's a bit harder to satisfy a spirit with a mind of his own, like me. I'd like to give to the pact maker as good as I take…but my conditions with Lia are pretty strict."

"It's been on my mind since earlier, but Lia, that's a cute nickname."

"Your Emilia-tan's even cuter, though. I should call her that, too."

"—Don't. Seriously. I'm begging you."

With puffed-up cheeks, Emilia cut into their silly games.

As Emilia returned, the spirits around her winked out; apparently Spirit Talk Time had come to an end. Subaru stood up and brushed the grass off his rear.

"Quality time over? That felt easier than I expected."

"I was mindful of you two, so I asked them to keep it short. We have things we need to discuss today."

As Emilia spoke, she offered up her palm; Puck leapt from Subaru, landing upon it. Puck's round eyes turned toward Emilia with what seemed like a small, satisfied smile.

"It's all right. I got a good feel for him, and I can't find one shred of malice, hostility, or intent to do harm. Subaru's a good boy, though his personality is a bit weird."

"Now wait a…"

Aghast at Puck appraising him to Emilia on various levels, Subaru could only gape.

"Why did you… Even if it's true, isn't saying it in front of him hurtful?"

"Oh, ah, that's fine! I'm a complete stranger to you, so of course you'd check me out. You're right to doubt. But that part at the end really hurt, Emilia-tan!"

Emilia quickly covered her mouth with a hand and made a pained smile at Subaru.

Subaru hadn't touched Puck all over without a reason. He'd expected this to come up. Emilia and the others weren't so careless as to accept Subaru without knowing a single firm thing about him. No doubt that partially explained Ram's and Rem's demeanor.

"That said, I don't have any good way to explain."

There was obviously no preexisting record of Subaru in this world. Explaining that he'd been summoned was a tough sell, with good odds he'd be treated as a lunatic.

That being the case, letting Puck get a good read on him was the best option. Words from Puck, trusted by Emilia and able to read conscious thoughts, were a lot more convincing than anything Subaru could come up with.

"It's all right, Lia. Oh, and I know what you were up to, Subaru. Naughty boy, using my mind reading like that."

"I'm honored. Let's get along famously, my friend!"

How Subaru addressed them put a look of shock on Puck's face; he then broke into a wide smile.

"It's been a while since I got this kind of treatment. I like it."

"I'd rather hear those words from Emilia-tan. Oh well, as they say, to take down a general, first take down his horse… Well, you're kind of a cat so does that still make sense? …I wonder?"

A surprised look came over Emilia as she watched Subaru put a finger to his chin and sink into serious thought.

When Subaru curiously raised his eyebrows, Emilia inhaled a bit.

"—Really, Subaru, you are so strange."

"Huh?"

"Giving leading looks to a…half-elf like me who speaks to spirits like it's a normal thing…it surprised me, even as a joke."

In his heart, Subaru countered, *Would you be as surprised if you knew it wasn't a joke?* But he forgot all about that as he fell for Emilia's charming smile.

This smile was on par with the one she'd given him when they'd exchanged names at the royal capital. It seemed fleeting and fickle, which only made his heart flutter all the more.

Her beautiful, flowing silver hair was as surreal as dew in the moonlight; her skin was as pale as the first snow. Her violet eyes seemed to hold Subaru's mind firmly in their spell and wouldn't let go.

He knew she was sublime, beautiful, with a heart of gold wrapped around an unshakable core.

Subaru wanted nothing more than to put his hands on his cheeks and give thanks to Mother Nature, but he abstained.

"Huh, wonder what's with those two?"

And, as Emilia mentioned something she'd noticed, Subaru looked toward the manor.

The twin maids were walking down from the mansion. Both gave formal bows before Subaru and Emilia, speaking in perfect stereo, not off by the slightest bit.

"—Master Roswaal, lord of the manor, has returned. Please come this way."

Their perfect combo surprised Subaru, but the maids' change of demeanor surprised him more.

Their earlier frivolousness was nowhere to be found, replaced by a sense of dignity befitting servants of the upper crust.

"I see. Roswaal... We'd best go see him, then."

"Yes, and he said to bring our Dear Guest as well, should he be awake."

Puck wriggled into Emilia's silver hair. Emilia's face stiffened a bit as she patted down her hair. Watching her from the side, Subaru cracked his neck slightly at being addressed.

"So, who is this Roswaal guy, anyway?"

"Lord of this manor... Ah, that's right, I didn't explain."

Emilia put her palm to her mouth as she realized her own slip.

"Err, right. Roswaal is... You'll understand when you meet him."

"You gave up on that explanation too fast! What, he's too plain to describe?!"

Emilia, Puck, Ram, and Rem all replied in unison...

"—No, the opposite."

Subaru's jaw dropped open in a face of surprise multiplied by four. The blue-haired girl gently closed his mouth from below with her hand before giving a solemn bow.

The pink-haired maid standing beside her motioned to the mansion.

"One cannot describe the likes of Master Roswaal with words alone. You shall understand when you meet him, Dear Guest. It is all right; he is a kind lord."

The twins met each other's gazes and nodded, with the repeated affirmation serving only to deepen his doubts.

With Subaru bewildered, Emilia looked like she grudgingly agreed with the twins as she gently reached out to him. Giving Subaru's shoulder a couple of pats, Emilia murmured in a grave voice.

"—You'll probably get along just fine, Subaru. He'll wear you out, though."

CHAPTER 2
THE PROMISED MORN GROWS DISTANT

1

In the dining hall the twins led them to, where breakfast was to be held, the girl with curly hair said in place of a greeting, "Watching from above, I felt…dismay at seeing your considerably disappointing head, I wonder?"

Emilia had split off midway to return to her room to change clothes, so at that moment, only Subaru and the curly-haired girl were in the dining hall. Subaru made a sour face at her sarcasm.

"What's with talking like that on a fine morning like this, loli?"

"What is that term, I wonder? I have never heard it, yet it feels distinctly…unpleasant."

"It means you're not on my list. I never go for girls younger than me."

"…Perhaps I should pity you for having insulted me so?"

Deliberately ignoring the sarcastic girl's words, Subaru looked over the dining hall.

A table covered in a white cloth was at the center; the plates had already been set. If one was set for Subaru, it was surely the lowest seat at the table.

"I don't know anything about table manners. How about I let you give me pointers?"

"Is that arrogance, I wonder? If you do not understand, simply say so and lower your head."

"If I could do that much, I might as well just sit in the big chair and really irritate you."

The girl shook with anger, her face going red as Subaru waved with a palm and sat in the big chair. It'd probably be Emilia or the lord of the manor who'd sit there, with fifty-fifty odds for each.

Seeing Subaru genuinely unable to get comfortable in the chair, the curly-haired girl shook her exasperated face.

"Well, fine. More importantly, have you no words with which to thank me?"

"Thanks? I asked for help just now and you brushed me off, didn't you? And what kind of person *asks* to be thanked? I'd wanna see the look on your dad's face for that one!"

"What are *you* angry for, I wonder?! I should be the angry one! After all I did…!"

They kept egging each other on.

The girl, her voice flustered at Subaru's reply, never quite finished her sentence. Mindful of the unnatural pause, Subaru prompted her to continue, but…

The door to the dining hall opened and the twin maids came in pushing a cart.

"Pardon us, Dear Guest. I shall set the meal."

"Pardon us, Dear Guest. I shall set the tableware and the tea."

The blue-haired girl laid out an orthodox breakfast menu consisting of salad, bread, and the like, while the pink-haired girl briskly poured and placed cups of tea. The warm scents made Subaru's stomach grumble out of nowhere.

"Whoa, not bad at all. Now this is a breakfast fit for nobility… I was worried it was going to be some weird out-of-this-world thing."

Subaru, worried that any strange thing could potentially be served here, was considerably relieved.

When he looked all around, he couldn't place anything in particular that seemed to pose physical or mental danger.

His enthusiasm rising, Subaru leaned back against the chair, making it creak. The sound echoed throughout the dining room, bringing a hint of annoyance to the girl's soothing face.

For some reason, Subaru couldn't resist needling the curly-haired girl. Wanting to see her soothing face break down further, Subaru, full of mischief, decided to move his butt all around the chair.

However, before he could do so, a new individual entered the dining hall, his happy-sounding voice interrupting everything else.

"Ohhh my. You certainly seem raaather spry. That is good, veeery good."

He was a tall man, at least half a head above Subaru's height, wearing his dark blue hair long to nearly cover his entire back. But his body seemed not so much slender as delicate, with his skin color ghastly pale.

Combined with the look of his face, he somehow seemed like some sort of pretty boy. The effect was further accentuated by his left and right eyes being different colors, the first yellow, the other blue.

—Well, it *might* have if he wasn't decked out in that weird outfit and makeup that made him look like a clown.

"...Man, you hired a jester to entertain us before breakfast? I'll never get how rich folks think."

Beatrice watched and commented.

"I have some idea what you must be thinking, but I shall not get in the way."

"Don't be that way, Betty. We're friends, right? Let's do some more small talk."

"What kind of relationship do you and I have, I wonder? Also, do not speak my name so casually."

The girl snubbed him with a shrug and withdrew from the conversation.

Subaru scowled at her behavior as the clown walking into the dining hall opened his eyes wide, looking at both her and Subaru.

"Oh my, it is raaare to see Beatrice here. Is it not fortuitous thaaat you decided to share a meal with me after so looong?"

"If that man over there is the only optimist, wouldn't that already be too many, I wonder? I wait for Puckie and Puckie alone."

Brushing off his chummy statement, the girl—Beatrice—shifted to behind the clown. The silver-haired girl, having finished changing her attire, entered the dining hall a bit after the clown.

"Puckie!"

Practically leaping from her seat, Beatrice ran over, her long skirt swaying. Seeing a smile like a flower in bloom come over her was so adorable that it made him forget how he'd pegged the girl as "cheeky."

Her gaze was trained on Emilia, but it was not Emilia who replied.

"Heya, Betty. It's been four days. Have you been happy and ladylike?"

Beatrice nodded at the words of the buoyant little gray kitty popping out of Emilia's hair.

"I have been eagerly awaiting your return, Puckie. You would enjoy spending the day together, I wonder?"

"Yeah, that'd be great! Both of us can take it easy for one day."

"That is wonderful!"

Puck leapt off Emilia's shoulder to land upon Beatrice's outstretched palms. As she caught Puck, Beatrice lovingly embraced him and ran around in circles then and there.

Subaru was struck senseless by the happy, carefree scene as Emilia walked over with a teasing smile.

"Tee-hee, aren't they merry? Puck and Beatrice are very close, you see."

"Nobody uses *merry* anymore..."

When Subaru gave Emilia his stock reply for when she used outdated words, Emilia went, "Mm?" and pointed Subaru's way.

"Er, Subaru, that chair..."

"Oh, right! Uh, it's not what you think. I mean, a cold chair really throws you off, so I figured I'd warm it up a little. It wasn't that I just wanted to sit where you usually sit, like an indirect sit-down, really."

"Sorry, I'm not really sure what you mean, but that's Roswaal's seat."

With Subaru's big scheme foiled, he slid off the chair in front of the wide-eyed Emilia.

"Oh, there's *no* need for *concern*. I see, your warmth may not reach Lady Emilia, but I shall treasure it *greatly*."

The clown reached out and patted Subaru's shoulder, smiling at him in consolation. The touch to his shoulder and the gently smiling, made-up face drew a sour frown from Subaru.

"This clown's acting real chummy. It's not polite to touch the dancing girls, you know?"

"Since when did you become a da… Er, no, Subaru, this man is…"

"My, my, myyy, I do nooot mind, Lady Emilia. Considering how he went from being at death's door to being in such high spirits, shooould we not be quiiite grateful?"

The clown's tone of voice excelled at getting on one's nerves, yet his statement was extremely sensible. The others continued to watch the clown as he slowly sat down in the chair—the very chair at the head of the table that Subaru had been seated in just before.

"Hey, now. Not that I should say this, but sitting in someone else's chair is gonna tick people off."

Emilia made an exasperated face at Subaru's statement as she murmured, "No need to worry about th… You, ah, really should introduce yourself to Subaru."

It seemed Emilia's exasperation was also directed toward the clown.

"What do you mean?"

"In ooother words, she meeeans…this."

The clown seated in the chair replied to Subaru's query as he spread his arms out wide.

"'Tiiis I, lord of this manor, Roswaal L. Mathers. It is goooood that you feel so safe and comfortable under my roof, Subaru Natsuki."

And so, the deviant noble dressed as a clown introduced himself in a lively manner thoroughly devoid of shame.

2

Beginning with Roswaal in the seat of honor, they sat in prearranged seats and began breakfast.

"Mm…this is better than usual…"

Subaru was admiring the food before his eyes reminiscent of salad and soup. Roswaal nodded back, seeming to take personal pride in Subaru's appraisal of the cooking as he looked at Rem.

"Mm-hmm, iiindeed, indeed. She may not look it, but Rem's cooking is quite something."

When Subaru looked at Rem, too, she made a fox sign with a hand. Subaru didn't know what it meant, but it might've been this world's version of making a V with your fingers.

Subaru made a frog with both hands in reply.

"So the blue-ha... Is calling you Rem fine? So you cooked this?"

"Yes, Dear Guest. Rem handles the meals in this household. Sister is not especially good at it."

"Oh-ho, so it's like, you twins have different specialties. So, your sister's really good at cleaning?"

"Yes, Sister specializes in cleaning inside and doing the laundry."

"So since you're good at all the cooking, you're not so good at cleaning and laundry, Remrin?"

"No, I excel at all domestic chores, including cleaning and laundry, more than Sister."

"What's she here for, then?!"

An older twin sister worse at everything under the sun than her little sister? This was a new one.

The older sister seemed to pay no heed to Rem's statement. Subaru couldn't prove it, but he guessed the words were true. So why wasn't Ram bothered by it at all...?

"So maybe it's different fields, huh? Ramchi does combat stuff and the other does more domestic stuff?"

"Not a baaad guess. Though Ram and Rem make a poor first impression because of their idiosyncrasies, yes?"

"Hard for that to stand out now when their master's so unique, Rozchi."

By *Rozchi*, Subaru was addressing the man in charge by a pet name, but Roswaal let the statement pass with practiced ease. Subaru had an ingrained tendency to get a rise out of people, but not so here. That said, the items on the menu vanished from the plates one after another before they knew it.

"It'd be something of a dilemma if the food wasn't good, but it's delicious, so no prob. Right, Emilia-tan?"

Emilia wiped her lips with a napkin, grimacing at Subaru's carefree words. Subaru tilted his head, wondering what was up, as Emilia exhaled slightly.

"You know, Subaru, you shouldn't speak at the dinner table. It's rude to Ram and Rem, who prepared this all by themselves. Without proper manners, you'll make blunders during important occasions, so…"

"No one uses *blunder* anymore… Table manners, huh. Kind of late to learn them now, though, right?"

Subaru delivered his cliché while motioning toward the dining hall with his hand. In spite of the spacious hall, Subaru was sitting right beside Emilia.

By rights, the two would be seated quite far apart to make full use of the dining table.

"But I moved closer because I wanted to eat with Emilia-tan. Roswaal didn't say he minded, so what's the big deal? I mean, you can give me any veggies you don't like."

"All right, you can have my green bepper— Wait, that's not the point. I'm being an idiot."

Subaru laughed, finding it cute how Emilia tapered her lips in a pout at being outdone in their verbal jousting.

After that, Subaru belatedly brought up an issue Emilia's words had raised.

"Incidentally, Rozchi, I thought I heard Emilia-tan say this household has only two maids working here?"

"Ahh, yeees, such is currently the caaase. Ram and Rem are the only ones left."

"Two people handling a place this huge? You'd think people would die from overwork no matter how good they are. That said… it doesn't feel like you're going to be hiring any new maids here?"

Roswaal was silent to Subaru's question, crossing his arms at the table. Roswaal's face displayed a smile, but the eyes with which he regarded Subaru had subtly changed.

"You truly *are* a mystery, having come to the house of Mathers at the far reaches of the Kingdom of Lugunica, yet you do not *know* the circumstances? Amazing that you made it past royal customs."

"Well, I am kind of an undocumented immigrant in a sense…"

Subaru's casual reply startled Emilia; she gave him a glare like she was scolding a young child.

"I can't believe it. If you say things like that so easily, bad people will make mincemeat out of you."

"Nobody uses *mincemeat* anymore."

"Don't joke about this. Hey, Subaru, is that really true? Is everyone where you come from like this, or is it really just you who doesn't know?"

Subaru, feeling bad at how Emilia was genuinely worried, reflected upon his own behavior.

"Err, more like my education's especially lacking. So if it's no bother, I really would be grateful if you filled me in."

"You seem an educated enough child to me from the big words you're using, but…"

"I mean, this here's my debut with high society. I mean, there're things you don't know either, Emilia-tan? Honorifics like that and extra-polite words seem to throw you off?"

"Err…you do have a point."

Emilia seemed to shrink at Subaru's observation. Seeing Emilia like that surprised him, but it was not the wilting Emilia who followed up but Roswaal, previously silent in the seat of honor.

"I do understand what you are saying, but Lady Emilia is cuuurrently studying such things, you seeee."

"Studying, huh. Wait, you mean we lost her when we were talking earlier?"

"You truly do have an active mind. It is because you think so much that you can make such thoughtless-sounding statements."

Subaru slouched from Roswaal's apparent praise before giving his own chest a thump.

"Thinking while you live is just common sense. It's the duty of every man to think on his feet for when the chips are down. That or your guts get spilled all over the floor."

"I feel like your guts kind of did spill on the... Ahem. Back to the other subject... Subaru, do you know this country's...the Kingdom of Lugunica's situation at the moment?"

"Not the smallest, tiniest bit."

"Hearing you say it like that, I'm shocked you've lived this long."

That doesn't sound like praise to me, Subaru thought while looking fondly at Emilia. He wasn't *trying* to arouse her protective instincts, but she was certainly giving him that mother-hen feeling.

"By 'situation'...you mean the country's in a bad spot?"

Roswaal carefully chose his words.

"A fairly difficult situation, yes, for Lugunica currently lacks a king."

Subaru's breath caught as it sank in. He gave the man in performer makeup a guarded look as he sat straighter in his chair.

"There is no need for suuuch concern. The gravity of the situation is alreeeady well known to the public, you see."

"Well, that's good. I was thinking I'd learned a dangerous secret and would never get out alive."

"It's sad you're hearing it first from us... Anyway, the nation's highly unstable right now," Emilia said.

I see, thought Subaru as that sank in. A kingdom without a king was in a very precarious situation. The sudden death of a king, from natural causes or otherwise, could shake a country to its core.

"But isn't that usually dealt with by having a child of the king inherit and take over?"

"Usually, that iiis the case. Howeeever, that went awry due to an incident half a year ago when a great plague struck inside the palace walls."

As Roswaal told it, they announced that the epidemic only affected those of a particular bloodline. And so, the king and his descendants dwelling in the castle perished.

"Can't blame them for getting sick and dying. But what's gonna happen to this country, then? If there's no royal bloodline, what, start a democracy and elect a prime minister?"

"I do not cooomprehend the latter part of your statement, but presently, a Council of Elders manages the affairs of the country, formed from great families decorating the kingdom's history. The country will continue to operate. However…"

After pausing a moment, Roswaal grew tenser.

"…a kingdom must have a king."

"I suppose so."

Even if just for show, you couldn't have an organization without someone at its head, let alone a kingdom.

"I see," reflected Subaru. "I've got the gist of it. In other words, the country has no king and is in a jumble while it's trying to pick a new one. Your relations with foreign countries are deteriorating and you're in international isolation. So a mysterious foreigner like me appearing is…super suspicious?!"

"Fuuurthermore, by making contact with Lady Emilia, you have become associated with the House of Mathers, you *see*… Though the evidence is circumstantial, that is all some would need to…"

Roswaal lowered his eyes and traced a line across his throat with his thumb. Though Roswaal looked like he was joking, Subaru suddenly broke out in a cold sweat.

He had a bad feeling about something. He'd picked up on it earlier, but it loomed larger and larger with each passing moment.

"Why is…the lord of the manor calling Emilia-tan *lady*?"

The golden rule of any household was that everyone paid respect to the person of the highest rank.

When Roswaal laughed, Subaru felt like the bud of anxiety in his chest had begun to bloom.

"Is it not naaatural to address someone of higher rank than I with proper reeespect?"

Subaru froze with his mouth open. He looked at Emilia so robotically that you could hear the gears turn in his neck. The girl, a grimace on her face, sighed with resignation.

"I don't want you to think I was pulling the wool over your eyes, all right?"

"—Err, in other words, Emilia-tan, you're…?"

Subaru stubbornly stuck to the nickname as she seemed to drive in the final nail.

"Currently, my title is royal candidate, one of those seeking to become the forty-second ruler of the Kingdom of Lugunica…with the backing of Roswaal's House, that is."

Her words made Subaru feel like he'd insulted Heaven itself.

3

—So the pretty girl he'd stumbled upon in the other world was a queen.

That word alone firmly established that this was a true-blue fantasy world.

Technically, she was a candidate to be queen. When he remembered his time in contact with her now…

"Man, three lives aren't enough to pay for this, are they…?"

"Sorry to surprise you this much. I really hadn't meant to keep quiet about it, but, well…"

"Hey, I'm not upset. You truly are as kind as an angel, Emilia-tan."

"Eh?!"

Subaru's overly direct words made Emilia's face look shocked, then scarlet.

"Well, you know, you're the reason everything's happened since I've been here, Emilia. You're seriously E M T (Emilia-tan's a Major Treasure), that's my honest opinion!"

"…Sigh. Now I think I understand how I got involved with you. You'll brush off anything from anyone. Let's just get to the point, shall we?"

Traces of redness still on her face, Emilia clapped her hands to reset the scene. Though still seated, the earlier sense of distance seemed to return; Subaru was forced to go along.

"I feel like I am interruuupting, but regardless, let us indeed get to the poooint, shall we? Is that fiiine with you, Subaru?"

"Based on my head not flying off my shoulders, I'm guessing it's nothing all that bad."

Roswaal whistled at Subaru's words. Emilia looked equally taken off guard, for both surely saw Subaru's words and actions as a sign that he had a firm understanding of their intentions.

Of course, both were reading far too much into it, but that flew way over Subaru's head.

"Well, that's what I guessed about the 'point' based on your telling me Emilia-tan's a royal candidate and why that's important, right?"

Emilia made a belated remark.

"...Subaru, are you actually smart, or are you simply wrong in the head?"

"Those are two extreme choices, you know?!"

Subaru agonized as Emilia stuck out her tongue at him a little. She was cute, so all was forgiven.

Notwithstanding Subaru's internal simplicity, Roswaal followed up after Emilia's "apology."

"Your guess is quite on target. This matter is deeply related to what shall become of you. Lady Emilia?"

"Mm, I understand."

Emilia, nodding when called, pulled out something and set it on the table. Her white fingertips pushed it forward. Subaru raised his brows when he saw it.

"—That's that badge from...?"

Glittering atop a white cloth, it was a badge with a dragon motif, a jewel embedded in the center of its maw. It was also the key item stolen by the light-fingered Felt, which Subaru had returned to Emilia, its proper owner, coming back from three deaths to do it.

The deep, serene twinkle of the jewel struck Subaru's eyes, filling him with newfound awe.

"The dragon is the symbol of Lugunica, you see, enough that it is known by the rather graaand name, the Dragonfriend Kingdom of Lugunica. Castle walls and weapons are often adorned with this symbol, but this badge is particularly important."

When Roswaal took a pregnant pause, Subaru looked at him to urge him to continue. Roswaal shifted his gaze to Emilia to suggest she proceed. Emilia closed her eyes as her lips trembled.

"It is one's qualification as a royal candidate—a test to determine if the person is worthy of sitting on the throne of the Kingdom of Lugunica."

Her statement, said in a strained voice, made Subaru's eyes go wide. The badge sitting on the table, a dragon with wings outstretched on the glittering jewel, supported the proof of her claim.

"H-hold on here… You *lost* the badge that proves you're a royal candidate?!"

"That's putting it rather crudely. A light-fingered girl stole it!"

"Same difference—!!"

With that great shout, Subaru smacked his palms against the dining table as he rose to his feet. The impact threatened to make utensils fall to the floor, but Rem's quick follow-up prevented that. Subaru paid that no heed as he spoke.

"Wait, seriously, what'd happen if you didn't have it?! That's, like, the type of item that's really, really bad to throw away, right?! They can't issue another one?!"

"Weeell, if a candidate loses it, it won't end with just talk and excuses, yeees?"

With Subaru all flustered, Roswaal adjusted the lapel of his unnecessarily large outfit as he spoke.

"A king carries the kingdom on his shoulders. It is thought that a person who cannot protect a single small badge cannot be entrusted with a responsibility as grave as an entire land."

"Well, that figures. If anyone knew, it'd be a huge scandal… Which means?!"

The strife in the royal capital over the stolen badge and the warm reception now—it could mean only one thing.

Subaru continued, "It's really bad if the public finds out you lost the badge. That's why Emilia-tan was looking for it all by herself."

Emilia replied, "…Yes, that's right."

"Felt was the one who stole it, but Elsa was the client, and *she* said someone else put her up to it…meaning someone's trying to stop Emilia-tan from becoming queen?"

"That wooould appear to be the case. There is no simpler way to disqualify someone than to steal the baaadge."

Inside Subaru, everything that had taken place the day before started to come together.

How Emilia stubbornly refused his help; Felt and her client, Elsa; Subaru being murdered three times over—all of it was rooted in the value of the badge. So, too, was why Subaru was there at the manor.

"Man, looking back on it, I did a super good job! Man, I need a bigger reward, huh!"

Subaru was full of himself now that he suddenly knew the importance of his own actions. He looked down at Emilia haughtily, wagging his finger teasingly. He was waiting for the punch line. But.

"Yeah, you're right. You've been a huge help to me, Subaru. So much that merely saving your life isn't enough. That's how much this means to me."

The way she lifted her hand to her breast, giving Subaru a serious look, put him at a loss for words.

The stiffness of his cheeks didn't match the tense, serious aura all around him.

—*Oh man, I seriously suck at reading the mood.*

Subaru's inability to read the tension in the air clashed with the serious look on Emilia's face. Finally, amid his great embarrassment…

—

"…What are you doing?"

"Er, my hand just kind of reached out."

With Emilia staring at him, Subaru had gently brushed his fingertips into her hair, not so much stroking her head as simply passing his fingers through the hair and enjoying the feeling.

"I'm an easygoing guy. I was thinking this would be reward enough for me."

"…You stroked Puck's fur, too. Subaru, do you have some kind of hair fetish?"

Subaru let out a yell at the harsh assessment.

"Hey, wait, fur and hair aren't the same thing at all! Your silver hair's really pretty!"

Emilia's silver hair truly felt smooth as silk; its soft charm bewitched Subaru in an entirely different way from Puck's fur.

But for some reason, Subaru's words made Emilia lower her eyes with a pained look. Subaru tilted his head, not knowing the reason for Emilia's action. His head was still like that when he felt a gaze from behind.

"Ah, perrrhaps we are in the way? We could leave you two to yourselves?"

"Your concern's the dictionary definition of *none of your business*. And it's still my turn to ask questions."

Subaru continued enjoying the feel of Emilia's hair as he used his free hand to point at Roswaal.

"I understand Emilia-tan being a candidate for becoming queen, but what about this business of you backing her?"

"You really aaare rather observant. You've picked up the preeevious matters quite well, though this is aaall second nature to any human born and raised in the city."

"I'm honored to have your praise, Count. Though simple anime and romance novels kind of prepared my mind for this fantasy stuff."

Like any reader, he'd been thrust into original scenarios with confusing, hard-to-remember world-building. Stuffing this level of background info into his head was no big accomplishment.

"Well, it is not something I was trying to conceal. My title is the Kingdom of Lugunica's...I suppose technically I am lord of the outer regions, but my role sounds better expressed as...court magician, perhaps?"

"Court magician...? So you handle magic use at the castle?"

Emilia picked up where Subaru's words left off.

"Yes. That's the magician of the highest rank... He's the foremost magic user in the entire kingdom."

She looked a little dissatisfied nonetheless. Roswaal seemed nothing but pleased with Emilia's reply, smiling as he brought some tea to his lips.

"So continuing the earlier topic, I stand in support of Lady Emilia's royal candidacy. I am the shield behind her, her patron, sooo to speak."

"Patron, huh."

A representative for those backing her. So that was the position of the man before his eyes.

Subaru looked anew at the tall man in clown makeup before gently trading a glance with Emilia.

"I don't mean to put this the wrong way but…Emilia-tan, you sure about this guy?"

"It can't be helped. He's the only one in the kingdom I can ask for support. In the first place, only a meddlesome eccentric like Roswaal would help someone like me, so…"

"Ah, I see. Process of elimination."

"Quiiite a conversation you two are having right in front of your patron, if I maaay say so…"

Perhaps feeling somewhat slandered, Roswaal gave off an adult chuckle rather than anger. Maybe he had really thick skin—that or he simply took pleasure in ignoring people.

"So, back to the point, Rozchi. I get that you're Emilia-tan's sponsor. It's cute how she goes from one extreme to another to hide how she's a bit of an airhead, but acting on her own like she did yesterday in the capital, that's kinda rare, huh?"

"I wooould call it unprecedented. Thooough Ram should have been with her…"

Roswaal made a strained smile as he shifted the topic to Ram. When Subaru looked at her, he saw she had the same hairstyle and face as Rem, standing beside her. At least you could nicely tell them apart by their hair color.

"Man, that totally smug 'I got away with it, just as I hoped' look gets on my nerves."

Whether she intended to reflect on her error or not, he had her over a barrel. However, Emilia raised a hand in her defense with an awkward look on her face.

"Um, it's not Ram's fault. Yesterday I split up from Ram because I…lost out to my curiosity and wandered all around."

"What's that doe-eyed little-girl excuse?! Emilia-tan being a big airhead doesn't change the fact that she didn't fulfill her lord's commands. Is that all right…?"

With Emilia trying to cover for Ram, Subaru pointed a finger from each hand at her before he shifted them over to Roswaal.

"You dooo have a point, thoooough I share responsibility for Ram's lack of discretion. But what are you trying to say, I wooonder?"

"Simple. You're the ones who dropped the ball by taking your eyes off someone important like Emilia-tan. That's where I came into the picture. I'm saying, if you had it all covered to begin with, none of this would've happened."

Subaru's little speech changed the looks on everyone's faces.

Emilia raised her eyebrows, one of the twins looked apologetic while the other glared with hostility, Beatrice still had her heated gaze trained on Puck while Puck was precariously stuck headfirst into the egg yolk on the dish before her...and Roswaal made a pleasant smile, nodding as if he agreed.

"I seeee. Certainly Lady Emilia's worth exceeds my considerable personal fortune. It is appropriate that you should seek a reward only from me, as her sponsor, iiis it nooot?"

"Yep. And you're not gonna say no, are you, Rozchi? I mean, I saved Emilia-tan's life and stopped her from dropping out of the royal selection. I'm totally her savior!"

Subaru rose from his seat and posed with a finger pointed up to the sky.

"I muuust admit that it is the truth. Now, then, would you care to elaborate?"

Roswaal, too, rose from his seat, looking down at Subaru from his superior height. Emilia looked worried as she watched Subaru and Roswaal stare each other down.

"Whaaat is it that you seek from me? I cannot refuse your request, if only to prevent this matter from becoming public knowledge. Nooow then, what is your desire?"

"Heh-heh-heh, that's a noble for you; you really get it. Whatever reward I want! And you can't say no, Rozchi! A man doesn't take back his word!"

"That is quiiite a saying! I see, a man should make no excuses. No reneging on his word."

Subaru's petty villain behavior made him hear his popularity meter drop in his mind, but the entire effort was devoted to dragging that one statement out of him.

Roswaal's consent made Subaru's inner self smile.

"I want one thing and one thing only. I want you to hire me."

Compared to the extended foreplay, Subaru's declaration was plain and simple.

The girls behind Subaru were in shock at his statement. The looks on the twins' faces became mildly conflicted, whereas Beatrice looked seriously perturbed. As for Emilia...

"I-it's not for me to say, but that's kind of..."

Her eyes were so wide that even the sublime beauty she was born with lost half its power.

"You're cute when you're surprised, but are you that against the idea?"

"It's not that; you want so little!"

It was like Emilia was angry for him as she slapped the table and closed the distance with Subaru.

"It's not just the thing with Puck, okay? It's...like when you asked me my name back in the royal capital."

Emilia listed the rewards Subaru had claimed to the best of her knowledge. Emilia knew what he'd done to get those rewards; she shook her head like she really didn't understand.

"You don't...understand how grateful I feel. I can't...repay you at all for saving my life and more, if you ask for so little!"

Emilia's inflection tapered off as she pressed a palm to Subaru's chest and lowered her head.

Hearing Emilia's lament, Subaru painfully understood his own thoughtlessness.

Emilia had always felt indebted to him. She wanted to pay him back in some suitable way.

But the same went for Subaru. Subaru had always been indebted to Emilia. And twice he had become indebted to her in a way he could never repay.

He could not repay kindness that had "never happened."

Before him, Emilia raised up her wavering violet eyes. Seeing the serious look with her plea, Subaru abandoned all thought of kidding around or papering it over.

Subaru decided to convey to Emilia how he really felt with all the seriousness he could muster.

"You don't understand, Emilia-tan. At the time, that was what I truly wanted from the bottom of my heart, you see?"

"—Huh?"

"At the time, I wanted to know your name. I think being in a new, uncertain land with no idea what would come the next day, if I'd stopped to think about it, there were lots of things I could've considered— But I'm a man who can't lie to himself."

It was a reward for which he'd died three times.

For nothing more than to see the smiling face of the silver-haired girl before his eyes and to learn her name.

—At that moment, there was no greater reward he could wish for.

"My request to Rozchi's like that, too. Right now, I'm completely, totally broke. Sure, I could ask for a pile of gold, but why not set myself up so I can make a living long-term?"

"…If you wanted that, you could ask to just live here for free, not as a manservant, you know?"

"Oh, I could've done that?! Hey, Mr. Roswaal, could you let me live as a fr—"

Looking at Roswaal as Subaru tried to amend his wish, the man crossed his hands above his head in an X mark.

"I shall honor the first request. A man does not take back his word, dooooes he?"

"Whoa! You're right! A man doesn't do that, huh?!"

Subaru tearfully found his request denied because *someone* had to open his big mouth earlier.

"And I thought for a moment there you seemed actually serious… I must have just imagined it."

"And then Emilia-tan lowers my rating! That's kicking me while I'm down!"

Subaru realized he'd passed up the chance to establish the perfect easy life in a fantasy-world environment. He didn't need to lower the beautiful girl's opinion of him on top of that.

"Anyway…that's how it is, so…I mean, Ramchi and Remrin must be straining to take care of this place all by themselves, so please let me work under them."

"It iiis true that is an actual concern… Though I beeelieve it is as Lady Emilia said, it is indeeeed asking rather little?"

With Roswaal showing a strained smile for once, Subaru put up his left and right index fingers and wiggled them.

"I'm a super greedy guy, actually. I mean, living under the same roof as a super cute, beautiful girl who's totally my type, what guy wouldn't want that? Close in body is close to the heart, and opportunities abound!"

"…I seeee, certainly it is as you say. It is rare one gets to work by the side of girls one is interested in, iiis it not? Quiiite pleasant for you."

"Well, besides."

Subaru stopped wiggling his fingers and used them to scratch his unkempt hair.

"Besides, you're not gonna let a guy you know nothing about like me just pack up and leave. And to me, the pros and cons say I should stay with Emilia-tan."

Subaru knew a few too many inconvenient things. He was declaring his belief that nothing good would happen to him if he left the manor without any means of protecting himself.

If Roswaal had never considered any such thing, no doubt he would have taken extreme offense. But in contrast to Subaru's awkward feelings about it, "Then it shall be as you ask—I hope we geeet along very nicely."

Roswaal's instant reply came with one eye closed, looking at Subaru with his yellow eye alone.

Subaru couldn't read what he was thinking behind that suspicious twinkle.

Incidentally, Subaru was very embarrassed inside from having made such a strong public confession.

But when Subaru timidly looked at Emilia's expression…

"Goodness, you really are a hopeless child… Did something happen?"

Her perfectly calm reply left Subaru at a loss for words.

Maybe he was overthinking it? This was just the result of his lack of experience with being around a beautiful girl.

"Man, dealing with a girl I like this much is gettin' me all worked up…"

Emilia, watching Subaru get fired up on a tangent instead of dealing with more pressing matters, murmured in a little voice, "Which one's more your type, I wonder…Ram or Rem?"

Emilia put a finger to her lips in a huff, taking what he'd said earlier *completely* the wrong way.

4

—With the long breakfast taken care of, the matter of what to do with Subaru was largely settled.

Seeing this, the first to stand was the girl with curly hair—Beatrice.

"I see the discussion is settled, so may I take my leave with Puckie, I wonder?"

Beatrice was quick to finish her own meal so that she could leave as soon as possible. Grimacing even then, she seemed about to leave without bothering to put her plates in order when Subaru wagged a finger at her.

"Wait, there's no need to be in that much of a hu— Hey, at least introduce yourself. I don't know what your place is here at all. You Rozchi's little sister?"

"Treating me as that *thing*'s relative? You are quite accomplished at angering me."

Beatrice let out a sigh full of disgust as Roswaal, thoroughly bad-mouthed, smiled in amusement. Subaru slumped his shoulders as Beatrice shot him a nasty glare when Puck spoke up.

"Betty's the librarian of the archive of forbidden books here in Roswaal's manor!"

"Puckie?!"

Just when it seemed like an argument was about to break out, the gray cat's statement tore it to shreds. Puck was busy nibbling on the heel of a loaf of bread glazed with sugar for a luxurious dessert.

"Sweet, tasty, meow…"

"Hate to bug you when you're on a sugar high, but could you tell me more?"

With Puck lost in a sweet daze, Subaru touched Puck's heavily sprinkled ear, urging him on.

Subaru was toying with it quite a bit when Puck raised his face from the plate.

"It's because Roswaal's a pretty accomplished magician, plus he comes from a pretty old family. There're lots of books here that aren't for other people to see. So, he made a pact with Betty for her to protect them."

"Yes, that's true. How is Puckie always so right, I wonder?"

Beatrice seemed to agree without thinking, speaking as her hand sprang out to Puck's other ear. A lovely look came over her as her fingers felt the fur of his ears.

It was the first time Subaru had seen Beatrice with an expression that suited her loveliness.

Subaru's breath caught. The odd girl out, Emilia tilted her head a bit as she watched.

"You two look like you're *really* getting along nicely while playing with the cute kitty there."

"Getting along nicely with this person is a little…!"

"How could I ever get along with this person, I wonder?!"

Subaru and Beatrice both shot down Emilia's idea. For his part, Subaru was hiding a blush; for her part, Beatrice looked quite serious.

"Hee-hee. I'm so scary, making two people at odds with each other into my slaves… Meow meow meow!"

Puck was busy being the literal center of attention when Emilia's outstretched fingers grasped him. Puck was in Emilia's fingers, unable to move, as she sighed.

"All that said, being the guardian of an archive of forbidden books… The sound of it really tickles a guy's mind."

Beatrice was giving Subaru a sullen look as he tickled Puck, but Subaru's suggestion softened her expression. She toyed with her own long rolls as she gave what was, for Beatrice, a frank reply.

"Perhaps you did not hear Puckie's explanation? It is the room you entered earlier."

"Oh, the one with all the books!"

Remembering the great volume of books chewing up all the floor space, Subaru could accept it being that kind of archive. On the other hand, the idea that all those volumes were somehow forbidden made him feel like it was a crime on a completely different scale.

"Don't tell me this loli's your unwitting partner in crime…?!"

"That word annoys me every time I hear it. And to answer your question, the very thought that I am an innocent victim annoys me enough, couldn't I just die, I wonder?"

"Don't be so prickly, shrimp. It takes calcium and a calm heart to get taller. If you were about as tall as Emilia-tan and me, we'd have quite a little love comedy going on here…"

He left Beatrice to stew indignantly at his comment as he gave Emilia an amorous glance. But Emilia let that comment slide and pressed a different issue with Beatrice.

"Wait a minute. Beatrice…don't tell me you let him into the archive?"

"…I shouldn't have to tell you. Why would I ever need to let in a stranger such as him on purpose, I wonder? No, he solved the riddle of the Passage all on his very own."

A vein bulged on Beatrice's forehead as she roughly stood up and pushed open the dining hall door.

Subaru, faced with the incomprehensible scene before him, asked like a complete idiot, "Ah? The hallway just…?"

Before his eyes, the open door that should have led to the manor's hall beyond had opened to a huge room lined with bookshelves. He almost swooned when he remembered that he'd seen it once before.

"This is the Passage. You are trembling as its sublime beauty burns itself into your eyes, perhaps?—Come on, Puckie."

Beatrice stepped into the archive of forbidden books, looking triumphantly at Subaru as she stretched out her hand. Puck leapt from Emilia to land upon her outstretched palm.

Upon this, Beatrice closed the door behind both her and the cat.

Ram didn't say a word as she opened the shut door. Subaru's eyes widened in total surprise.

"Whoa, that's incredible."

Beyond the door, closed so roughly a moment before, Subaru walked with his own feet into the hallway beyond. The scene before him a moment before was like a mirage.

"I see. In other words, magic makes it so any door here can connect to any room. Pretty neat for recluses who need to find the john in a pinch."

Emilia seemed a bit thrown off.

"You actually look less surprised than I expected. What's a recluse?"

"A guardian who sacrifices himself holding down the fort at home, waiting for weary family members to return."

"Er...that sounds noble. Are you a recluse, Subaru?"

Emilia was full of concern when a puff of smoke interrupted her and Subaru, tickling his nose.

"Achoo!"

"Yes, *yes*, shall we continue the introductions? Ram, Rem."

"Pleased to make your acquaintance. I am Rem, employed as chief maid by this household."

"Nice to meet you. I am Ram, working as an ordinary maid in Master Roswaal's mansion."

Subaru crossed his arms.

"Wow, you sisters suddenly got nice and formal. Well, not that I'm one to talk, but..."

The twins joined hands and looked at Subaru.

"But Dear Guest...or rather, Subaru, you are our coworker now?"

"But Dear Guest...or rather, Barusu, you work under us here now?"

"Hey, Big Sis. You're throwing my name back in my face here."

That was the one thing you absolutely did *not* do at your first formal introduction. Of course, there was no way for Ram or Rem to know of that rule of Japanese society. Subaru endured the mockery as he turned toward Roswaal.

"So that's my standing, huh? Not so much a butler as an apprentice maid?"

"In this situation, your doing odd jobs at their discretion seeems best. Dissatisfied…?"

"If I was gonna be dissatisfied I'd have only myself to blame. Well, had to be done, so no regrets. Take good care of me, my seniors. I'm gonna work super hard and break a leg!"

"Break a leg."

"So it would seem."

The three seemed to instantly agree on the never-before-raised term. With a *yeah!* Subaru raised his hands and they high-fived each other. They were already getting along.

"Harmonious relations are a beautiful thing. As your employer, I think it iiis just fine, so long as there are nooo ill feelings, yeees?"

"For some reason, we kinda get along. A lot better than that loli! Way better than with her!"

"You really don't want to be seen as Beatrice's friend, do you…"

Emilia's pitying murmur signaled the end of the gathering.

5

"Well then, shall we be off, Barusu?"

So spoke Ram, commanded by Roswaal to be Subaru's personal tutor. Her little sister, Rem, was off to the side meticulously cleaning up the dining hall; Ram made no effort to help as she reached for the dining hall door.

"So you intend to call me that full-time, huh?"

"Yes, I do, Barusu. Master Roswaal commands it, so I shall show you around the mansion. Can you at least make sure not to wander off?"

"I'm not Emilia-tan, so I won't let curiosity get the best of me."

Emilia's cheeks puffed up at being teased about getting lost in the capital.

"Su-ba-ru!"

Emilia was about to split off to continue studying various ceremonial roles, mandatory for a royal candidate. Subaru was making a point of burning Emilia's beauty into his eyes before she left.

"Well, with minor regrets, let's be off. Lead the way."

"Yes, let us, Barusu. Until later, Lady Emilia."

Ram held the hem of her skirt, bowing courteously as she left. Subaru started to follow behind her.

"Subaru. I will, too, but…try hard, okay?"

"Wow, I'm super happy to hear that. I'm really pumped for this!"

Mimicking Ram, Subaru held the collar of his track jacket as he bowed. Emilia shot him a strange look as he did so before leaving the room. Ram had a grimace on her face, waiting as he walked into the hallway.

"That's quite a sour face, Big Sis. I was just playing around a little. I'm not so ignorant of maid culture to the point that I think a maid is the same as a manservant. Oh yeah, what about clothes?"

He didn't think it was very likely he'd be starting life as a servant in his tracksuit.

Prompted by Subaru, Ram put a hand to her mouth and nodded.

"Certainly, clothing is very important. Let's see, clothing in your size… Yes, we should have some."

"Awesome. Okay, let's get me changed, then. I think formal actually suits me pretty well. Let's make me a refined, high-quality man!"

Subaru smiled with a thumbs-up and a twinkle of his eyes when Ram led him upstairs to take his measurements.

"The servant quarters are on the second floor, so you'll change there. Your clothing size should be similar to Frederica's, who quit several months ago."

"Huh, interesting timing to quit. This Frederica…is a woman?"

"Her dimensions should be right about the same as yours."

"But she's not the same gender, right?"

Ram stopped walking and gave Subaru a cold look. She looked tired as she put her hand to her forehead.

"Clothing that is formal, refined, and high quality...which of these do you have a problem with?"

"How about all the above?! Emilia-tan looked like she was gonna pay me and everything, so why do I have to borrow a maid outfit?! What if people think I'm some kind of weirdo?! I don't want *that*!"

A trip to a fantasy world without any special talents, save cross-dressing. Subaru would almost have rather died. But, since Subaru had a frightening ability, death was no consolation.

Guided by Ram, he continued to the west side of the manor. Roswaal Manor had a main wing in the center, with a corridor connecting it to the east and west wings. The dining hall and Roswaal's private study were in the main wing, whereas the empty servants' quarters were on the western side.

"An empty room on the second... Yes, any room that has no plate above it is fine. Pick whichever you wish for your private quarters and I shall drop off your change of clothes there."

"Okay, roger that. Hmm, which one..."

Having been granted private quarters in the mansion, Subaru surveyed the candidates from the end of the corridor onward. Having said that, surely only the locations differed; the contents would remain the same. Being near the stairs was convenient, so...

"All righty, I'll pick this room over h—"

He opened the door with no special consideration. At that moment, he spied what looked like a loli playing with a kitty cat in a library.

"*Fuwaah,* you're so wonderful, Puckie. Your fur is the best fur ever..."

The girl with the long curls noticed Subaru and slowly shifted her gaze toward him. Subaru looked back at Ram, standing in the corridor, as she shook her head. Subaru gave her a big thumbs-up.

"Don't worry, I won't say a thing. That feeling turns all of us into blithering idiots..."

"Could you cut short the magnificently stupid statement and *close the door already*, I wonder?!"

"*Gyaha!*"

Some invisible power, likely something magical, threw Subaru back, and he flew hard into the corridor wall. The impact to the back of his head made Subaru's eyes spin as he saw out of the corner of his eye the door slam shut with a ferocious sound.

Shaking his head, Subaru retraced his steps to complain about the violence of a moment before.

But when he opened the door, an empty room within greeted him. The Passage had done its magic.

"Once Lady Beatrice conceals her aura, one cannot know which door it is. She will not emerge unless you go opening every door in the entire mansion."

Ram spoke like he should bluntly accept defeat. From behind, she patted his shoulder. That feeling made Subaru admit he had lost this—

"Oh *man*, she annoys me. She acted like I did something wrong there!"

Or not.

Brushing off Ram's hand, Subaru turned and sprinted down the corridor full force. In front of wide-eyed Ram, he ran straight to the door at the other edge of the hallway.

"Here!!"

"—*Hyah?!*"

The girl yelped as the gray cat made a sound of admiration.

"Impressive, Subaru."

This time, seeing Beatrice's face rocked at his having broken the Passage a second time, he instantly made a roll into the archives so that she couldn't blow him out again.

Beatrice's eyebrows rose with anger at something one simply did not do in any library, never mind these archives.

"You are kicking up dust!"

"Well, you should've dusted it better, then!! And you don't bring cats into the library anyway! You get claw marks all over the covers!"

"It's fine, Lia trims my claws really short!"

The odd man out, Puck's casual murmur failed to reach Subaru and Beatrice as they argued. They looked ready to shout loud enough that the echoes would carry through the entire mansion.

Ram, belatedly entering through the door leading to the archive of forbidden books, looked at the arguing parties and said in a small voice, "If not friends, you certainly are birds of a feather."

Roswaal Manor seemed to shake from their combined shouts.

"—Absolutely not!!"

6

And so, Subaru's life as a servant started with a bang.

With the conclusion of the unexpected session with Beatrice, Subaru used a dressing room to put on the servant's attire that Ram had given him. It was a white shirt with a black jacket and matching pants, doing no violence to Subaru's preconceived image of a butler. The problem lay elsewhere.

"Hey, Ramchi, I put on the outfit, but…"

Ram, waiting outside the dressing room until he'd finished, entered when called.

"Though I'd like to say something about how I've been addressed, is there something wrong with…?"

Ram, complaining as she made her way in, stopped mid-sentence as she got a good look at Subaru, putting her hand to her forehead.

"Indeed there is. Your shoulders, and also, your legs are too short."

"You mean my height?! The shirt's fine, but the jacket's real tight on the shoulders. I'm decently athletic, not that it gets me anywhere, but this super tight top makes me look like a macho man here."

Just as Ram had indicated, the shoulders were stiff because the sleeves were a poor fit. In particular, the armpits were far too tight for his shoulders to move. Subaru wondered if this was a natural problem when dealing with hand-me-down servant uniforms.

"I can roll up the sleeves, but the top's no good like this. I suppose I can handle shortening sleeves on my own, but…"

"So you have unexpected talent, Barusu… We cannot have you working in such a sorry outfit. It will bring the manor's, and Master Roswaal's, standards into question."

"He dresses like *that* and he worries about standards?"

Though Ram had a neutral expression, the tilt of her head made plain her displeasure, so he shut up. Subaru's "zipping" his lips with his finger brought a sigh out of Ram.

"We can do nothing for what is inside, but we can at least make you look presentable. At any rate, let's leave the shortening of the legs for later and just fix the top."

"Easier said than done, though? I don't have any experience with that, either."

Maybe I could manage anyway, voiced Subaru as he assessed the limits of his sewing skills, but Ram countered, "No need for concern. Rem, come over here."

"Come over here…? She's not gonna pop right in just 'cause you…"

"You called, Sister?"

"Waaaaah!"

As soon as she was casually called, Rem appeared right beside them, giving Subaru quite a fright. It was as if they were playing a joke.

The twins tilted their heads in unison as they watched Subaru's shocked, frozen reaction.

"What are you so surprised for?"

"What are you so scared for?"

"I'm not s-scared! Just a little surprised! That Twin Power thing's really something!"

Maybe it was some kind of twin "sympathy" they talked about on those supernatural investigation shows; that thing where they could read the other even when apart.

Seeing Subaru so shaken, Ram made a *hmph* sound.

"Of course it is no such thing. I spotted her happening to walk by and called out to her. Perfect timing."

"That last part sounds like it's rubbing it in somehow?"

Ram cut in.

"So what is it you need? I do not have much time to waste on Subaru."

"That uncaring attitude really hurts, geez! I'm the new guy! Be gentle!"

But the truth was that Rem was indispensable for maintaining the manor. Delaying her for any real length of time was surely a bad thing, yet Ram looked at Rem, pointing to Subaru as she stated, "Rem, surely you have noted Barusu's pathetic appearance?"

"His shoulders rotate oddly and his legs are too short. Also, his face is terrifying. And?"

"You just had to poke at two things I can't do anything about!! It's not like clothes; you can't change how your face looks no matter how hard you try!"

The sisters ignored Subaru's complaints as they continued to converse. Subaru, the odd man out despite being the subject, was left with nothing better to do than to roll up his sleeves.

"Barusu, hand Rem your jacket. You will have to do without it until tomorrow morning."

"That's a big help, but…sure about this? You've got a mountain of work, right?"

"Of course I am quite busy. However, handing it over saves time and trouble later."

"Ahh, right. Please and thank you."

Swayed by the sound argument, Subaru stripped off his jacket and handed it to Rem. Upon taking the jacket, Rem pointed to the dressing room and motioned with her chin for him to get in.

"I need to take your measurements. You can't take them yourself, can you?"

"…I feel sorry for making you go through all this trouble."

"I do not mind. Someday, you shall repay me for this. With interest."

"That doesn't sound quite right, but you seem dead serious. So scary!"

Subaru and Rem left the haughtier-than-thou Ram in the corridor and went into the dressing room.

The dressing room held not only servant uniforms but various changes of clothes for Roswaal as well. Everything felt like it came straight from a circus dressing room.

When his gaze left the area with lord's attire of rather poor taste, several more flowery outfits drew him in. One of them was an outfit he'd seen at the royal capital, so these were no doubt outfits for Emilia.

"I'd love to have her model all of those, twirling around and show-ing them off…"

"What are you mumbling about? Get over here, please."

Summoned by the especially sharp voice, Subaru obeyed without further kidding around. The middle of the dressing room had no booth for trying on clothes, but it did have a divider for that pur-pose, and there awaited Rem with a slender measuring tape. The elaborate imprint on the tape marked it as a high-quality item.

"Stand straight over there. Stretch out your arms so I can measure your arms and shoulder height."

"Okay, roger that. Thanks."

Turning away from Rem, Subaru reached out both arms as she had instructed. Subaru stretched his short frame as much as he could while Rem wrapped the tape around his arms and back.

Subaru's shoulders quivered with a sensitive sound when he sud-denly became aware of her soft touch and breathing.

"Please do not make strange noises, Subaru. It is unpleasant."

"I couldn't help *that*! This is tough on a guy on more than one level!"

Faced with Rem's cold, heartless words, Subaru searched his mind for any change of subject.

"By the way, there's Rozchi's and Emilia-tan's clothes in here, but I don't see any dresses for you, Ram, or the loli. They in another room?"

"Lady Beatrice changes her clothes in her private quarters. Sister and I do not wear clothes other than these, so we do not require dif-ferent outfits. We change in our own quarters."

Subaru raised his eyebrows at Rem's matter-of-fact reply. Then Rem, having just finished measuring him, wrote something on a nearby memo. Subaru crossed his arms and looked at her.

"You don't have any other kinds of outfits, so what, it's all maid outfits? What about when you go out and days off?"

"It is no hindrance to our work here at the manor or when accom-panying Master Roswaal in public. I think it is a quite logical way to present our status without need of an explanation."

"Logical ain't the point here… I think a beautiful girl has a duty to wear pretty clothes and bring joy to others."

"Sister may be another matter, but no one would be pleased were I to dress up."

"Maybe I would?"

"Would pleasing you do me any good, Subaru?"

"Maybe it'll make me work harder at the servant's life. That's logical, isn't it?"

Rem had the slightest look of surprise at Subaru's comeback. Subaru, pleased at cracking her neutral expression, twisted the corners of his lips into a grin.

"I do not know why you would go so far as to say that, Subaru."

"Even your hairstyles and outfits are the same! Your personalities are different so at least pick different clothes! ...Or something like that. I mean, the maid outfits look good on you, and it does kinda work for twins like you girls."

In her current outfit, she was cute with room to spare, but their attire was identical down to the haircut. Precisely because they were twins, he wanted to see some *individuality*, the essence of human emotion.

That was how Subaru felt, but...

"—ness."

"Eh?"

"None of your business. What is wrong with my being the same as Sister?"

It was hard to believe, but Rem's expression was more glacial toward the wide-eyed Subaru than before. Subaru unintentionally hemmed and hawed, the exchange of small talk until just earlier seemingly long forgotten.

"...Let us go back and not speak silly things. I cannot leave Sister waiting any further, and there is a great deal you must learn, after all."

Her demeanor permitting no dissent, Rem turned her back on Subaru and headed to the room's entrance. Subaru, more confused than before, walked behind her as he murmured.

"That's being a little too into your big sister..."

He sighed, concerned about where his relations with the seemingly unflappable girl would go.

7

With the measurements done, they linked back up with Ram in the dressing room, and Rem went her separate way.

In spite of being pressed by work, Rem said, "I will re-stitch your jacket overnight and deliver it before morning once it is done."

She shot Ram a look rich in meaning as she left. Their eye-to-eye message system made Subaru give Ram's shoulder a soft poke.

"Hey, what did Rem say with that eye-contact thing just now?"

"She said, 'Subaru gave me perverted glances when we were alone'... You beast."

"So you got that much from just th— Hey, don't back away, that hurt my feelings!"

Though Ram's retreat from Subaru, clutching her own shoulder, pained his heart, his time as a servant at the manor finally began in earnest.

The west wing contained the servants' quarters, spare furniture, and normal books not meant for the archive. In contrast, the east wing had suites for welcoming visiting nobles, with rooms for entertaining guests and other facilities, with few functional differences from the main wing.

"You have now toured nearly all the manor. All that remains are the gardens outside the buildings and the front yard between the manor and the gate. You can see those later. Any questions so far?"

"Shouldn't the tour have been something Emilia-tan would've done?"

"Not at all, since we will be getting to work immediately."

During the guided tour, Ram's personal disposition and Subaru's penchant for stopping and going off on tangents made her easily fend off Subaru's latest line.

Subaru wasn't sure if that meant the last several hours had brought them closer or he'd simply dug himself into a deeper hole, but...

"My chores for today are maintaining the garden and front yard and checking the surroundings. I will be assisting in preparing lunch, and at Eight Solartime, I must wash the silverware... You shall assist me, Barusu."

"Sure thing, but what's that Solartime you mentioned?"

It was a term he'd heard when he'd awoken that morning. He'd guessed that *Solartime* referred to time during the day, but...

"So Eight Solartime indicates the time... Do you have a clock or something?"

"*Clock...?* If you mean a magic time crystal, they are all over the mansion, including right over there."

Subaru looked where Ram pointed and saw a crystal emitting a dim light. The crystal hung from the upper part of the mansion's wall—pretty much right where a big clock might be back in his world.

Subaru squinted as he stared at the flickering green light emitted by the crystal.

"It's a little weird, but I guess it's just another clock. How do I read it?"

"Solartime is Wind Time from zero to six, then Fire Time for the next six. Lunartime goes from Water Time to Earth Time— To not know this, are you some kind of barbarian, Barusu?"

"An actual barbarian wouldn't answer yes to that, you know?"

He hated hearing it, but Subaru's lack of common knowledge made that appraisal hard to shake.

Thinking back, there was a magic time crystal in the room Subaru awoke in, too. Subaru felt that the crystal had been a lot greener then.

"So, what, the color gets brighter as time passes?"

"...Wind Time is green, Fire is red, Water is blue, Earth is yellow. Anything else you want explained?"

"I'm okay with the time stuff now. Solartime and Lunartime are kind of like AM and PM from the sound of it."

No doubt he'd have to endure many other clashes with what passed for common sense in a fantasy world.

Subaru crossed his arms and nodded. Ram seemed tired as she put a hand to her forehead.

"It's hard enough to train you for the job from scratch, but having so little common sense... When did I go from domestic help to an animal trainer?"

"It's scary just to hear words like *animal trainer*, so maybe you could pick different ones, boss?"

Ram's eyebrows twitched at being called *boss*. Feeling that she either didn't care or wasn't too bothered, Subaru switched gears a bit.

"By the way, there were only you two taking care of the place earlier, but it wasn't gonna be like that forever, right? I mean, you had that maid who quit before?"

"...Master Roswaal has relatives living at various lesser manors, so most of our coworkers have come from there until now. Rem and I work here at the main residence so that we may attend to Master Roswaal personally."

"Main residence and lesser manors... So, um, this is the main residence?"

"Master Roswaal is head of the Mathers family, so of course he lives at the main residence. And I say relatives, but his relations with the other branches of the Mathers family are not particularly deep."

Perhaps Subaru should have expected that a nobleman like Roswaal would have a complex relationship with his family. Now that Subaru was working for the man, he couldn't consider himself a bystander in that; besides, he was closely related to Emilia, a royal candidate.

"Even if you're just looking after Rozchi, this mansion's too huge for two people to handle, right? Can't you hire more people?"

"—Circumstances make that impossible at the moment. Also, the time for idle talk is over."

Ram clapped, signaling the end of that line of discussion as she calmly walked forward.

Subaru wanted to ask her more about stuff, but he could do that and pick up more common knowledge as he worked. He needed to put his back into the work first, to keep her happy if nothing else.

"Haven't worked like this before, but I feel really positive for some reason. I guess it's the beautiful-girl thing?"

"Flattery will get you nothing. No kindness, no mercy."

"You should learn a little modesty from your little sister, geez!"

Subaru threw that out, still chewing over the conversation with Rem back in the dressing room.

8

"Oww—!"

Subaru was half in tears as he yelped at the fresh wound, wet with red blood.

Ram, engaged in the same work right beside Subaru, narrowed her eyes as she watched him wave around his bleeding left hand.

"That is what thoughtlessness gets you. Basuru, do you know the meaning of *improvement*?"

"But this is the first time I've dealt with any tableware that's not chopsticks!"

Subaru stuck his cut finger into his mouth as he complained, his cheeks puffing as the metallic taste filled his mouth.

They were in the kitchen, shortly before noon. After wrapping up in the garden with Ram, the two returned to the dining hall to help Rem prepare. That being said...

"I understand me, but making your big sister peel stuff, too? I mean, where's the dignity?"

Ram was quick with a counter.

"We have worked and lived together a long time, so we divide work by our specialties. This is not my place to shine."

"I thought I heard earlier that she's better than you in every area, though?!"

He'd heard earlier how Ram came in behind Rem at cooking, cleaning, washing, sewing, and pretty much every other chore. Ram did seem pretty experienced at peeling veggies, though.

"Are both of you going to be done soon?"

Rem spoke, seemingly wide-eyed at the two she'd entrusted the peeling to as she put them to shame with her ferocious meal preparation. Rem's practiced hand was far beyond the norm, making her cooking feel like a type of highly polished performance.

…Completely unlike the other two, doing menial work off in a corner.

Rem looked back as she poured ingredients into a huge frying pan and mixed them. Silently looking over her big sister peeling and Subaru bleeding, Rem nodded like nothing had happened.

"As usual, Sister, the sight of you peeling vegetables is worthy of a painting."

"Your favoritism is so obvious, it's refreshing! I'd love a comment for the work I'm doing, too!"

"I feel sorry for the farmer who grew those vegetables."

"Stop, you're wounding me!"

Rem was looking at the atrocious wreckage of the vegetables Subaru had peeled. The potato-like vegetables had been cut down roughly halfway, yet, skin remained on them. Furthermore, fairly deep cuts to his hand had left the table wet with blood.

Ram, peeling her potatoes very prettily, glanced at the still-bleeding Subaru and offered advice.

"You handle a knife poorly, Barusu. You're cutting yourself because you're moving the knife, not the vegetable. When peeling, keep the knife steady and rotate the vegetable around."

Her form was excellent; her peelings had no interruptions from head to tip. She continued, "I will have you know, my specialty is steamed potatoes."

"You actually looked proud when you said that! Damn it, just watch. My beloved blade Shooting Star will put you in your place!"

Frustrated, he picked up the knife and tightly grasped the wooden handle. It was a completely ordinary knife for peeling, but from that day onward, it would be Subaru's precious Shooting Star.

"Uoaaah—!"

Raising his voice, he hunched over and held the knife steady, rotating the vegetable just as Ram had advised. The first cut was still rather deep, but he was surprised inside at how smoothly the rest went.

When he glanced over, he saw Ram looking proud of Subaru doing as she had instructed.

Genuinely grateful, Subaru concentrated on peeling without a word, when suddenly—

"...What? If you stare at me like that I'm gonna start blushing."

Subaru looked up when he realized it was Rem who was staring at him. Rem looked slightly taken aback as she tried to counter. But whatever she was trying to say, Ram's words interrupted.

"—She is staring at how pathetic you look, Barusu. In particular, your head is quite lacking."

Her words made Subaru tilt his head.

"I thought this haircut was a lot better than it used to be, though..."

"At the very least, it deserves a failing grade, given that you are a servant... Right, Rem?"

"...Ah, yes. I suppose so. It does seem just a tiny bit lacking."

"Looks like it really bothers you! Geez, sorry!"

Their plainspoken low assessment of the work he'd taken some pride in put Subaru down a bit. As Ram watched Subaru, she made a *hmph* noise through her nose.

"Incidentally, Rem handles people's hair here at the manor. She dresses me and does my hair every morning, you see?"

"Yeah, that's how you twins are the spitting image of... Wait, that sounds wrong?"

The way she said it just then made it sound like Ram did all the work by herself. But faced with Subaru's retort, Ram folded her arms and boldly replied.

"It is exactly as you think, Barusu."

"Help out your little sister a bit, geez!"

Ram's boldly declaring herself to be the good-for-nothing older sister made Subaru shout with a look of feigned shock. Then, Ram stroked the pink hair that Rem had combed, looking at her younger sister.

"Rem, would you mind giving Barusu's hair a little cut?"

"Now hold on, having a girl playing with my hair is really gonna throw me off here!"

"Sister...?"

Ram's sudden suggestion threw off both Subaru and Rem. Ram trained her red eyes on her sister's questioning look, slightly lowering the tone of her voice.

"…You were looking at Barusu because of his hair, yes?"

"…Yes, that is correct. A little combing and styling would make it look much better."

"You should let her do as she says, then. Rem's hands are heavenly, I assure you."

"That makes it sound like a kind of perverted request, you know…"

It seemed like the older sister was giving Rem the excuse to indulge in her unexpressed interest.

Maybe it was an issue of personalities. Unlike Ram, already giving Subaru no quarter, Rem apparently hadn't decided yet how she should act toward him. Subaru agreed with the need to close the distance, but…

"If you don't want to, then you don't have to. I kind of hope you do, though!"

"No, not at all. It is true that it bothers me slightly, very slightly, just a little."

Knowing that it was *really* bothering her, Subaru lost more confidence. He thought he was just indulging in *his* individuality—but with such thoughts on his mind, three voices sounded as one.

"—Ah."

The edge of Shooting Star shifted from a potato to Subaru's thumb. Subaru yelled out as he shallowly peeled the wrong kind of skin.

"Whoaa! Oh man! It took off a little—!"

"It seems it is displeased to be called your 'beloved knife.' Since your love is so one-sided, perhaps you should try calling it your favorite knife instead?"

"Sister, the water is boiling, so let's put in the vegetables you cut—"

"You two love hazing the new guy, don't you?!"

Their prioritizing of the work was admirable, but Subaru lacked the mental strength to praise it.

9

—And so, half a day flew by.

"So tired—!"

As Subaru spoke, he flopped completely onto the bed, all his strength exhausted.

He was in the servants' quarters he'd been given. From that day onward, it would serve as Subaru's private quarters and sleeping space. It was a frugal room with a cheap bed, desk, and chair, so of course it lagged far behind the standards of the guest room where he'd been a patient.

"Well, the expensive stuff is really stifling, so this is A-OK…"

Burying his face into the pillow, he decided it still smelled and felt up to high-class standards. Now that he was off work, Subaru quickly changed from his uniform to his tracksuit, intending to go to sleep in clothes that he was more accustomed to.

"Man, they worked me to the bone. Work's hard work. I seriously get why Dad and they are so awesome in the working world. Even one day of this is nothing to sneeze at."

He let out honest admiration as he loosened his creaky body, thinking back on his first day at work.

Sure, there were lots of little details he didn't know, but he was still depressed at how bad a job he'd done.

The saving grace was perhaps Ram's attitude as an instructor.

"She's blunt and to the point, but she's gentler and more polite than I expected, really… Ah?"

He lifted his face at the abrupt knock on the door. As he did so, he heard a voice from the door's direction.

"It's Rem. Subaru, is now a good time?"

"Ah, sure, sure. I'm not doing anything weird, so come on in!"

"That makes it sound more suspicious rather than less, but pardon me."

Rem opened the door and entered the room, still dressed in her maid outfit. For a moment, Subaru raised his eyebrows at Rem's visit, but he understood the reason as soon as he saw the black jacket she had in her hands.

"Wait, you don't mean you're done already? This redefines the words *fast job*."

"It is nothing so grand as re-tailoring it altogether. I would have to take more care if it were one of Master Roswaal's outfits, but this will do for you."

"That made it sound like you, um, really cut corners?"

Rem made no reply as he took the jacket, briskly opening it and putting his arms through the sleeves. Before, the outfit's armpits were too tight and his shoulders could barely rotate, but…

"I hate to admit it, but you did it perfectly. My arms can go round and round… Ah, does it look good on me?"

"When combined with the rarity of your gray-colored clothing, nobody else's strange outfits could compare."

"Okay, that didn't sound like a compliment. Guess even I can tell that much!"

Having the manservant's jacket over a T-shirt made Rem's assessment a natural one. Indeed, it must have taken considerable effort not to laugh. But…

"What shall we do about the cuffs?"

"Cuffs… Ah, you mean for the pants. Crap, I forgot. With a needle and thread I could do it myself, though."

"I have brought some with me. Shall I adjust them now?"

It was a good-faith suggestion with no apparent ill will from Rem's side. She'd slipped in some choice words with it, but that was her style, so he let it slide.

Either way, Subaru wanted to repay the favor somehow.

"Okay, hand the needle and thread over here. My sewing skills are gonna get a whole new grade today!"

"I should expect more from the person who had showed such dexterity while struggling to peel vegetables for dinner today?"

"Keh-keh, underestimate me while you can. And by all means, prepare to be shocked!"

Looking like she was giving up on Subaru, sky-high with confidence, Rem took a fantasy-world sewing kit out of a pocket and handed it to him. He took it, finding that the contents matched up pretty nicely with what he could expect from home. With a practiced hand, he passed the thread through the needle and pulled the cuffs of the trousers up over his knees.

"Mmm, hmm, *mm-hmm*."

As Subaru made a singsong sound, Rem let out a sigh of admiration.

"...I am shocked. You really do have experience."

Subaru moved the needle in a brisk, lively fashion. Before he finished humming, he pulled it up.

"Okay, one side done. Take a good look. I sewed it right, didn't I?"

Subaru stretched out the pants to show off his own work. Rem drew in her chin in plain acknowledgment.

His mood improved by the reaction, Subaru began working on the other cuff when Rem spoke abruptly.

"Ah...Subaru, about the conversation at noontime..."

"Mm, noon? Noon, what happened then?"

"Ah...er, if you have forgotten, it's quite all right."

Rem made a small shake of her head in front of Subaru, who still had his head down. Narrowing his eyes at her reaction, he recalled that they'd discussed fixing his hair when preparing dinner.

"Oh, about the hair? I half thought that was a joke. You gonna do it?"

"No, I just thought it was very impertinent of me. You may be a coworker, but you are also Lady Emilia's savior, so our positions are different."

"That kind of stiff attitude will just crimp my style... Wait, that's what you think?"

Her statement, that she couldn't treat him as a simple coworker because they stood apart, stuck in his ears.

Seeing Rem raise her eyebrows at the question, Subaru began roughly tugging on the hair on his head.

"To be honest, I'm not good at picking up on stuff like that. Sorry to...make you worry about it."

"No, I am simply saying it cannot be helped. Please forget about it."

"I can't just let that go so easily. People are petty like that. Now, then..."

Subaru put a hand to his forehead, lowering his eyes as he looked at Rem. She seemed not so much regretful about her slip of the tongue as she seemed chastened by Subaru's admonition. That helped him decide what to say.

Subaru lifted a finger as he made a suggestion.

"Okay, I'll give you my one condition. If you're okay with that, I'll totally forget what you just said."

Rem closed her eyes briefly before nodding with a look of resignation.

"Condition...you say? I understand. I will hear you out."

Subaru made a strained smile, not intending to draw out that big a reaction, and then said...

"If you fix up my hair and give it a little brushing, I'll forgive you."

"..."

Unable to take Rem's silence in the face of his counteroffer, Subaru raised his voice.

"The silence is kind of painful to me here, you know."

Rem's pale blue eyes reflected Subaru in them as she sighed a little.

"Lady Emilia already pointed this out, but you desire very little, Subaru."

"That's weird. I thought we'd be making up instead of you getting all shocked like that..."

"As I have heard from Sister how you gave her perverted looks when you were alone, I was rather resigned to something less decent."

"Slander's a horrible thing!!"

He was scared that Ram's gossipy statement would make sparks fly with Emilia in short order. He'd have to establish a direct lifeline with Emilia before that could happen.

Subaru was still plotting countermeasures against Ram in his head when Rem grasped the hem of her skirt.

"I accept your condition—I shall go along with your idea."

And so, with a prim and proper bow, she accepted his suggestion for smoothing things over.

Her performance drew a laugh out of Subaru as he looked down at his hands.

"Hey, I wrapped up shortening the legs while we were talking. I did it right, huh?"

The work complete, Rem took hold of the trousers, acknowledging his work...

"...Yes, you did. You get full marks for sewing. But much like yourself, I do not think it will be of use, Subaru."

...then poured cold water all over him.

"Huh?! I thought we just made up here?!"

Combined with Subaru's retort, the earlier awkward atmosphere had fully lifted.

Subaru returned the sewing kit to Rem before stroking his own forehead.

"So, about my hair...when do you wanna do it? It's tough to do it today 'cause it's so late."

"That is true. I would like to get it done as soon as possible, but I will be working in the evening for several days...unfortunately."

"We'll just have to make the time. Man, it's really been a while since I had my hair styled!"

He'd been cutting his own hair since he got into middle school, nearly five full years earlier. He was good enough to do it by touch without using a mirror.

"Well then, it is getting late, so I will excuse myself. You will be working in the morning as well. Can you wake up on time on your own?"

"Honestly, not all that sure there. I'm good at waking up if I have a clock, but there's nothing like that here, so maybe not? Don't you have roosters or something?"

Faced with Subaru's unreliable reply, Rem reluctantly launched him a life raft.

"...This seems severe, so Sister or I shall wake you in the morning."

"Seriously? I feel bad to use my seniors in place of a clock, but..."

"It shall do us no good to have you sleep into the afternoon, after all."

"What kind of oversleeper do you take me for?!"

"Someone who could sleep away the entire day, I imagine?"

It took a while for Subaru to realize that this was a joke, by Rem's standards.

After the banter, Subaru thanked Rem as she left for accepting his suggestion.

She passed through the doorway and waved a hand as she went out of sight.

"Whatever comes out of their mouths, they're sisters through and through, huh."

Rem was superficially polite as she slipped in the dagger; Ram was arrogant. But just the same, they were considerate to the point of overbearing, something Subaru thought was highly desirable in coworkers.

10

—Later.

"*So* then, how was Subaru after all that?"

It was evening—the sun had already set in the west, just as the crescent moon took its place in the night sky—when the secret report took place.

It was a large room. The center had a table and tall chairs for receiving guests; farther within, the room was furnished with a chair and desk for its owner to conduct his writing affairs. The ebony desk had sheets and feather pens strewn over it, beside which stood a cup that was still steaming, a gentle aroma wafting up from it.

This was the uppermost floor in Roswaal Manor's main wing, the private study of its lord, Roswaal L. Mathers.

His voice was like a whisper, but it reached its mark with no difficulty. Of course it did.

The small body of Roswaal's speaking companion was sitting right across his lap.

"It's been five days since that spectacle—time enough for you to see how this shaaall proceed?"

"I suppose so— He is no good."

Ram heard her master's voice in her ear as he stroked her pink hair. Roswaal and Ram were the only two people in the room; there was no sign of the twin's "other half," Rem.

Put simply, that day's report was about the issue of Subaru and Ram's education of him. With her stating that his education was going most poorly, Roswaal stared for a moment before laughing.

"Ahaaa, is that so. Completely useless?"

"Barusu really can do nothing at all. He's no good at cooking, clumsy at cleaning, and the very thought of entrusting laundry to him disturbs me. He's oddly skilled at sewing, but besides that, nothing can be left to him alone."

"In a place with so many girls, that, too, is a grave matter, is it nooot?"

At that age it cannot be helped, Ram seemed to say with a strained smile, looking up at her master as she thought back on the details of the previous four days. In that brief but vivid time, even a stranger would have noticed the grimace replacing Ram's graceful, neutral expression.

"It is quite raaare to see such a face on you. Is he so worthless?"

"Worthless through and through. It is not that he is clumsy; it is that he does not know. I cannot but think he was raised poorly. However, he is also lacking in culture."

"So haaard on him."

Roswaal held back a laugh. Ram sighed a little, shifted her position in her master's arms, and sank farther against him. He gave Ram's pink hair a good stroke with his palm.

"So, Ram, the important part— Do you think he is involved?"

Roswaal maintained his smile, his tone of voice unchanged from before. The subject was unstated, but she knew what he wanted to hear. Ram closed her eyes, thinking for a little while.

"I cannot rule it out, but I think the possibility is low."

"Hmmmm. Why is that?"

"He stands out too much to have been sent to infiltrate this House… Not in a good or b… No, in an especially bad way… In the first place, Barusu himself is…"

The words seem to pour out of her mouth.

It was, in a fashion, a reply to his question, so Roswaal greeted her answer with a satisfied smile. It was the smile of a master that said: *It makes perfect sense.* Though the smile was not being sent her way precisely, Ram realized her cheeks were burning nonetheless.

"I see, and I must agree with that. Meaning he truly is a benevolent bystander."

As Roswaal spoke, the chair creaked as he shifted positions. He

turned opposite to the desk, straight toward the large window through which shone the moonlight.

Roswaal's oddly colored eyes seemed to twinkle; the corners of his lips rose at the scene below.

"I muuust say, he certainly doooes not discourage easily."

The private study overlooked the manor's garden. There, in one corner of it, he saw a black-haired boy speaking and laughing with a silver-haired girl. As was typical, the young man made one-sided conversation, but the girl didn't seem to mind.

"How chaaarming. I no longer possess such passion."

His words were like a soliloquy, but Ram looked into Roswaal's eyes from close up as she replied.

"Women are happy when they're pursued."

But in contrast to the luster in her eyes, Roswaal's eyes narrowed in a teasing look.

"Perhaps you measure Subaru higher than I thought?"

"...He is no good at all, but I do not think poorly of him. He knows nothing related to the work, but what he simply does not know, he can be taught."

Responding to the dissatisfaction in Ram's eyes and her chilly voice, Roswaal used the hand with which he had brushed her hair to caress her cheek. Ram seemed too enchanted to speak as Roswaal pondered her reply.

It was rare for Ram to speak of others like this.

Her unexpressed counsel to her master was, *Let us get to know him better.* It seemed the two maids were quite fond of the black-haired young man. *There is beauty in enthusiasm,* Roswaal thought with a nod.

"Based on my position, I shooould probably intercede, yeees?"

Roswaal commented as he looked down on the cute rendezvous in the garden with his yellow eye alone.

"Both are such children. Nothing will happen regardless."

"You do have a point."

Faint laughter filled the private study as they pulled the curtain over the window overlooking the rendezvous between the boy and girl below.

—What happened after that, not even the moon was given the privilege to see.

11

With the moon still lingering in the center of the night sky, Subaru was full of optimism.

He stretched out the wrinkles visible through his manservant outfit's sleeves and checked how he looked in the window. It'd already been four days since he was wearing these clothes, so he thought it was about time he felt used to them.

"Not bad, not bad at all. I can do this. Right out of the bath, I look fifty percent sexier in the mirror. I feel like this is gonna work!"

Whether it was objectively 50 percent was another question, but it was important to reassure himself.

Trying to at least surround himself with an attractive aura, Subaru took a long, shallow breath and stepped forward. He was walking on the shortly mowed grass of the garden, heading for a green-covered corner lined by high trees, a place where the blessings of the moon were all the more remarkable.

There sat a girl, her silver hair twinkling in the moonlight as a pale light surrounded her.

Subaru now knew that the firefly-like pale glow actually came from spirits. That fact added to how watching the surreal scene bewitched his heart, like a demoness that wouldn't let go. He unintentionally stopped in place, his breath catching.

Perhaps sensing him, the girl's closed eyes abruptly opened. The two amethyst jewels caught sight of Subaru approaching.

"Oh, hi. R-real coincidence bumping into you like this?"

"You come like this every day, you know. As for coincidence… don't we live under the same roof?"

One glance from being spotted before he could speak threw Subaru off his game; for her part, Emilia sighed at the already typical line from him. Undeterred by his slip, Subaru smiled at Emilia.

"Hearing the words *under the same roof* really gives me a tingling…"

"The word *tingling* really sends a shudder up my spine. For some reason, I don't like it."

With Emilia staring up at him, Subaru scratched his cheek and sat next to her like it was perfectly normal. They were a mere three hands apart, proof that the sense of distance between them had lessened.

Emilia, by now used to Subaru sitting next to her, did not bother to point out the distance.

Between her daily morning ritual and mealtimes, his sitting beside her was something she now took for granted.

It was unclear whether she was silently permitting it or simply giving up on forbidding it, but either way, Subaru was happy to be so close.

"So, what are you doing?"

"Mm? An extension of the morning routine. I can meet most of them in the morning, but I can meet some of them only at night, so..."

Subaru nodded in response, readily accepting Emilia's reply.

He was finally accustomed to living in a world where time was measured in "day" and "night."

Incidentally, daily life over a twenty-four-hour period was largely as one would expect. Living in accordance with the body's internal clock brought a sense of tranquility like nothing else.

His four days of training as a manservant had also been four days acquiring that world's common knowledge. That said, learning servant work came ahead of academics, so his overall comprehension was still rather thin.

"Gives me new perspective looking back on my school days with the weekends off..."

Subaru had often disparaged his Spartan instructor during the last four days. But such one-sided comments from Subaru still furthered the friendly conversations he had with Emilia at night.

Subaru silently watched the side of Emilia's face as if bewitched by the dreamlike scene.

Emilia suddenly commented, perhaps finding it rare for Subaru to be lost for words.

"It's no fun to watch, is it?"

How Emilia somehow sounded apologetic made Subaru sit up and shake his head.

"Nah, I could never be bored being with you, Emilia-tan."

"Wh—"

The straight-hitting statement made Emilia's breath catch as her cheeks reddened. Seeing Emilia's face flushed from the surprise attack made Subaru redden up to his ears.

After all, the line he'd said just then had been the complete, literal truth.

Subaru rapid-fired his words as if trying to explain away his blushing.

"Ah, er, I mean, we hadn't had a chance to settle down and talk for days, right?"

Emilia nodded in full agreement.

"Th-that's right. Seems you've had quite a time learning how to work at the manor… You've been working your heart out, huh?"

"Hearing that makes me so happy I wanna cry…"

Glossing over the atmosphere, they buried that topic in a deep hole and turned it into an unintentionally bittersweet moment.

Assessments of Subaru's work over those four days had been rather harsh, and even if he managed to somehow bribe his superiors, it would not change his score of "totally useless."

Subaru's first job, since he was lacking ability in the domestic fields of cleaning, laundry, and cooking, was to acquire the skills required of a servant at a manor. His current grade for all of the above was stuck at C.

"Shortening the sleeves of my uniform and putting buttons on an apron got me top marks, but that's it."

"You really are exceptional in only one area."

"Well, I tried to grow up to be a guy with an edge instead of perfectly round and flat…"

Subaru's skill at sewing was a product of how his parents had raised him, but he, too, wondered what in the world they'd been thinking.

Emilia, not knowing of Subaru's introspection, gave honest praise for his self-confidence.

"I see, is that so. I'm glad that you're confident in something, too."

Subaru made a rather conflicted smile at the sight of Emilia being happy for him.

"Besides, it's not like you're awful at the other jobs. Ram and Rem keep this quiet, but they have been praising you, you see…"

"Seriously? So I'm making ground even with my seniors here? So, what, cutting myself with the knife, knocking over the bucket, and messing up the laundry, it all raised my relationship points?!"

"I think you should reflect on that just a little."

Emilia made a pained smile at Subaru's stating his glaring failures. Her violet eyes gently narrowed, looking at Subaru, examining him carefully at close range.

"But work's hard every day, isn't it?"

"Super hard, totally tough. It makes me wanna borrow Emilia-tan's arms and breasts and lap for some low-stress healing."

"Yes, yes. If you're making light of it, you must be all right."

Emilia reached with a fingertip and gave Subaru's forehead a light push. Subaru, weak to the pressure, could not resist Emilia's fingertip, making a showy tumble backward onto the grass.

He let out a pleasant sigh as he felt the soothing coolness of the grass and gazed up at the star-filled sky. A world without city lights made Subaru appreciate the beauty of the stars and the moon in the sky more than ever before.

"—The moon's so pretty, isn't it?"

"There are some places you just can't reach, right?"

"I wasn't asking for it at all, and you hit me with something like that?!"

"What, did I say something bad?"

Subaru's attempt at dropping a romantic line fell flat due to cultural differences in a different world. He pressed a hand over his heart to show he was apologetic, startling Emilia.

"Ah…"

"Oh, darn it! I was tryin' to hide that…"

Subaru tried to hide his blushy smile as he moved the hand Emilia was staring at behind his back... The left hand that had borne the brunt of his repeated failures at work.

Subaru stuck out his tongue to try to gloss over it, but Emilia lowered her eyes with a serious look.

"So, everyone else is working hard, too."

Emilia's murmur sounded like she was criticizing herself.

Subaru silently acknowledged what Emilia was thinking as she spoke to herself like that.

Subaru wasn't the only one learning something at Roswaal Manor. Emilia was in the middle of absorbing a wide variety of things that she had to learn as a royal candidate.

Subaru and Emilia were after much different things. To compare the pressure on the two of them was nearly outright rude.

Bearing such heavy burdens must have been exhausting. Perhaps Emilia carried worries that she couldn't discuss with anyone.

Belatedly, Emilia asked a question.

"...How about I cast a healing spell?"

"Nah, it's fine. I'd rather not heal it and leave it like this."

"Why's that?"

"Mm, it's hard to put it into words... It's kinda a sign of how hard I've worked?"

Subaru thought that they weren't typical words coming from him as he strongly clenched his beat-up hand.

"I don't mind working hard as much as I thought I would. Being able to do things I couldn't do before...it ain't bad. It's hard, it's really tough, but it's kinda fun. I mean, Ram and Rem are surprisingly strict, that loli's annoying, seen less of Rozchi than I thought I would, though..."

"Roswaal would probably get prickly if you told him that."

"Nobody uses *prickly* anymore..."

Subaru bent a hip to emphasize his bending the conversation. Then, rising to his feet like a spring-loaded doll, he brought his right hand to his forehead in a tidy salute toward Emilia.

"Well, just need to knock down the problems one by one. I mean, this is the only place for me to live... Either way, it's fun, see?"

In his original world, living "easy" had been just fine with him. But he couldn't expect that kind of peaceful daily life in this world. Hence, Subaru sought as much "ease" as he could.

Having been senselessly tossed into that world, one could call it Subaru's stubbornness toward his fate.

Subaru's display of determination made Emilia's expression freeze like time had stopped. Only her eyes moved, blinking several times over, before a smile suddenly came over her.

"That's right. Yeah, I think that, too... Goodness, Subaru, you're such an idiot."

"Wait, isn't that reaction weird?! Shouldn't we be falling back in love or something?!"

"I wasn't in love to begin with! You really are such a... I'm an idiot, too."

Subaru looked hurt at the exaggerated reaction. Emilia's final murmur never reached him.

Emilia's smile deepened. The softness of her charming smile was as if the earlier pressure on her was long forgotten, like Subaru had unintentionally bewitched her with his own spell.

He couldn't express how Emilia looked at that moment with mere words like *pretty* or *cute*.

"E M D (Emilia-tan's Majorly Divine)!"

"I'm genuinely grateful and you joke about it like *that*...?"

Emilia tapered her lips in a slightly annoyed pout and pushed a finger into Subaru's forehead again.

It was likely not Subaru's mere imagination that these occasional touches carried more warmth than they had before.

"Having said all that...it's nice that you're trying hard, but how'd you get your hand all beat up like that, anyway?"

"Oh, this one's simple. This afternoon, I tagged along when Rem went shopping at the village close to the mansion. The kids were playing around with me when this little dog-ish thing chomped on me."

"So it's not the product of hard work?!"

"Nah, it's so big you can't notice the traces of hard work... I didn't think I was the type animals hated, though..."

Back in his own world, children and little animals loved him—that, or he just looked like a pushover. That made the former result odder still. But his effect on kids was still going strong.

"The village kids... They smacked me, kicked me, and blew snot on me, too. That sucked, damn it."

"Somehow you seem good at looking after little kids, Subaru."

"That's taking it the wrong way, Emilia-tan. Winning them over now means I'll reap the rewards when they grow up. I'm a long-term thinker, see."

"Yes, yes. I will admit you're honest about your petty stubbornness."

Emilia, accustomed to Subaru's silliness, let it roll over her as she stretched and looked up at the sky.

"I'd best return to my room now. How about you?"

"I can't sleep by Emilia-tan's side, so I'll head back, too."

"You get that job only when you've polished your skills with your current work."

"Now you said it. Just watch, they're gonna write legends about me...!"

Subaru took Emilia's words to heart, burning with enthusiasm. Emilia made a strained smile as Subaru looked back and raised a finger.

"Ah, right. Would you come with me tomorrow when I give the village brats some payba—er, a lovey-dovey da—er, go to watch the cute little animals?"

"Why did you correct yourself several times...? And, ah, I..."

Emilia lowered her eyes, seeming hesitant as she murmured, "I don't mind going with you, and I'm curious about that small animal, so..."

"Okay, let's go, then!"

"But it might be troublesome for you to have me with you like..."

"Got it, let's go!"

"...Are you really listening?"

"I'm listening! I could never let a single word or phrase from Emilia-tan escape!"

"Oh, Subaru, I just hate you!"

"Aaa! Aaa! Sorry, what was that?! I can't *hear* you!"

How Subaru covered his ears, spectacularly taking back what he'd said the moment before, made Emilia break out in laughter, all ills forgotten. Then, she wiped a teardrop from her eyes with a finger as she looked at Subaru.

"Goodness…but only after I finish my studying and you finish all your work, Subaru?"

"Oh yeah! Roger that! I'll so totally get them *done*!"

With the date arranged, Subaru made a dramatic fist-pump pose.

Watching Subaru's self-satisfied look, a charming smile came over Emilia as she let out a little sigh.

"I was thinking, watching you makes my worries seem so small, Subaru."

"No way?! I mean, you might become queen; worries and social stress like that would turn my stomach inside out!"

Emilia, unable to hold back any more, burst out laughing, her mirthful voice making Subaru laugh, too.

The two laughing like that announced that their rendezvous for that night had come to an end.

Let it be noted that there was one final exchange.

"Come to think of it, why are you dressed like that after work?"

"Ah, I thought it'd make a good impression on you… So, what do you think? Pretty handsome, huh?"

"Mm, I suppose so. It has that 'I'm a capable servant' look."

"Well, there you go crushing my hopes!"

12

Subaru had his hand on the door, peeking in as he spoke in a casual voice.

"Huh, do you actually sleep right, loli girl? If you stay up too late, you won't grow as tall as you should and you'll end up as an adult that short."

Beatrice replied with resentment in her voice.

"…Do you breach the Passage as if it is a matter of course, I wonder?"

She sat on the wooden stool well within the archive as she glared at Subaru.

"Did you have a reason to come see me, I wonder?"

"Not really. I thought I'd say hi before I went to bed. I was gonna give up if I didn't get it in three tries, but I got it in one, so…"

"Truly, what kind of intuition do you have…?"

Beatrice had a tired look as she pulled on one of her rolls. When her fingers released it, the stretchy, elastic roll bounced the other way. The sight struck Subaru profoundly.

"Can I try it, too?"

"Only Puckie may touch the likes of *me*… Would you go away already, I wonder?"

"Not fair only you get to play. Oh well. I'm in a good mood, so I'll forgive you."

Still buoyant from the promised date, Subaru headed out as Beatrice glowered at him. But the moment before the door closed, he thought he heard a voice speak with a lonely echo.

"—That has nothing to do with me."

The voice tugged at him.

"Huh, gotta open the door so I can give her a good comeback."

The once-open door to the secret archive now led to a simple guest room once more.

He tried opening and closing the door in front of him to see if he could catch it connecting to the archive again.

Rem looked beside herself as she watched Subaru there, opening and closing the door.

"…What have you been doing? Checking the condition of the lock?"

"Oh yeah, I thought I heard a creak in the hall the last few nights… So that was you, Rem?"

Rem was carrying a silver tray with nothing on it in one hand as she watched Subaru feel up the door.

"Is something bothering you?"

"Nah, this led to the archive of forbidden books with the loli girl till just now; it's gone, though."

"Did you want something from Lady Beatrice? You could ask me if you prefer...?"

"Just saying hi before going to sleep. Nothing...big."

The phrase he heard from Beatrice just before the door closed was on Subaru's mind, but he shook his head—it wasn't something he needed to press her about at the moment.

"What, you're still working, Rem? Better turn in. Morning's coming quickly."

"I'll sleep after I do the dishes. At the moment, Sister is serving tea to Master Roswaal, you see."

"What the heck are those two doing at a time— Ah, well, that's fine."

It was almost past midnight; he didn't much care for Roswaal and Ram having a private chat, discussing some lively topic between just the two of them.

Not my business to say, though, Subaru reflected. He suddenly realized that Rem was watching him. Her pale blue eyes were staring in the direction of his head.

"Don't suppose chances like this come up much. Doesn't look like it bothers you any, though."

"...No, until now it has not bothered me that much, or somewhat, or even a little bit."

"Geez, downplaying a bunch of times back-to-back makes it sound like it *really* bothers you!"

The sharpness and intensity of Rem's gaze increased to the point that his capacity for speech faltered.

Subaru wrapped up work rather late and Rem had been constantly busy, so few opportunities presented themselves. *What the heck,* thought Subaru with a grimace when Rem raised her hand a bit.

"If you like, how about I do it now?"

"What... Now? It's pretty late, isn't it?"

"A quick cut and wash will not take very long. If I do not, I cannot fulfill the cherished desire you confided in me from your own lips, Subaru."

"*Cherished desire* is a little much!"

For such a neutral expression, Subaru saw Rem's eyes brimming with fierce determination. Subaru scratched his face, realizing it must have annoyed her quite a bit over the last four days.

He wanted to do something about that annoyance if he could, but—

"Sorry, Rem. I've made a promise to go out with Emilia tomorrow. I've gotta get up early and take care of work quickly, so I really can't do it tonight..."

"Is that so... No, I was being unreasonable. I'm sorry."

Using the just-made promise as his reason for putting off the promise he'd made to Rem before, at his own suggestion, weighed on his conscience. But Rem was a practical girl and tried to take Subaru's circumstances into account.

Feeling guilty about Rem's position, Subaru felt his words left a bitter taste in his own mouth when suddenly, "How about tomorrow night?"

"...At night, you say?"

"My condition for the promise with Emilia is getting all my work wrapped up. There's no special work scheduled for tomorrow afternoon, so after that, since it's still on your mind..."

As he spoke, he was truly shocked with himself for arranging dates with two girls on the same day. Not that his feelings toward Emilia and Rem were in the same vein to begin with...

With Rem, he felt fondness toward a fellow coworker. He still didn't really know how he felt toward Emilia.

Faced with Subaru's suggestion, Rem closed her eyes and made a small nod.

"Understood. Tomorrow night it is. This is a firm promise, you understand?"

"I don't know why it bothers you *that* much, but yeah, a promise it is. Tomorrow night, then."

He thought about making it a pinkie promise, but he hesitated, not knowing if such a thing existed in that world's customs. As he hesitated, Rem made a polite bow, turning around with a small flutter of her skirt.

She departed with quiet, gliding steps. Subaru watched her go before heading back to his room, biting down a yawn as he mentally went over his schedule for the coming day.

"I have to thank the kids for creating the reason for a date all the way to the village tomorrow. Oh, before I do that, got to find out where the best flower gardens are…"

As he entered his room, he held his nose high and puffed out his chest, full of hopes and dreams for the coming day. Subaru stripped off his butler uniform, giving himself a makeover with the tracksuit as he crawled into bed.

As his head hit the pillow, his eyes were open, thoughts racing about the next day, not conducive to sleep at all.

Faced with his mind betraying his body, Subaru immediately switched mental gears and resorted to his secret weapon. Namely…

"One Puck, two Pucks…"

In the back of his mind, little gray kitty cats were running around and frolicking as he counted them one by one. Subaru linked his fantasy Puck to the real one, letting his memory of the fluffy feline lead him to a happy place. His mind slowly sank, pulled into dreamland.

"One…hundred and four Pucks…"

Picturing a fluffy paradise, warmth enveloped his mind—and finally vanished.

13

As Subaru awoke, he felt like his consciousness was rising as if poking his head through the water's surface.

Suddenly released from the suffocating feeling, his eyes opened, waiting several seconds to take in the world. He felt like he'd woken up in a different place than where he'd gone to bed.

He felt sunlight burning his eyes. Subaru sat up his slightly sluggish body and shook his head.

His head was a bit heavy. Perhaps he was tired from not being entirely used to his new life yet.

But this was not the day for such weak thoughts.

Wide-awake, Subaru went over the date promise he'd made with Emilia the night before. "That's right, Subaru Natsuki—today's the time to leap into action!"

The day was a day with a happy future. A day he'd awakened to crisply, a day of promised victory. But…

"—"

Pink-haired and blue-haired twin sisters looked upon Subaru's determined face in surprise.

Subaru, blushing to the tips of his ears, buried his face in the pillow to hide it.

"What! You were there?! Then you should've said something! Aw man, I'm so, so embarrassed!"

The fact that they'd stopped rousing him awake two days before made him careless. To think that both of them would visit on that particular morning…

As usual, the twins' expressions did not change much as Subaru groaned on top of the bedding. Though it did seem like they were fighting the temptation to point at him and break out laughing.

"Er, hold on, you two. I mean, that reaction kinda hurts. I'm a delicate soul here. There are other reactions, right?!"

He was looking forward to their at least engaging in the cold verbal abuse to which he was accustomed.

—Subaru realized afterward that it was quite awful for him to actually be *looking forward* to the verbal abuse.

"Sister, Sister. He's greeting us as if he knows us somehow."

"Rem, Rem. He's greeting us in a very chummy fashion."

It didn't feel right. Their murmurs brushed against something in the back of Subaru's mind.

"Er, ah? Something weird? My seniors coming to wake me up is one thing, but playing pranks on me is bad taste, you know?"

Certainly the two were always blunt, but—something felt off.

As Subaru spoke, he began to realize why he felt that something was off with them.

—Their eyes.

The way they looked at Subaru. The familiarity from the previous night was gone; they'd gone back to treating him like a complete stranger. Then, decisive proof came flying at him.

"Sister, Sister. Our Dear Guest seems to be a little confused?"

"Rem, Rem. Our Dear Guest seems to be a little touched in the head."

—Subaru was aghast at being called "Dear Guest."

The polite echo made Subaru feel like something sharp had gouged out the back of his stomach.

Subaru pressed a hand to his chest to hold back the phantom pain. He didn't know what it all meant. Their reactions, it was as if—

"You two... Ha-ha, this really isn't...funny..."

With both of them still looking at him like a complete stranger, Subaru abruptly brought up his left hand to block them from his view. But Subaru instantly regretted doing so...

...because he saw that the bandage on his left hand was gone.

The rough fingertips from kitchen work, the callouses from handling knives in ways he wasn't used to, the bite marks from the puppy that had bitten him while the children toyed with him—they, too, were gone.

—Somewhere distant, he heard what sounded like a bell tolling.

The ringing came over him in a rush, crashing against him over and over again like a wave.

Subaru didn't realize that the pain that came with the sound was from him pulling out his own hair.

The temple of his head really hurt; he felt a hot, nauseous feeling in his nose. But Subaru's mind focused instead on the sharp pain and taste of blood from biting his own lip, as if he were using it to drown out the sense of loss that felt like someone had carved out his internal organs.

The facts at hand forced Subaru to accept reality.

Feeling his eyes grow hot inside, Subaru buried his face in the pillow for an entirely different reason than before.

—For he absolutely, absolutely did not want anyone to see his face at that moment.

Not the people he'd grown so fond of.

Not the people who'd seemed to grow so fond of him.

He absolutely didn't want to cry in front of people looking at him like he was a stranger.

"Why'd I…go back?!"

—And so, Subaru was dragged back into the loop anomaly that had brought him so much suffering.

For the second time, his first day at Roswaal Manor began—

CHAPTER 3
THE SOUND OF THE CHAIN

1

"Dear Guest, Dear Guest. You look rather unwell. Are you all right?"

"Dear Guest, Dear Guest. You look like your stomach hurts; did you soil yourself?"

As Subaru hung his head in shame, the sisters called out with voices of concern.

They were familiar voices, even after such a short time. The voices were sometimes annoying, sometimes relieving, voices that he could trust.

—But now those voices sounded entirely different, ringing harshly against Subaru's eardrums.

Responding to the feel of their gazes, Subaru put his breathing in order and lifted his face.

"Sorry to…make you worry. I'm just a bit…dense when I'm waking up."

Somehow, the rage surging within him had dissipated while he pressed his face into the bedding. Though the initial shock had subsided, he felt as if he were bound with silk string, a sense of loss that made him feel a sob rising from his chest.

—Thinking how wonderful and infuriating it would be if only this was all just some mischievous trick Roswaal was playing on him. The pretense in his own mind making him feel somewhat better, Subaru opened his eyes and looked straight ahead.

"—Ah, that's right."

After an instant, the blurry world became clear and reality forced itself upon the young boy.

Subaru saw the twins standing on both sides of the bed, their hands on the bedding. The familiar faces of Ram and Rem were gazing expressionlessly at Subaru, as per usual.

Neither pair of eyes contained any emotion toward Subaru whatsoever. The four days that he had lived with them, growing closer to each other bit by bit, had evaporated like morning mist.

"Dear Guest—?"

With bewildered voices, both of their lips wove the words in unison.

Their gazes chased after Subaru, now sitting up in bed. But Subaru, seemingly feeling a chill in the air, obeyed his feeling of unease and rose in great haste, putting distance between them.

"Dear Guest, you mustn't move suddenly. You are not yet well rested…"

"Dear Guest, it's dangerous to move suddenly. You have not yet soundly rested…"

Subaru's body reflexively pulled back from the two girls and their concerned voices. The cold response made their eyes tighten with hurt looks, but Subaru was too frantic to notice such a thing.

He was having a very hard time dealing with the feeling that he knew them but they did not, in turn, know him.

It was only a few days prior that Subaru had the same feeling in the busy street, the back alley, and the dilapidated shop.

But it was completely different now. The situation was different. The time was different. The experience was different.

It wasn't like when he'd redone things with Emilia and Felt when he'd barely known them.

Certainly he'd done some arm-twisting to redo things with the people he trusted. But now, faced with having people he knew turn back into strangers, Subaru was gripped by an unshakable, faceless terror.

The maid twins before Subaru's frightened eyes had begun to sense that something was terribly wrong.

Silence descended upon the room. Neither side could say or do anything. That was why...

"Sorry—I can't do this right now!"

...Subaru's action, gripping the doorknob and practically falling into the hallway as he rushed out, was just a moment faster than the twins' move to stop him.

Subaru ran, the bare soles of his feet soaking up the cold of the hallway, drawing heavy, ragged breaths as he went. He ran fiercely, in a daze, with no particular destination in mind.

He ran. He fled. Yet he didn't comprehend what he was running *from*.

All he knew was that he couldn't bear to remain in that place a moment longer.

Subaru ran down a corridor lined with similar-looking doors, his strides still tenuous, like he was about to fall over at any moment.

Then, out of breath, Subaru put his hands on a door as if it led right to it—

—and, as he tumbled in, he was greeted by the great mass of bookshelves in the archive of forbidden books.

2

With the door shut behind him, the archive was completely sealed off from the outside world.

The only remaining way to intrude into the room from the outside was to open every single door in the entire mansion.

Subaru no longer sensed pursuit. He slumped his shoulders, leaned back against the door, and sank to the floor.

He wasn't squatting, and yet, his knees were shaking. So were the fingers he stretched out to try to hold them in place.

"If I were playing paper sumo, I'd cut some crazy lines right about now, ha-ha..."

Even his self-mockery had no bite to it. His dry smile seemed to contain nothing but hollowness.

The scent of old paper in the air of the calm archive gently sprinkled a sense of ease and tranquility into Subaru's mind. Though Subaru knew it was shallow comfort, it was the only thing he had to cling to at the time.

One after the other, after another...he desperately took deep big breaths.

As Subaru gasped like a fish out of water, a scornful voice spoke from within the archive.

"—Quite a rude thing you are, barging in without so much as a knock."

There was a footstool sitting straight ahead from the entrance, well inside the dimly lit room. A girl sat upon it.

It was Beatrice, guardian of the archive of forbidden books, keeping her distance from Subaru, the same as always, not a single hair of difference.

With a loud sound, Beatrice closed the book, altogether too large for her tiny body, and looked at Subaru.

"I wonder, how do you breach the Passage...? This makes twice now."

"Sorry, a little while is fine, so let me stay here a bit. Please."

Subaru put his hands together, bowed his head in supplication, and closed his eyes without waiting for her reply.

—*This is a quiet place with no one here to bother me. I've gotta get a grip on the facts. What's my name, where am I, who are the two twins from earlier? What's the name of the girl in front of me, and who is she? This weird room? The four days I spent? The promise I made, to be with someone, tomorrow, who—*

"Oh yeah, Emilia..."

He recalled her silver hair, twinkling under the moonlight, her bashful smile...

He remembered the promise he had made with Emilia, with the moon and the starry sky shining above them...

"Beatrice…"

"…Are we close enough for you to be calling my name, I wonder?"

"You said I breached the Passage just now, and once before, too?"

Beatrice made a sour look at being addressed like an acquaintance and having a question foisted upon her. However, Beatrice valiantly maintained her poise as she replied, "You and your thick skull barged in here not three or four hours ago."

"The time I came in, messing with your setup, and you got mad so you bullied me. Got it."

Though there was no strength behind it, he did not neglect his sarcasm toward Beatrice, getting further under her skin.

—Subaru had encountered Beatrice three to four hours earlier, she'd said.

Her words could only mean when he had first awakened at Roswaal Manor, when Subaru had, without any thought whatsoever, broken through the looping corridor on his first try. When he next awoke that morning, Ram and Rem were in front of the bed.

"In other words, this is the…second time I woke up in the manor, then."

Subaru gathered up memories from all over the place to piece together his circumstances.

The only time the twins had both been present when Subaru woke was *that* morning. They'd alternated after that. Furthermore, the first day was the only time when he'd had the social status to use the bed in the guest room.

"In other words, I went five days ahead, and I've gone four days back…?"

Just like in the royal capital, Subaru had gone back in time. That summed up his present situation.

But understanding it was one thing; accepting it was something else.

Subaru clutched his head and tried to think of what could cause him to go back in time.

When Subaru had gone back in time at the royal capital, it was triggered by death, which he'd dubbed Return by Death. He'd decided that, having died three times over before saving Emilia, he'd left that loop behind.

In point of fact, he'd spent five days at Roswaal Manor in absolute peace and quiet, hadn't he?

And then, poof, suddenly going back in time—he hadn't received any warning whatsoever.

"Did the conditions change from before…? I made myself think dying sent me back, but maybe it goes back on auto after one week…? No, if that were the case, then…"

If that was so, there was no reason for him to have awoken on the first day at Roswaal Manor at all.

The principles underpinning going back in time remained unclear, but loops like the one at the royal capital surely followed certain rules.

One rule was definitely the place where you were reborn. If Subaru hadn't been freed from that loop, he should have awoken right in front of the owner of the fruit shop with the scarred face, as he had three times over.

"But it wasn't a scarred middle-aged man, it was those angelic maids. Guess I've moved on up…"

That part made him feel like he'd traded Hell for Heaven.

With several pats, Subaru felt up his own body and ensured that he was uninjured. You wouldn't think anything had happened.

"But if I died, how did I die? Everything was normal before I slept during the fourth night. At any rate, it didn't feel like any situation I'd die in my sleep before reaching the fifth day."

He wondered if instant death without any conscious knowledge of it whatsoever was truly possible.

He tried to picture dying from poison or gas in his sleep, but that meant being assassinated.

There was no reason anyone would assassinate Subaru, so the preliminary conditions simply hadn't been met.

"So does that mean it's a forced loop unless I reach clear conditions…?"

If you looked at it like a game, it was like a Game Over that happened if you didn't trigger the necessary flags.

Not knowing who'd put up the flags or why was bad enough, but not knowing the triggers—that was pretty dismal game design.

"Besides, I'm the kind of gamer who gives up quickly and runs off to read a strategy guide…"

A scornful smile came over Beatrice as she watched Subaru sink into an ocean of introspection. She sounded bored when she spoke.

"It's become rather boring around here with all the mumbling you've been doing. Death this, life that—this is why humans are so boring, I suppose. It's all deceits and conceits to the very end. This is why I can't hold a conversation with your kind."

It was a blunt, even cruel way of blowing him off. But Subaru was relieved that Beatrice's attitude hadn't changed a bit. He rose up, dusting off his rump as he turned to face the door.

"Leaving, I suppose?"

"There're some things I've gotta figure out. I'll leave moping around for sometime later. Thanks."

"I have done nothing at all… Would you leave already, I wonder? I really must readjust the Passage."

Though there was not even a sliver of gentleness in her tone, for some reason, Subaru found that reassuring.

Beatrice herself may not have had any such intention, but Subaru felt like her words were pushing him onward. He twisted the doorknob; a cool breeze blew as he took his first step outside.

The wind made his short hair sway; he covered his face with an arm as he felt a faint prickling in his eyes.

Then, the wind stopped, he felt grass under his bare feet, and his breath caught a bit as he spotted the silver-haired girl in the garden, making his heart leap for joy.

"Ahh, she really is so radiant."

Well, this is a nice touch, he thought, internally pouring out a string of invectives at the cheeky guardian of the archive.

"—Subaru!"

Upon noticing Subaru, the girl's violet eyes opened wide as she urgently rushed to his side. Those three bell-like syllables pouring from her lips were in the highest pitch she could make.

Subaru spontaneously shifted his feet toward the fast-approaching girl. As she gazed at him from head to toe, the corners of her eyes descended in relief. But she immediately snapped back to her senses and returned to her normal look.

"Don't make me worry like that. Ram and Rem were really worked up, running all around the mansion making a big fuss because you ran off right after you woke up."

"Rare for them to get that worked up, huh. And sorry. Beatrice held me up for a bit."

"Again? I heard she picked on you once already before I got up, but…"

As Emilia's beautiful face drew near with an expression of concern, her defenseless look made Subaru reach out his hand to her, as if his own weak heart were trying to cling to her for support.

But it was far too abrupt a place for it. If he did that, calming down in the archive would lose all meaning. It wasn't his goal to make a scapegoat out of Beatrice.

All Subaru could do, seeing Emilia's anxious face, was respond with a vague expression.

It wasn't very Subaru-like behavior, but Emilia's formality didn't permit her to dig much deeper.

Of course it didn't. Emilia hadn't spent a single hour with this Subaru since meeting him; there was no way she could know that.

The four carefree days Subaru and Emilia had spent together had been tossed into the gutter; four carefree days that had really happened, that Subaru knew but Emilia did not.

"What is it? Is there something on my face?"

"Yeah, there are cute eyes, nose, ears, and mouth all over your face… Er, I'm glad that you're all right."

Emilia's face, scowling as if to complain about the initial sweet talk, immediately nodded at the last part.

"Yes, I'm quite all right, because you protected me. How about your condition, Subaru?"

"Ah, all good, all good. Thanks to blood loss, mana drain, and the shock from when I woke up, I'm a bit weak and my mind feels like it's been beaten with a bat, but I'm feeling good!"

"I see, that's won— Eh? That sounds like you've been taking a beating all over..."

"I'm *fine*. See?"

He spread out both arms and turned all around to show Emilia that he was in good health.

He did seem to be returning to top form, bit by tiny bit. The gears were turning, the tongue was moistening the lips; he had to start being Subaru Natsuki.

"Well, that's fine and good... Er, are you going back to the mansion? I have a little bit of business, actually."

"Ah, chat time with the spirits, huh? I won't be in the way, so can I stay? And lend Puck to me, would you?"

Emilia tilted her head and spoke as if speaking down to a child.

"That's fine, but you *really* have to stay out of the way. This isn't a game."

Emilia's sisterly behavior was just so adorable that it made Subaru's spirit burn with determination.

"Okay, Emilia-tan, let's get this show on the road! Time is short, the world is big, and our tale has just begun!"

"I suppose s... Eh? What did you say just now? Where did this 'tan' come from...?"

"It's okay, just go with the flow!"

With Emilia expressing surprise at his intimate pet name, he pushed on her back as both headed to that spot in the garden.

Her losing the will to keep "correcting" him and grudgingly accepting how he spoke to her had been one of the bonds built up between them during those four lost days. Emilia still wore a face of resistance as Subaru walked behind her and murmured very quietly.

"—We'll get them back."

As they stopped, he gazed at her long silver hair, and then shifted his eyes to the sky.

—He spitefully looked at the sun rising in the low sky of the east.

This and four more and he'd be right at the appointed hour.

All he needed to fulfill the promise with this girl like the moon was to greet the arrival of the sun.

—He had time. And he knew what the answer would be.

"I dunno who's got it in for me, but I'm gonna take it all back and make you cry. Don't underestimate how tenacious I can be after I fell madly in love with the smile I saw that night."

He shook a fist toward the sky and declared war to no one in particular.

It was Subaru's first declaration of open defiance at the "summons" and "loop" that had brought him to that world.

He had begun his battle against the second loop. All so that he could move past his week at Roswaal Manor and learn how those days would continue.

And to protect and fulfill the promise he had made that night—

3

Subaru's caustic words to the rising sun raised the curtain for his second "first day" at Roswaal Manor.

All he had to do was see the sun rise five times.

Subaru's plan was to spend the intervening time doing the same things to the fullest extent possible.

In accordance with his resolution in the garden, Subaru's final objective was to fulfill the promise he'd made to Emilia on the final day. To do that, he had to get to that fourth night and make that promise once more.

This was because he'd concluded that loops were, to a certain degree, set in stone. If he followed the same path, the story would "conclude" at the same place.

If things followed the same flow as before, it was a natural result. Factoring in the thought processes and behavior patterns of the people involved, things would surely head to the same place. To Subaru, the important thing was to redo everything and change up only the end result. That was the best way to proceed he could think of.

In other words, the best way to reach his objective was to see the loop through. With sublime mischief, Subaru resolved to save and load his way forward, leading events to the conclusion he desired.

"So, what is this...? Did I mess up somewhere...?"

In the steamy bath, Subaru opened his mouth wide and blew bubbles as he looked back on his first day.

As far as his plan was concerned, everything after that moment of resolve that morning had been a complete disaster.

First, he'd finished his daily morning routine with Emilia and awaited Roswaal's return to the manor before speaking to him in the dining hall.

Put bluntly, he didn't have confidence he could reproduce all the fine points of an in-depth conversation, but surely he'd touched on all the high notes from last time. He'd got to touch Puck as a reward, addressed Emilia like a friend, discussed Emilia's candidacy for the royal succession, and determined where he stood in relation to Roswaal Manor.

Just as before, Subaru had charmed his way into becoming an apprentice servant at Roswaal Manor. Afterward, he'd gone off with Ram to be shown around the manor and begin his first day of work, but that's when things went off the rails.

Subaru, his face the only part not submerged in the bath, let his chin ride upon the water of the tub as he murmured with dismay.

"Then why was everything different from last time? I feel like a student who went through all the trouble of writing cheat sheets when they changed all the subjects on the test... What was the point of redoing it?"

Subaru's whole plan had been to redo everything exactly as he'd done before. However, the details of the training for his new post and the duties Ram had imposed on him were completely different from before. He felt like it went from Odd Jobs 101 to Odd Jobs 401.

"They were still all odd jobs, but...there was waaaay more to them than last time."

Perhaps he needed to look at it as trusting him with higher-level work and more of it?

"Last time everything just ran me ragged, but this time it was hard as nails... Damn, I thought it was gonna be easy, all the same stuff."

Subaru was not merely venting complaints at his expectations being so cruelly disappointed. He'd decided he really wasn't in a good situation.

This was the result of his trying to spend his time like before. With so many details of his first day altered, he could not rationally expect things would be like last time on the second and following days.

Overlooking the fine details, he was terrified that a much larger problem might yet rear its head.

"I still don't have any real clue why I went back this time around..."

This time, he'd gone to sleep "normally" and woke up having gone back in time. Unlike the death loop he had been in before, he had no way to avoid something he couldn't anticipate. Just the thought of it made his head hurt.

"With this many differences, can I rely on my memory at all...?"

He thought back to that fateful day when he met Emilia in the capital.

A mountain of little details differed, but things were still proceeding in largely the same direction. He didn't know how to escape from the big event. The only thing that stood out differently from the last time in Subaru's mind was the promise he'd made with Emilia.

Surely, if he made it that far, he'd be able to change the results and get past this.

Subaru sank into the bathtub, put his thoughts in order without a breath of oxygen, and poked his head out of the bathtub once more.

"Well, hello. Maaay I join you?"

The sight of the bare-naked nobleman before him, hands on his hips, made Subaru deeply regret that he required air.

They were close enough to touch as he stood in the nude, his crown jewels swaying between his legs as he looked down at Subaru.

"It's currently occupied. I refuse."

"The facilities in my own manor are my personal belongings, are they nooot? Allooow me to freely enjoy them."

"Then don't ask. You don't need my permission to get in the tub!"

"Oh my, so haaarsh. You do not understand. The bath is certainly my personal possession..."

Roswaal went down on one knee as his hand reached out and gently lifted Subaru's unresisting chin.

"...but in the capacity of my servant, are yoooou not as well?"

Chomp.

"No hesitation, I seeee."

After biting the creepy fingertips holding his chin, Subaru swam backward, putting distance between Roswaal and himself.

The bathroom's size was firmly in the realm of "stupidly huge," with a tub as broad as the oldest, best bathhouses. Plainly, it was the habit of nobles to use an excessively large amount of space, but he had to admit that monopolizing all that space felt pretty satisfying.

"Another twist I didn't expect, geez..."

—During the previous four days, he hadn't encountered Roswaal in the bathtub even once.

During the last loop, Roswaal had been extremely busy; the two barely saw each other. No doubt the twins had tended to his needs, but Subaru barely had any contact with him outside of mealtime, their initial meeting excepted.

"Damn it, every little thing's happening in completely different ways than what I expected..."

"Althooough I know not what troubles you, not eeeverything in this world goes according to plan."

Roswaal moved to Subaru's side as he spoke of it being a tough world. He leaned back against the wall of the bathtub and let out a long sigh, somehow looking like any other man in the world enjoying the pleasures of the bath.

"I only just noticed, but I guess even you take off your makeup for hot baths."

"Mm? Aaahh, that's right. Oh my, Subaru, I wonder iiif this is the first time you have seen my face unadorned?"

"I suppose it is. I'm like, you look totally normal. No need to hide your face like that."

"Cosmetics is a hobby of mine. 'Tis nooot out of any need to hide my face. It is not as if the curl of my lips or the arch of my nose are abhorrent to the eye... Oh my."

"Don't look at me while saying that stuff. Make three doe-eyed blinks and I'm keeling over here and now."

Being born with bad looks was a serious drawback when making first impressions. And if Subaru wanted to complain about the face he was born with, what could he say? He looked exactly like his mother.

Remembering his parents, Subaru had a conflicted look on his face as Roswaal changed the subject.

"Aaare you getting along nicely with Ram and Rem? They've worked here for quite a while, so they are suuurely passing things along to their junior?"

"Well, I haven't talked to Rem much, but I'm getting along well with Ram. If anything, Ram is a bit too friendly. Even with us senior and junior, she hasn't treated me any differently from when I was a guest."

"Weeell, Rem will make up for that shortcoming. It is only right sisters support each other. Those two are verrry well suited for each other in that sense."

"From what I see and hear, Ram's the weaker sister, while Rem always covers for her."

In every sense, it was clear which twin sister had the superior ability at domestic work. Rem had first-rate skills across the board while Ram would have needed to work hard to come close to second-rate. Normally, that setup would give Ram an inferiority complex, but....

"But all I hear is, 'Ram's amazing because she's older.' Being so bold is unreal."

"If you wish to speak of being bold, I think you are quiiite the specimen? But I see. I wonder if you replied and said the same things to her? It is quite a thing you are treading upon without reserve, which is quite maaarvelous."

"The emphasis there doesn't sound like praise at all, you know?"

Subaru didn't hesitate to intrude on other people's personal turf because he was so bad at reading the mood. That aloof disposition made it easy for him to get isolated. You might say that it was his bad habit to get on other people's nerves.

At Subaru's reply, Roswaal closed his right eye and looked up at the ceiling with his yellow left eye alone.

"It is not sarcasm. I truly believe it is a gooood thing. Those girls are a little too perfect for each other, you see. Quiiite likely, some things change only when someone comes from outside and gives a liiittle…push, yeees?"

"Something like that, huh?"

"Something like that, indeeeed."

The two immersed themselves into the bathtub up to their necks, letting their entire bodies soak up the sensations. A little after that, Subaru raised his eyebrows, remembering something.

"Oh, right. Ros, there's something I wanted to ask you. Is that all right?"

"Weeell, if it is within my vast personal knowledge, I wooould not mind."

"That's the most roundabout way of saying 'I'm really smart' that I've ever heard. But ah, anyway, how is this bath heated?"

Subaru knocked a couple of times on the bottom of the tub as he addressed what had been nagging him the whole time.

The bathtub Subaru and Roswaal were soaking in was made of stone; its pleasant smoothness made him think of marble. The bath was in a corner under the mansion, and of course it was for both genders. To begin with, everything in the bath was swapped after each time, so he had no special sense of fulfillment from getting in after Emilia.

Subaru added a thought.

"Not that I'm boiling in here. I just noticed before I got in."

"From time to time, your inquisitive spirit truuuly astounds me. I wonder if it is youth…although I wonder if I would have had that thought when I was your age?"

Roswaal seemed to see a rare dazzle in Subaru's youth as he nodded.

"Regardless, the answer iiis quite simple. You seeee, there is a fire-attuned magic crystal under the bathtub that heats it. When triggered by the mana of someone entering the bath, it activates and brings the water to a boil. Surely you used such a thing in the kitchen?"

"So that's how that pot worked. I was wondering how you cooked here without gas."

After Rem had made brief use of it, it'd been Subaru's turn to peel vegetables. In the first place, not understanding the meaning of words like *it runs on mana*, spoken like an obvious, everyday thing, probably meant the dawn of Iron Chef Subaru was still a long time away.

"I mean, if it's mana, does that mean only magic users can use it?"

"Nooot at all. All life forms have 'gates.' Nooo plant or animal is an exception. If 'twas not so, we could nooot achieve a society built on the use of magic crystals."

Subaru puzzled over the new piece of vocabulary. Roswaal, watching Subaru like that, cleared his throat and raised a finger.

"Very well, shaaall we indulge in a lesson here? I, teaching magic tooo you, the somewhat unenlightened?"

"I'll ignore the way that stuff came out and accept with grace."

Responding to the lecture proposal, Subaru turned to face Roswaal, who was kneeling in the center of the bathtub. None of that changed the fact that both were buck naked.

"Verrry well. First, the basics. Subaru, you know what a 'gate' is, do you not?"

"No, you say it like it's obvious, but you don't know what you don't know…"

"Your voice sounds very low all of a sudden. So you do not know of gates…or shall I saaay, totally? Mm, did I use that correctly?"

Roswaal checked on the proper use of the word *totally*. Among all the little expressions Subaru had imported that originated from his world, he'd used that one especially frequently, so Roswaal was quite accustomed to it.

Subaru gave Roswaal full marks for good usage. After making a high five, they returned to the lecture.

"So, what is a gate, anyway? Is that something you have or don't have?"

"Put very simply, a gate iiis a doorway that leads inside your own body. Mana enters through the gate; mana leaves through the gate. A basic rule ooof life."

"Ahhh. It's like a faucet connected to MP..."

He grasped Roswaal's simple explanation. So that was a gate; his ears had heard the term several times over. So it was pretty much what he'd guessed.

"So if everyone has a gate, I have one, too?"

"Weeell, you surely would, if you are confident that you aaare human. So, are you?"

"There's no purer human that's been thrown into another world, ever. Totally normal. Totally mob-grade."

Situations that required combat strength to bust through them were completely new to him. His scientific know-how was fairly below average; his hand-eye coordination was pretty high, but his endurance was a sore point. His Acquired Skills were Sewing and Bed-making.

One-way trip to becoming cannon fodder.

But Subaru wasn't hung up on that; this was the second thing to be happy about since arriving in a different world. Enthralled by the word *magic*, his heart thumped, his eyes twinkling with hope.

"Of course the first thing I'm happy about is meeting Emilia, but this is pretty awesome! Finally, I can fulfill my dream of being a magic user... I've waited my whole life for this!"

"Weeell, I am glad speaking of magic pleases you so, but becoming a magic user is largely dependent ooon fortune. In the first place, the properties of gates matter a great deal. You are uuunlikely to be as blessed as a genius such as I. I boast only because I must."

Roswaal's behavior made Subaru hear a little *ding* as a flag rose in his mind.

In spite of Roswaal's overwhelming confidence, he didn't know that Subaru, soaking in the bathtub in the nude before his eyes, was a "guest" summoned from another world.

Tradition held that those summoned from another world possessed special abilities. So far, weapon skills were out, intellect was out, his luck modifier was either zero or somewhat negative, but: magic!

"My new hope is in your hands, Rozchi. Magic, magic, let's talk magic some more! There's a magic wave here, and my twinkling future's surfing on it!"

"Is that sooo? Then let us continue. Did you knooow that magic has four basic affinities?"

"*Nope!*"

"Ahaaa, it feels good to have someone so senselessly, pointlessly guileless and ignorant before me, so I shall explain. The four elements of mana are fire, water, wind, and earth. Dooo you understand?"

"Got it; these are the basics, huh? Consider them absorbed. Go on, go on!"

Subaru's request seemed to rub Roswaal the right way, so he nodded and continued his explanation.

"Fire element relates to temperature. Water element regulates life and healing. Wind element functions outside the bodies of living things. Earth element functions inside the body. So, most affinities are divided by these four categories, aaand normal humans have an affinity for one of the four! Incidentally, I shall have you know I have an affinity for aaall four."

"Whoa, the boasting's annoying but I'll praise you anyway. That's fantastic! How do you figure out someone's element?"

"Naaaturally, a magic user as accomplished as I can discover that through mere touch."

"Seriously?! This is what I've been waiting for. Well, do it and tell me!"

As Subaru begged like a puppy that hadn't been housebroken, Roswaal gave him a halfhearted look and pressed his palm to Subaru's forehead. The eyes of both completely nude men twinkled at the scene.

"Well, if you shaaall excuse me. *Myon myon myon myon...*"

"Whoa! A magical sound! Total fantasy immersion!"

Subaru was taken in by the invigorating scene before his eyes, forgetting his many sources of worry for that moment.

—Magic. Finally he, having been summoned to another world, would get fangs of his very own.

His eyes twinkling in certainty of his hope, Subaru awaited the results of the scan.

"—Yeees, I see."

"Here it comes! What, what is it? Maybe fire element that burns like I do? Or water for when I'm calm and composed, the coolest guy in the room? Or maybe wind because of my refreshing nature, like the breeze blowing through the grass? No, no, it's gotta be earth for my being such a laid-back, big-brother-type nice guy, definitely!"

"Yes, it's Dark."

"None of the above?!"

Doubting his ears at the scan result, his reaction was like someone being told he had cancer.

Roswaal then spoke in a grave tone that seemed to fit that image perfectly.

"You are completely, uuutterly Dark. Your connection to the other four elements is quiiite weak. Put differently, though, this iiis exceedingly rare..."

"So what is Dark, anyway?! It's not in the other four categories? Some kind of reject?"

"I did not mention it, buuut there are also elements beyond the basic four, namely Dark and Light. Hoooweeever, very few people have those affinities, so I diiid not bother to explain."

Meaning Subaru was far, far off the beaten path.

Hearing Roswaal elaborate made Subaru feel less buffeted and calmed him down.

Yes, this was a rare, limited element: in other words, a special power!

"It's gotta be a really awesome element. Like some super-special power that comes only once in five thousand years."

"Yes, Dark element magic is quite famous…able to obstruct an opponent's vision, sever him from sound, slow his movements, and the like. Rather convenient uses."

"I'm a Debuffer?!"

A Debuffer was a specialized support class dedicated to so-called debuffs—skills that weakened the enemy.

He'd had his hopes up that he could use magic of peerless, legendary destruction, able to rend the sky and split the earth, but Roswaal was breaking it to him that his magic would have crowd-control and attribute-lowering properties.

He really did seem apologetic, so it was no doubt the truth.

"Summoned from a world without weapons skill, intellect, or cheat codes…and a magical element for debuffs…"

"Incideeentally, you have no talent for magic. If my limit is a ten, yours is about three."

"I wanted to hear that even less! This place is forsaken by God and Buddha!"

Subaru opened his mouth and made a loud groan as he immersed himself in the bathtub. Until a few moments before, it had been a theoretical hope, but expectations, once sprouted, were not so easy to brush aside.

"Well, using it at all is good, I think… Or maybe being a debuffer makes me kinda cool…?"

"Putting aside the level of coolness, there is nooo harm in learning. If you wish to use magic, by all means, learn. Fortunately for you, there is indeeeed a specialist in Dark spells here at this mansion."

"I see, that's it! I suppose I should be satisfied with learning magic for situations where you wanna slow someone down. Okay, let's get this show on the road!"

Subaru was eager to have Emilia guide him into magic, drawing both of them closer together. His prior goal of following the same route as last time was long forgotten.

"You seem to harbor a misunderstanding, buuut the specialist in Dark spells is nooot Emilia, you know?"

"The *heck*?! Are you enjoying playing with someone's heart like this?! So who's the specialist, you, the elite magic user with all elemental affinities?! This sucks!"

"It is Beatrice."

"That's worse!!"

With a great *kerplunk*, water spray leapt everywhere as he let loose his loudest shout of the evening.

4

"Damn, that was all over the map. Damn that Roswaal, working me up and down like that like I'm on Buddha's palm!"

In the washroom, Subaru's face was red as he put his hands through the sleeves of his change of clothes. With the affinity scan in the bathtub ending in dejection, Subaru got out of the bath first.

He'd been worked up during the conversation with Roswaal, but his face felt heavy from the effects of the long bath. After all, it hadn't been a full day yet since being healed from his wound; he had to expect some anemia.

"Plus I'm gonna have serious aches and pains tomorrow. Ugh, damn you, Ram; you remember this, just because I'm better than last time doesn't mean you have to work me like a dog…"

"I will remember that as you wish."

"Fwaaaah?!"

The timely reply, coming just as Subaru was leaving the washroom with his laundry in a basket, surprised him enough to make him jump. As Ram stood in the corridor before the washroom, his underwear, scattering out from the bouncing basket, fell to her feet.

"My goodness."

Ram crouched, plucked Subaru's underwear off the floor, and stuffed them into a garbage bin right beside her.

"There's a guy carrying a basket heading to the laundry right in front of you, y'know?!"

"I'm sorry, I was gripped by psychological distaste the instant I picked them up. I had to get rid of them without a single moment to spare."

"Considering all that, your form was very relaxed, huh?!"

Subaru tearfully recovered his underwear from the garbage bin and turned to face Ram. Seeing Ram serenely standing in the hallway, he tilted his head and wondered what she was up to. Ram seemed to reply to his unasked question.

"Unfortunately, I have already bathed, so my clothes will stay on no matter how long you wait."

"I didn't say anything!! And ain't that backward for a maid?!"

"I jest. I am simply waiting for Master Roswaal to finish before helping him dress."

"That's pampering him a little too much. I'm sure he can dress himself."

Apparently, in this world, there existed people who'd never in their lives worn a single shoe without a servant slipping it on their foot. Roswaal surely fit the bill.

"Don't tell me you both help him put on that weird makeup. My low trust's falling even further."

"There shall be no rudeness toward Master Roswaal in my presence. Next time I shall spank you."

It felt like a warmth-filled warning, but seeing that she wasn't kidding, he knew he ought to take it to heart.

In point of fact, Ram had explained his chores at the mansion with great care and patience, but she had a look that suggested she'd make him work in the hog house if he asked her the same question twice.

"I'll save myself the grief, then... If you'll excuse me. See you tomorrow."

"Basuru, what are you doing later?"

"I'm just heading off to sleep. Morning comes early after all? Damn it. Those mornings are really tough."

At Subaru's reply, mixing rebelliousness with weakness, Ram nodded a bit and closed her eyes.

Subaru was just about to ask the silent Ram if there was something she wanted to say when she opened her eyes.

"Wait in your room, then. I'll be there later."

Subaru's response sounded very obtuse.

"—Huh?"

5

Subaru Natsuki, as he'd declared several times over, was firmly in Emilia's corner.

Perhaps it was because he'd never encountered such beauty, either in this new world or the one from which he came, but Emilia stood out in Subaru's mind.

It was partly pure physical beauty, but also the beauty of each and every action.

Consequently, there was simply no room for anyone else in his heart, no matter what she looked like.

"That's why this perfectly made bed has one purpose: for me to get a good night's sleep!"

Subaru forcefully thrust an accusing finger at his bed, venting to no one in particular.

Subaru, having returned to his room after leaving the bath, had wasted all the intervening time on putting his bed in order. He'd abandoned his laundry, working up quite a sweat in spite of having just bathed.

"There's no deep meaning to it. No deep meaning to it! Mundane thoughts out, mundane thoughts out. Calm down, calm down. One Emilia, two Emilias, three Emilias… Is this Heaven?!"

"Be quiet, Barusu. It's night already; do be quiet."

"Yikes!"

He made a large leap and slammed into the wall. Ram, having opened the door without a sound, was standing at the entrance to the room.

"And just after I told you to be quiet. You are hopeless."

"What's with rules that apply for only you?! Anyone would jump from that! What do you want from me here?!"

Ram made a muted *hmph* at Subaru as he vented. Subaru, struck by the humiliation of not being worth a proper word, had no good option left but silence.

Then, cutting in front of the silent Subaru, Ram entered the room—and headed straight to a writing desk in the corner.

It was something every room was supplied with, but to Subaru, who couldn't read that world's books, it was a worthless piece of junk, so he had not turned in the desk's direction until then.

"What are you standing there for? Come here, Barusu."

Subaru made a dispirited face at being spoken to like a dog being taught manners, but he was resolute to not get wrapped up in Ram's pace. Besides, screwing around was Subaru's job.

He headed toward her with a steely resolution to not be swayed no matter what wacky statements she might dish out. Subaru felt like he was going to war as he stood before Ram, puffing out his chest.

"And? What impossible trial awaits me this time?"

"What are you talking about? I told you, sit down quickly if you want me to teach you how to read."

"That's news to me!"

His steel heart was instantly shattered.

Subaru could not hide his unease at having his hardened resolve so easily broken. He sucked in his breath as he beheld the pure white note page spread atop the table, joined by a feather pen and a reddish-brown bound book.

Apparently, this was neither a joke nor a prank; she truly intended to teach him how to read.

"But why now, all of a sudden…"

Ram's reply to the bewildered Subaru's question was extremely straight and to the point.

"I realized while watching you work today that you could not read. So I will teach you. If you cannot read, I cannot send you to buy groceries or leave you notes."

Ram showed Subaru the red-bound book as his mouth flapped like that of a fish caught off guard.

"We shall begin with a simple picture book meant for children. I will accompany you for study every night from now on."

No doubt it was an offer he should be grateful for, but Subaru's bewilderment was stronger than his gratitude at that moment.

Like the events that unfolded in the bath, this situation was one that was unthinkable last time. And, according to Subaru's senses, his intimacy with the twins still fell far short of what he'd experienced on the fourth day last time.

"Why are you being nice to me like this?"

"It is obvious. I… No, it is to make things easier."

"Man, you're hard-boiled. You didn't even say what you corrected…"

"It is only natural. As your work increases, mine decreases. If my work decreases, Rem's work will naturally decrease as well. It's all for a good cause."

"That means a ton of work falling on me, though?!"

"…?"

Ram tilted her head like she couldn't understand what he was getting at. He was at a loss for words.

But even if he was at a loss like this, he was happy that Ram was showing him such concern.

"Okay, roger that. Let's get this studying started, shall we?"

"Since you already have the spoken language down, it should not be all that difficult. After all, now is the time to correct your vulgar word selection."

"Tossing in insults with your help, huh?"

As he spoke, he sat down at the desk and completed preparations, feather pen in hand. With light and rather smooth and speedy strokes, he wrote his first words one ought to use to commemorate a visit to another world.

"Subaru Natsuki enters stage left… There we go!"

"You do not have the free time to be scribbling. Time is limited. Morning comes quickly, after all."

"Well, this is actually my mother tongue… Guess it wasn't obvious, huh?"

He'd held out hope that their being able to talk might mean she'd be able to read his writing, but nothing so convenient unfolded. Just like Subaru, she was unable to read the other side's language.

"First, we'll begin with basic I-script, moving on to Ro-script and Ha-script after you've perfected I-script."

"So there're three types, huh? Sucks to hear that."

It was tough to have your spirits discouraged right before a lesson in a new language. He recalled how foreigners felt when trying to clear the high hurdle of the hiragana, katakana, and kanji when learning Japanese.

"You can read the picture book by grasping I-script. Time is limited to one hour. Tomorrow is another day, and Ram is sleepy, too."

"That last bit sounded like the real story. Not that I mind…"

"I think my honesty is one of my selling points."

He didn't know if her unhesitant reply was serious or a joke. It really felt like she meant it, so Subaru dove right into the script lesson.

Fundamental to learning any new language was grasping the characters through repetition of the writing process. He copied the basic characters Ram wrote down, filling the page with them. It was enough drudgery to break him, but it was necessary, indispensable labor. Subaru felt fatigue and sleepiness pile up when, seized by a somewhat mushy feeling, he conveyed his honest thoughts to Ram.

"Y'know, even if you said it's to make things easier for you, I'm still glad."

The feather pen made a faint sound as it ran along the paper. Subaru thought back to the four days from last time while writing down the same characters page after page.

Now that he thought about it, he was chasing after Emilia every day whenever he had the chance, but he'd spent the most time with Ram during that period.

Subaru was basically an amateur at all the chores of the mansion. Of course teaching him was bone breaking, all the more so because Ram was doing that on top of her regular duties.

The burden naturally fell on Rem as well. In addition to that, he hadn't had much contact with Rem during those four days. Subaru knew that the highly competent Rem was covering for a portion of her sister's chores, so Subaru owed her for indirectly shouldering his burden, too.

"Honestly, I didn't think you liked me that much."

It was natural that educating a useless newbie like Subaru was a pain. Certainly that was the opinion Ram voiced, but Subaru felt used to it already.

"I hate to weigh you down, but thanks. I want to be useful as soon as possible."

Subaru was thanking her from the bottom of his heart for then and for the future. For her part, Ram quietly went...

"*Guu.*"

...making a cute sleeping sound atop the immaculately made bed. The feather pen made a sharp sound as it snapped.

6

Subaru, surrendering to his sudden impulse, opened his mouth wide and yawned.

He brusquely wiped away the wetness from the corners of his sleepy eyes and stretched all the way up. The sinking sun of the evening sky had left an orange tint as its parting gift to the leisurely passing clouds, thanking them for another day's work.

Subaru watched the clouds as he rotated his arms, legs, and neck to make sure everything was in working order. Effects remained from heavy labor, but he didn't feel the same fatigue that he had on his first night.

No doubt it wasn't that his body had grown tougher; rather, he'd become more accustomed to his chores, the greater efficiency leaving him less beat.

Since his body didn't get any stronger with Return by Death, he had to rely on learning through experience.

"Sorry to make you wait, Subaru— Are you all right?"

"Mm. Yeah, I'm totally okay. Finished your shopping, Rem?"

"Yes, no holdups. It seems you were rather popular."

Holding a carry bag containing the things she'd bought and complimenting Subaru was the blue-haired girl—Rem.

Wearing her maid uniform, Rem was holding down her wind-blown hair as she looked at Subaru—his servant's outfit stained with mud, dust, tears, and snot—with a slightly hardened expression.

"Kids have taken a liking to me since way back. I guess they really fell for, you know, motherly stuff that I just can't keep bottled up?"

"It's because children are just like animals and naturally decide a hierarchy. They instinctively recognize whether it's appropriate to make light of a person or not."

"That doesn't sound much like praise!!"

Sharp comments like that were what made him accept that Rem and Ram were actually sisters.

Ram was direct; Rem was roundabout. You had to have a thick skin to stick around them. Of course, their job was one that could not be accomplished without physical toughness as well.

The village closest to the mansion where Subaru and Rem were at was called Auram.

Though Roswaal dwelled in the hinterlands, he was nonetheless a minor lord possessing several pieces of land. Everywhere within them, and Auram Village was no exception, the residents welcomed Subaru and Rem like it was the natural thing to do, speaking to them in a very friendly manner.

Apparently, just the fact that the twins spent a lot of time in contact with them in the course of shopping meant word of Subaru's existence had passed around. The shock at the speed rural rumors traveled surprised Subaru, but still, though it was awkward, Subaru was happy for the warm welcome.

"Having said that, what's with those brats getting all clingy like that... Don't they know that touching everything just gets your fingers burned? Can't they tell I'm putting out a hard-boiled aura here?"

"It seems your pretending to be a 'motherly' adult kept you quite busy all by yourself."

"The 'by yourself' part sounded a bit sharp there, but it would've been nice being busy without getting mobbed like that. I really should've stuck with you going shopping..."

Since Subaru's inability to tell ingredients apart made him useless, Rem had him kill time in the village while she was shopping. The kids found him and he was immediately abducted.

"Man, they just don't have any respect. That's why I can't really get to like kids."

"When it comes to lack of respect, you look plenty childish to me...?"

"A very sound theory! Having said that, I think taking someone for granted from the get-go is a little different... Ram's really good at that, though."

"Sister is incredible."

They were speaking past each other somewhat. The way Rem seemed full of herself as she boasted about her sister, plus the fact that her sister wasn't watching, made Subaru surmise they were her true feelings.

"Feels like Ram's personality causes a lot of conflict, though."

"Her unflinching demeanor is part of her charm. It is not something I can pull off..."

Subaru, hearing a sad undertone to the words she added at the end, knit his brow but didn't press the point.

With Subaru suddenly at a loss for words, Rem seemed to snap back to normal as she changed the subject.

"Come to think of it, how is your studying going?"

"I'd like to say...steadily, but it's not as simple as that. Stuff like this needs time to slowly nurture and develop...just like love!"

"As long as you don't give up midway."

"There wasn't much tenderness in that comment just now!"

Seeing that his shout brought a slight smile to Rem's face, Subaru also smiled in relief.

—It had already been four days since Ram had offered him personal lessons. He'd heard Rem might take over, but she hadn't actually assumed the instructor's position as of yet.

Ram being that busy meant that the burden on Rem was all the greater.

Subaru kept smiling and waved to Rem, who was acting slightly hesitant for once.

"Don't worry about it. I'm not going to give up or disappoint Ram. I just wish she wouldn't fall asleep on my bed in the middle of the lesson. It's really distracting."

"Sister is probably acting that way to spur you forward."

"Man, your total worship of your sister is way past normal. Totally demon possessed."

"Demon possessed…?"

Rem tilted her head at the latest word trend Subaru had coined.

"Like possessed, except by a demon instead of a divine spirit. Demon possessed. It works, huh?"

"Do you like demons?"

"Better than gods. I mean, gods don't give you anything, but a demon will have a good laugh with you over a chat about the future."

Talking about the last year seemed especially popular with them. Subaru remembered the image of the Red Demon and the Blue Demon hugging each other as they laughed themselves silly, when he suddenly realized there was a definite smile carved upon Rem's face.

"Whoa…"

He'd seen her faintly smiling several times over, but this was the first time he'd seen a real smile on her face. Subaru didn't know what had tickled Rem's thoughts, but he snapped his fingers.

"That smiling face is worth a million-volt skyline."

"I will tell on you to Lady Emilia."

Subaru straightened himself and meekly pleaded for forgiveness.

"I wasn't trying to hit on you!"

Rem lightly raised her eyebrows toward Subaru.

"What happened to your hand?"

"Mm? Oh, that mangy mutt with the kids went all chomp-chomp on me."

His left hand, covered in bite marks, had already stopped bleeding, but it still looked somewhat pathetic.

Incidentally, it was only after he returned to the mansion that he realized that the middle of the back of his servant outfit was stained with snot.

"May I heal that wound?"

"Eh? What, you can use healing magic, too, Rem?"

"Only simple magic up to first-aid level. Perhaps you prefer Lady Emilia?"

"Mm, that is a pretty attractive suggestion, but…I'll pass on both."

Subaru declined her offer while gazing at the bite marks on the back of his left hand.

He'd decided that scars, in a way, were a good thing. The fact that everything, up to and including his scars from the previous loop, had vanished when he'd begun this play-through weighed heavily on Subaru's mind.

The presence or absence of scars was a great way to tell if he'd done a Return by Death or not. If the dog hadn't happened to bite him, he'd have been forced to cut himself with a sharp feather pen.

"Well, it's a mark of honor. No one lives as prettily as on the day they were born."

"It is said that scars are a man's medals, though all you accomplished on the battlefield were mistakes."

"That might have a kernel of truth, but don't say stuff so cold, geez!"

The way Rem tilted her head and looked at him indicated she didn't realize what a venomous tongue she had. That was even scarier.

"Besides that, I've cut my hand lots of times in front of you before, so why offer to heal me all of a sudden? I mean, you never offered to do it before?"

"That's because I thought you'd forget if it didn't hurt, so you should keep the wounds as a warning."

"That's educational policy straight outta Sparta… So why'd you offer now, then?"

He wanted to know the reason why this case was different from the others, making her unable to let this one go.

After Subaru posed his question, Rem kept her silence for a while.

Looking at her face from the side, Subaru thought it might have to do with the little smile from earlier.

"The futon flew on. The kitten catnapped. Who's the one who said a pun?!"

"Did you suddenly go wrong in the head?"

"You're jumping to conclusions. No, I thought I'd find out for sure why you were all smiles earlier."

Though, considering her reaction to the demon talk earlier, he thought it could be that, too...

"I thought you'd really go for cheap gags. So I wondered if I tried it, maybe it would put you in a good mood and make you want to be nicer to me, or something like that."

"Do not expect you will get a chance to have me heal your wounds ever again."

"You're that angry?!"

"I have been this angry since earlier from your bad-mouthing Sister behind her back."

"I do that a lot lately!"

The look Rem shot at Subaru grew sharper still thanks to that last comment.

Fearful, Subaru gave up on apologizing, closing his mouth and gazing at the sky. Evening was slowly giving way to night. That was when he felt his limbs stiffen.

—After all, it was his second time in that world reaching the fourth day.

"So the challenge is to get to tomorrow morning safely—but before that..."

...Before that came another important challenge: making sure that he actually had a promise with Emilia for a date to begin with.

7

For the second time, Subaru Natsuki was approaching his greatest crisis during his first week at Roswaal Manor.

With things having gone so much against his experiences during the first loop, he couldn't really call it smooth sailing, but the greatest danger was indeed that moment.

And so, with a slight blush, Emilia said to him...

"So, since Ram and Rem both said they weren't going to show their faces here tonight, I've come to supervise your studying in their place. Not that I can do much to help..."

...and cutely stuck out her tongue.

With Subaru sitting facing the desk, having Emilia sitting on the bed, watching him like a hawk, was ferociously whittling down his endurance.

—Here was a cute girl in the room of a teenage boy, just the two of them, late at night like this… Surely no one could blame Subaru for losing his concentration as he struggled against his baser instincts?

"Hmm. You're taking studying more seriously than I expected, Subaru."

Subaru was desperately chanting *innocent* inside his head, unable to feel innocent at all, when Emilia got up and voiced her admiration. Apparently she'd bathed just earlier; the faint hint of warmth hovering around Emilia, mixed with her own scent, were two more sharp blows to Subaru's state of mind.

Subaru fumbled with his notebook as he opened it to show Emilia where he'd gotten in his studying.

"R-right now I'm learning basic I-characters by writing them. My current goal is to read this picture book for kids, since it's mostly written in I-script."

"Hmm, the goal is a picture book… Ah!"

"What, it's got an interesting story or something?"

Emilia lightly shook her head at Subaru as her hand stopped midway through browsing the picture book he was using for reference.

"Well, nothing big, but yes, a little. When you can read this, too… Yeah."

Audibly closing the book, Emilia sat on the bed once more and got comfortable. Subaru was unable to conceal how Emilia's refined but unguarded nature left his mind all jumbled.

"Normally I wouldn't be doing this for someone I met only a few days ago, but I'm giving you special treatment…to thank you for your hard work."

"Sheesh, that's not a whole lot of thanks, Emilia. If you want to show your thanks, how about a massage? Something to melt away and heal all the aches and pains of a hard day's work, *geh-heh-heh*."

Emilia clapped her hands as she scolded him.

"That sounds perverted somehow, so no. And don't change the subject. Keep going, will you?"

Subaru turned back toward the desk as he fought his worldly desires.

Subaru chanted *innocent, innocent* in his head as he wrote the characters onto the notebook, driving out idle thoughts as he focused his head on one thing at a time.

"Goodness, you can do it just fine if you don't let yourself get distracted."

"That's because I lose track of everything around me once I'm into something. That's why I'm straight-like-an-arrow aimed at the person I like!"

"Hmm, is that so? It'd be nice if the person you like notices that sooner rather than later."

Certainly, Subaru's statement had been very frivolous, but Emilia brushed it off like it had nothing to do with her. The fact that she clearly didn't see herself as the target of Subaru's affections gave him no route to follow up.

"Hey, Subaru… Why don't you take work as seriously as you do studying?"

"My motto is to be diligently un-diligent…is what I would say, but this isn't the right mood for that. Uh?"

"It's a serious matter—Ram was complaining about it a little, too. From time to time it feels like you're holding back."

Naturally, Emilia's words and expression both held distaste at having to convey such a message. Hearing this, Subaru could make only a pained grimace, for she had hit the mark.

Ram was correct in her assessment that Subaru was holding back from work, for the truth was that Subaru wasn't taking the work seriously.

More precisely, he was deliberately trying to produce the same outcome as the last time. Compared to last time, when he hadn't learned the first thing about being a servant, Subaru was at least a little bit better. His slight adjustments hadn't escaped the veteran maid's attention.

"...So you do feel guilty about it. It feels like you're honest to a fault in some odd places, Subaru. You're not slacking off studying, after all."

"Well, there's some little circum... I guess that's not an excuse. I'll put everything into it starting tomorrow, so please forgive me, Your Highness!"

"Mnn, I have no objections... Ah, was that a little off?"

Emilia cutely tilted her head, perhaps wondering if she'd been a little too haughty.

Subaru, relieved at seeing Emilia's stance softening, firmly resolved to honor the pledge to Emilia he'd just given.

At the very least, there'd be no need to copy the last time after that night was done.

He'd work very hard to repay the debts he owed to Ram and Rem from over those four days.

...Not that he thought easing up on the brakes would turn everything around overnight...

"Feelings are real important here. I want my renewed hard work to completely provoke those two sisters!"

"And there, another splendid moment *completely* wasted... Are you finished studying?"

"I managed to get today's part done! Hey, Emilia, would you listen to a little request of mine? I'd like a reward for working hard from tomorrow on, so...?"

"A reward? Just so you know, I don't have a lot of money I can spare."

"Wow, you sure were brought up strict. Now, now, just hear me out. I'll work seriously starting tomorrow, so...let's go on a date!"

Subaru posed with a full smile and a thumbs-up as he made his proposal to Emilia.

Faced with the greatest smiling face in Subaru's arsenal, Emilia's big eyes blinked slowly.

"Um, what's a date?"

"Heh. A date is when a guy and a girl go out all by themselves. What happens between them, only the Goddess of Love knows!"

"Then you went on a date with Rem today, Subaru?"

"Nooo, an unexpected counterattack?! Please, that didn't count, that didn't count!!"

Certainly that counted as going out with a beautiful girl, but Subaru was hoping for something a little more mutually involved than buying groceries for the household.

"I understand you want to go out with me, but where?"

"Actually, there's this village close to the mansion with this super lovely mutt. It has flower gardens, too. I wanna use my metia to record for all eternity you standing among the blooming flowers."

Subaru went to a corner of his bedroom, where his shopping bag with his few, precious possessions from his original world were stored. The cell phone and cup of ramen were still in there, having survived the ferocious combat at the fence's shop.

"If the battery holds up, I wanna fill the whole memory card with pictures of Emilia..."

"Ah...the village, huh?"

In front of the person who wanted to drag her out from her daily routine, Emilia put her hand to her cheek, deep in thought. Subaru recalled that she'd hesitated considerably before the last date invitation, too.

Somehow he'd gotten her to say yes the last time. Subaru made his teeth shine to recreate that memory.

"The dog's super cute. Let's go!"

"But it might cause you quite a bit of trouble, Subaru. The villagers...."

"The kids there are completely innocent, totally a bunch of angels. Let's go!"

"...All right already. It can't be helped. I'll just have to go with you."

"The flower gardens are magical and wonderful and... Wait, seriously?"

He was struck senseless at how Emilia seemed less resistant to the idea than last time.

Subaru was still thrown off as Emilia tapered her lips and drew in her delicate shoulders.

"If that'll make you work hard from tomorrow on, I'll go with you. So don't go drifting off anywhere, okay...?"

"Nope, nope, will do no such thing! My soul's already burning with determination to finish all my work perfectly!"

"Your soul's burning for something like that?!"

Emilia's shocked face at Subaru's burning drive sent them both into laugher.

After laughing like that for a while, Emilia nodded a bit and got up from the bed. She passed by Subaru's side and looked out the window, making a faint, charming smile up at the sky.

"Mm, the stars are so pretty tonight. It'll probably be clear tomorrow, too."

"—Yeah. It'll be a day I'll never forget."

"There you go again, Subaru..."

Emilia turned around and leaned against the windowsill as she began to admonish Subaru for his frivolity. But her tongue stopped moving when she saw the expression on Subaru's face.

—No doubt it was because, when she hadn't been looking, Subaru's expression had become uncharacteristically serious.

"If you stay here too long, I'm gonna end up falling asleep and mistaking you for a squeeze pillow till morning..."

"Just now... Ahh, it's nothing."

"You know, if you suddenly stop talking like that, it really makes guys nervous...?"

Emilia, perhaps set off by his probing the deeper meaning of her actions, remarked, "It's *nothing*!" as she left the window and cutely strode past Subaru. She went straight to the doorknob before looking back.

"Now then, Butler Subaru. Work hard come tomorrow. Rewards come only to children who work hard for them."

She made a light wave of her hand to bid him good night, followed by a smile and a toss of her hair. Without waiting for Subaru's reply, the silver silhouette vanished past the doorway.

He could stretch out his hand, but it could not reach. All that remained in his room of the lovely girl was the faint scent of her perfume in the air.

But—

"Hold on, hold on, seriously? Geez, I'm getting real popular here. Seriously."

The promise had been made once more. Now, Subaru could challenge the night again.

It was six hours to get through the fourth night. Six hours before the promised morning of the fifth day.

"Now, Mr. Fate, let's *do* this—"

8

Subaru was sitting on the floor with his back against the bed, anxiously passing each moment as he waited for daybreak.

The coldness of the floor hadn't really registered in the two-plus hours he'd spent sitting there. But Subaru's body was extremely, almost excessively aware of the cold. The reason was simple.

"Who could sleep with his heart pounding like this anyway?!"

His heartbeat was fast and loud, making large thumps that he could swear were ringing in his eardrums. His senses were keen to the point of feeling his blood coursing through his whole body; his fingers throbbed nonstop like they were numb.

"Here's what I get for looking forward to the promise with Emilia. Geez, I haven't had this much trouble sleeping since before that picnic in first grade...and I ended up oversleeping for the school trip. Really takes me back..."

His reminiscing distracting him somewhat, Subaru glared at the sky he'd been looking up at for hours on end.

—*Still a long time*, he belatedly thought.

It was about four hours until morning. He didn't feel sleepy whatsoever, but remaining on guard for whatever might occur had frayed his nerves. Thinking of the possibility of an attack made it impossible for him to focus on anything else to kill time.

Besides, continuing to think was the only thing Subaru could do.

He'd redone the last four days, as in, four days for the second time.

There were numerous differences in discord with prior events. They had heavily affected the path he'd taken to reach that night.

But Subaru had surely checked off the majority of the events in his memory.

However, what nagged at him was that he still didn't have a clue how to avoid causing a new loop.

Relations with Emilia were good. He felt like relations with Ram and Rem were getting better, but…

He hadn't encountered Beatrice since that night.

The last time, it wasn't for long, but Subaru had been in contact with Beatrice. Setting that aside, he had barely seen Beatrice this time around. Strict time management had prevented him from exchanging more than a few words with her.

"Just like before, she gave me a good tongue-lashing just from seeing my face, sheesh…"

He didn't recall having much discussion with her, but it was most certainly Beatrice's being there that had saved Subaru's mind from shattering when confronted with facing his "second" first day.

It was the sheer normality of how she blew him off that made Subaru feel calm enough to find himself.

"I should've thanked her for that somehow."

Not that Beatrice would appreciate what he was thanking her for, and no doubt she'd make quite a sour face if he did, but Subaru still wanted to share his thoughts with her.

With a smile, he thought back on the thorny conversations the two had instead engaged in.

If he made it to the next morning, there would be lots and lots more that he could accomplish.

He had things he wanted to say, not just to Beatrice but to Ram, Rem, and even Roswaal. Of course, he wanted that to be after first exhausting ten thousand words on Emilia.

Looking back on it, he had to smile. Putting last time and that time together, it was eight days all told.

Maybe it was the mushy feeling inside him that made his eyelids seem a bit heavier, though there were still three whole hours until morning.

"This isn't an MMO. It's no joke if I fall asleep here…"

He rubbed his eyelids as the sudden sleepiness faded away. But the sleepiness had come with a chill; he made a bitter smile as his body began shivering out of the blue. He cradled both shoulders, trying to raise his body temperature. But the chill wouldn't leave him no matter what he did. Still, the sleepiness gradually got worse.

—Subaru, so gripped with optimism, realized that the situation had changed.

Looking closer, he saw that the skin under the sleeves of his track jacket had goose bumps all over. Chilled to the bone, he couldn't stop shaking. It wasn't normal. The season of this other world was like late springtime in his own world. The days were almost too warm for long-sleeve shirts. So why were his teeth chattering like this?

"This is bad; don't tell me this is…?!"

Feeling a chill that came not from cold but from fear, Subaru nervously put his hands on the floor. But with the shaking already spreading through his whole body, his arms could not support him. When he got up, his knees felt creaky enough to break apart; Subaru was aghast at how sluggish and nauseated he felt.

"S-somebody…"

Subaru's heart rate, so strong just earlier, had weakened, and his breathing was hard as he left the room. He wanted to call for help, but his raspy voice caught in his throat. His legs were cramping as if his lungs weren't accepting oxygen from the dry air that hovered in the dark corridor.

This is bad, was the thought that dominated the back of Subaru's mind. He didn't have any tangible understanding of what was happening to his body. The one thing he *did* know was that his life was in danger.

Subaru sluggishly walked forward, groaning as he made his way toward the stairway going up.

Each step through the familiar passageway was labored enough that it seemed to shave off another piece of his soul.

"Haa…haa…"

Reaching the stairs, he climbed up one step at a time on hands and feet. He wondered how long it would take him to reach the top. Just thinking about it deflated Subaru as he crawled deeper into the hallway.

The insides of his body seemed to be melting; he felt like everything was turning into some kind of soup. The vomit that welled up dripped from the corner of Subaru's mouth onto the corridor; his face was stained with tears.

Subaru, crawling so pathetically, had only one thing, one person, in the back of his mind.

—*Emilia. Emilia. Emilia. I have to get to Emilia.*

Responsibility, or perhaps duty—Subaru was driven by an emotion he couldn't put into words.

In that moment, Subaru had none of the self-preservation instinct common to all species.

Subaru, crawling his way to Emilia's room, was already barely breathing. His arms too weak to bear the weight of his body, he leaned against the wall and slid his way forward. Anyone watching would have felt less pity than disgust at his having lost the dignity of walking upright like a man.

"—"

His whole body was sluggish. His breaths were ragged as his ears continued their high-pitched ringing.

So it was pure happenstance, one might even say dumb luck, that Subaru noticed the strange sound.

—The sound he noticed was like the clank of a chain.

Getting a bad feeling, he stopped moving. His shoulder slid down the wall; he pressed his head against the floor.

"—Uh?"

The next moment, an impact blew Subaru back.

Subaru's body, flopping to the floor but a moment before, flew. He bounced several times, his face literally wiping the floor, as Subaru realized something had hit him incredibly hard.

There was no pain.

However, he felt a malaise like everything from the tips of his fingers and toes to the middle of his chest had gone through a blender.

"What happ..."

What happened, he started to say as he tried to put his hand to the floor to lift himself.

But his shaking hand had no strength to grip the floor. That was strange. He had no balance. His right arm was working so hard; what was his left arm doing? Where'd it run off to?

Annoyed for no tangible reason, Subaru glared at his useless left arm.

—That was when he realized that everything left of his shoulder had been torn off.

"—Ah?"

Falling on his side, Subaru gazed dumbfounded at his amputated left arm.

A large quantity of blood gushed out from the wound carved into him that had sent his left arm and shoulder flying, dyeing the hallway red.

A moment after he noticed the existence of the wound, Subaru was wracked with pain like lightning coursing through his whole body.

Subaru, no longer able to process the pain and heat, flailed around like a stranded, dying fish and slammed himself against the ground several times, too choked up to even scream.

His vision faded, with red and yellow light mixing together as Subaru's consciousness faded from the mansion.

I wanna die. I wanna die. I wanna die. I wanna die. I wanna die. I wanna die. I don't wanna live. I just wanna die. I'll die soon. I'm dead. I don't know anything. Everything's far off. Can't remember anything. Don't care about anything. Just let me die already.

As if responding to Subaru's earnest plea—

"The sound of a chain..."

That faint sound was the last thing he heard before his skull was smashed, granting his wish.

9

"—!!"

Waking up screaming was an experience that was bad for the heart.

Subaru, thrusting off the sheets as he woke, breathed raggedly as he absorbed the shock.

"L-left hand… It's here; it's here, isn't it?"

He stretched his left hand into thin air as if grasping for something with it.

His severed, blown-off left side was intact. Clutching his right arm to confirm it, too, was there, the sense of loss Subaru absorbed for a while made him shake and feel sick to his stomach.

Subaru felt like his heart was wrenching as he looked at his restored left hand.

Of course, there were no scars, either, not from being blown off, not from the dog biting the back of his hand.

"I've gone back again…"

The vanishing scars meant that Subaru had lost his bout against fate.

He'd gone back in time. Perhaps one could instead say that he'd been given another chance for a rematch.

At any rate, he had to confirm the time—and as he arrived at that thought…

"Ah, sorry. Good morning."

Subaru finally realized that the twins were clutching each other in a corner of the room as they watched him.

Like small animals keeping their distance, neither replied to Subaru's completely out-of-place greeting. Subaru scratched his head as he wondered what he should do.

Ram and Rem had no doubt forgotten about Subaru. That pained Subaru's chest somewhat, but Subaru ignored the pain and formed a smile.

He'd show his sincerity as the first step to getting along. After all, even if they'd forgotten him, he hadn't forgotten them.

"Sorry for the trouble. Subaru Natsuki, rebooted and ready to go!"

Subaru strongly rose from bed, standing and pointing his index finger to the heavens.

Disregarding the twins' surprise at his sudden approach, Subaru remained in his dramatic pose and said, "By the way, what's the date and time?"

—And so began his first day at Roswaal Manor for the third time.

CHAPTER 4

A DEADLY GAME OF TAG

1

—Looking back on his memories of the four days, Subaru came to a conclusion.

"So when I went back the first time, it was debilitation causing death in my sleep..."

As Subaru waited for morning, he'd been assaulted by unbearable cold and sleepiness. That feeling of having his mental and physical strength drained away was plenty strong enough to shave away his life in a short time.

Someone hit by that while asleep and defenseless would simply never wake up.

"But what about the sound of the chain...?"

He couldn't come up with any connection between that chain sound and his debilitation hypothesis.

It was a sound specific to long, heavy metal chains. That was probably the deadly weapon that had carved a chunk out of Subaru.

Just remembering the injury made his lost body parts throb and go numb. Though his body hadn't experienced it, his soul was rejecting the memory.

"So there was an…attacker, then? Not that I know if the debilitation and the chain were by the same person."

What he'd gleaned this time around was only enough to judge there was a perpetrator.

Someone had attacked Roswaal Manor on the fourth night. Subaru's name was on the list of pitiful victims. He didn't know if any other residents of the manor were on it.

"If I'm included, it's probably everyone. No doubt related to Emilia's royal candidacy, just like with the fence…"

But having thought that far, Subaru clutched his head. He'd come to understand there'd be an attack on Emilia and the others. That much was a success.

"But even if I know it, I don't have any proof to explain it with, and I'm too green to have any way to stop it…"

You could say that the problem with Return by Death was that you had no way to explain the information you got before you died.

That went double for a prediction of an attack on the manor. Even if he got Roswaal to take countermeasures, it wouldn't help if the attacker changed his plans.

Beyond that, there was the option of driving away the attacker himself, but Subaru's low combat ability and ignorance of the opponent's capabilities ruled that out.

It'd probably end like last time: him crying like a baby while getting beaten to death.

"I'm just too pathetic. Plus I didn't see the opponent's face or weapon. A total dog's death, geez…"

He couldn't begin to plan to drive off an opponent he knew nothing about.

Beatrice, seated in the middle of the room as Subaru paced around her in a circle, spoke with ill humor from the bottom of her heart.

"—You are so gloomy I could die. Either stop right now or I shall blow you away. Choose."

Subaru glanced back at the dangerous look Beatrice was giving him and innocently stuck out his tongue.

"Sorry, sorry. But for some reason, making something other than my head turn around gets my head turning, too. So let it slide, okay? We're buddies, after all."

"Is there such a relationship between us, I wonder? We have met only twice, after all?"

"The heart speaks louder than words. I mean, you did let me in here."

"You broke through the Passage all by yourself, I suppose. It is really quite unbelievable."

In typical fashion, Beatrice did not hide whatsoever her hostility toward Subaru. Subaru had made his way to the forbidden book archive on the morning he woke back up, feeling saved by her cold demeanor once more.

He'd meant to see it through, but being treated by Ram and Rem like a complete stranger was hard, after all. Unlike last time, he'd properly excused himself as he left the room, but it was truly the only place he could cling to.

"Well, I won't cause you any trouble. Let's have some tea and take it easy."

"We shall do no such thing. You truly are irritating."

The corners of Beatrice's lips twisted in annoyance as she toyed with one of the curls of her hair.

Watching Beatrice like that, Subaru suddenly had a thought.

"Come to think of it, you don't look like it, but you're a magic user, right?"

"Your choice of words offends me. Will you not associate me with such second-rate imbeciles, I wonder?"

"…You don't have many friends, do you?"

"How did you leap from that subject to this one, I wonder?!"

"Er, I don't have any friends, either, so I picked up on it, but that's not good for you. Being so high-handed at such a young age is going to affect you later in life. Should adjust that now while you can."

Feeling the glare of Beatrice's reddened face, Subaru coughed to clear the air. There was something Subaru really wanted to ask Beatrice, the magic user with the dissatisfied look on her face. And that was…

"Is there magic to…weaken someone and kill them in their sleep?"

Subaru wanted to clear up whether the debilitation inflicted on him was via magic rather than poison or illness.

In hindsight, he suspected that the terror and lethargy assaulting his entire body had been caused by magic.

For one thing, he didn't know of any disease with an onset that rapid that debilitated and killed you within hours. Even if it was another world, it was still a little hard to believe.

He'd thought about assassination via poison, but he just couldn't put good odds on it. When you added the fact that someone had bludgeoned Subaru to death, attacking both with poison and by weapon just didn't make any sense.

Listening to Subaru's question, Beatrice raised her eyebrows and shrugged her small shoulders as she replied.

"Such things do exist."

"They do, huh?"

"It is closer to a curse than a spell, I suppose? Shamans specialize in such arts, as suits their devious natures."

Bewildered, Subaru added the new profession *shaman* to his lexicon as Beatrice raised a finger and elaborated.

"Inflictors of curses, or shamans, hail from the nation of Gusteko to the north and practice an offshoot of magic and spiritualism. They are all worthless sorts unable to use their talents for anything better, I suppose."

"But how do you call someone who can kill someone else with a curse 'worthless'?"

"Because that is all they can do—curses have no use except to inflict harm on others. That is why they are the pettiest of all mana practitioners, I suppose."

Apparently, aversion to the dark arts was so ingrained that Beatrice could not hide her disgust. Subaru wasn't trying to stick up for curses, either; he simply craved all the information he could get, visibly prodding her for more.

"So curses can do things like what I said earlier?"

"I believe they can. But are there not simpler methods than a curse, I wonder?"

"Simpler?"

"I believe you have experienced it already."

As Subaru inclined his head, Beatrice turned her palm toward him with a cruel smile. The malevolent smile that in no way suited a little girl clued in Subaru as to the true meaning of her words.

"You mean...I could've died from that invasive mana-drain thing?!"

"Mana is the force of life itself, I suppose. Had I continued draining you so strongly, I could have indeed weakened you until you died. It is a much easier and more reliable method than relying on a shaman."

"So that thing you used at our first...I mean, the first day! You mean one slip and I was a goner?!"

"I held back because having your husk in here would be too much trouble, I suppose."

"Don't say husk! That sounds like I'm a bug!"

Subaru himself wondered why he felt such tranquility there when Beatrice truly thought of him as nothing more than that.

"Don't tell me you were the one who killed me..."

"It would be more peaceful if I had killed you and we weren't having this conversation. Unfortunately, I am quite busy, so I lack the time to bother to kill you, I suppose."

Beatrice held her hands behind her back, striding past Subaru to stand before the bookshelf. The hem of her goth loli outfit quivered as the little girl stretched, trying to get to a place just a little bit higher than she could reach, when...

"Is it this one?"

"...The one next to it. Give it to me already?"

"Yeah, yeah."

Subaru took the unexpectedly thick tome off the bookshelf and handed it to Beatrice, whose cheeks were puffed out. Beatrice kept up a sullen look as she accepted the book from him, not speaking a single word of thanks as she sat on a stool in the center of the room.

He'd seen her several times like that in the archive of forbidden books. It probably suited her better than an actual chair.

"What kind of book are you reading, anyway?"

"One that contains a method for driving an insect out of a room."

"A bug in an archive, huh… Sounds horrible. What kind?"

"It has large black eyes and a foul mouth. Also, it thinks rather highly of itself."

"That's pretty specific for an insect, there…"

He looked around the area, thinking of driving it off straightaway if he could.

As Subaru twisted around his neck, his eyes fell upon the book once more. Beatrice went, *Ahem.*

"Is there still something you want, I wonder? If not, could you please go?"

"Ah, er… Right, is that mana drain something anyone can do?"

"Should I feel slighted, I wonder… In this manor, only Puckie and I can perform such a feat. Even Roswaal cannot."

"Huh. I thought he said he could do it all."

So Roswaal was indulging in vanity? That or mana drain was an unexpectedly rare skill given the simplicity of its effect.

"Anyway, um, don't go sucking people dry too much, okay? Especially me—I'm seriously short on blood right now, so I'd weaken and die pretty easily."

"Ah, because the flesh was all restored but the blood was not? Well, I had no obligation to go that far regardless."

To Beatrice's declaration, made with a shrug of her shoulders, Subaru tilted his head and went, "Mm?"

The grammar she'd used just then implied something rather odd.

"The way you said that just now, it sounded like you closed my wound. Don't tell me you're petty enough to take credit for Emilia's work?"

"That half-baked little girl lacks the power to heal a fatal wound.

She and Puckie stopped the bleeding, but I healed the wound… What of it, I wonder?"

"Er, I'm seriously super conflicted here!"

The circumstances of Subaru's recovery had been exposed in highly unexpected fashion.

Subaru had been absolutely certain that Emilia had healed his wounds just like she'd done in the alley previously, but…

Though he narrowed his eyes suspiciously and made a look of doubt, Beatrice was unmoved.

Barring her being a liar of exceptional gall, the truth was no doubt as she'd spoken.

Meaning Beatrice was…

"Then you're a big filthy liar! Lot of gall you have there. Bottom-of-the-barrel personality!"

"And you have quite some gall to not politely accept the generosity of others!"

Subaru's rude statement and Beatrice's angry shout resulted in a staring contest between them, one Beatrice finally resolved by sending Subaru flying back with magic until he smacked into a wall.

As Subaru bounced off the wall and rolled head over heels before her, Beatrice slowly stroked one of her long curls.

"Could you finally leave, I wonder? Your hands aren't shaking anymore, so it would seem you've put your fears behind you."

"…So you noticed, huh?"

"You were trying to hide it, I suppose. I'm offended you tried to play me like that."

Beatrice made a bored-sounding snort and shooed away Subaru with her hand like he was an annoying insect.

Her words and how she lifted her hand before Subaru's face made his fingertips forget to tremble.

He'd died a total of five times so far, but he most certainly wasn't used to it. Quite the opposite; the more times he died, the more the accumulated experience made his knees quiver from his raw fear of experiencing death again.

That went double for the cause of death being first-degree murder.

Upon his return, Subaru's heart creaked from despair; surely no one could blame him for his courage not reaching the tips of his fingers and toes.

"Guess there's no more time for excuses. Man, you're not nice at all."

Sighing away the last cobwebs, Subaru got up and reached toward the archive's door.

Subaru looked back and made a bitter smile toward Beatrice, who wasn't even looking at him.

"Sorry, but thanks. See ya next time."

"I shall take more mana from you next time, so could you simply stay away, I wonder?"

Her eyes remained fixed on her book as she verbally brushed him off. Feeling Beatrice's attitude spurring him onward, Subaru turned the knob and slipped through the Passage. Then—

"Wait, the insect from earlier—don't tell me you meant me?!"

"You want to leave not on your feet but through the air, I suppose?!"

And so, he flew out of the Passage.

2

In the garden, the silver-haired girl looked down at him.

"Er, may I ask if you're all right?"

"That kindness alone heals my wounds. That much is no lie."

Subaru slumped his shoulders as he spoke.

Sent flying by Beatrice's magic, Subaru had been rammed through the Passage and shot out of a second-story terrace window facing the garden, tumbling onto a flower bed below. He'd almost died from a domestic dispute.

"The theory that *she* killed me is getting more and more convincing…"

"I think Rem fertilized that flower bed with manure yesterday…"

"Whoaaaa, three-second rule—!!"

Having been thrust into the flower bed for more like thirty

seconds than three, Subaru leapt out. He desperately tried to brush the mud—and perhaps things other than mud—off him as he stood before Emilia at an oddly close distance.

"It doesn't count! It doesn't count, right?! That was yesterday and all!"

"Well, just think of it as: When bad luck is with you, good luck is not far away."

"And Emilia's already in Consolation Mode!"

As Subaru wiped away small tears with his sleeve, Emilia, a bitter smile on her noble face, must have felt pity for him as she touched the pendant between her breasts.

"—Puck, wake up."

The green crystal flared lightly, responding to Emilia's call. The light formed first the contours, then the full image of a little cat that materialized and rested on Emilia's palm.

The little kitty heavily stretched its little body, looking like it was making a yawn.

"Mm, good morning, Lia. Ahh, Subaru's up already."

"Good morning, Puck. Sorry to wake you all of a sudden, but could you wash Subaru, please?"

Puck, watching with one eye as Emilia pled her request, suddenly oohed as he looked in Subaru's direction. Looking at Subaru's mud-covered appearance, he nodded, apparently agreeing with the girl's request.

"Time for a bath, then. There!"

"Bath is putting it mildly. I... Whoa?!"

As Puck thrust out both hands, the dazzling, pale light that came from them turned into a large amount of water the next moment, slamming into Subaru's upper body with incredible force, scrubbing away all the world's impurities.

"That's a water cannon—!!"

"Whoops, I threw off his balance a little."

With Subaru's body turning around from his upper body being bathed in water, Puck adjusted the water flow in the other direction with a little too much oomph. Subaru was unable to resist being turned right to left, round and round.

"See? You're all clean now. Isn't that nice?"

"Wh… When you play with me like that…my heart goes…round and round…"

Subaru, sitting on a soggy patch of grass, was groggy with his eyes still spinning. He wiped his face with his soaked sleeve and somehow rose up despite his wobbly state.

"Man, if you're that rough, I'll start seriously thinking you're the culprits?"

"I'm not sure what I'm being suspected of, but I'm deeply, deeply hurt… *Nyaa?!*"

As the little kitty floated in midair, pretending to be upset, Subaru pressed a finger to his narrow forehead and turned him toward Emilia as he cried out.

Somehow, this was the most frivolous, wonderful reunion he'd had so far. Putting aside that Emilia should have been tearfully rushing to greet Subaru upon his revival from mortal injury…

He wondered what he should say as his first step to resolving the situation—

"*Bwa.*"

"Huh?"

"*Bwahaha!* I'm sorry, I can't, *ah-ha-ah-ha-ha-ha*! What are you two doing… Ah, my sides hurt; I'm going to die…"

Suddenly Emilia, unable to hold it in any longer, burst out laughing, driving away all his worries.

As Emilia pointed at Subaru, who looked like a drowned rat, her normally neatly arranged expression was gripped by mirth. The unexpected reaction made Subaru look at Puck, who was floating right beside his face.

"Well, my initial bad impression's all gone! Thanks for the assist, Dad!"

In response to Subaru's impudent suggestion, Puck puffed out his chest haughtily.

"Who are you calling 'Dad'?! You won't have my daughter that easily!!"

Upon hearing this, Emilia's loud, laughing voice filled the whole garden.

3

Having finished her laughter, Emilia was watching Subaru as she spoke.

"I heard Ram and Rem were heading for the garden, but they're a little late…"

Emilia was still wiping the vestiges of the tears from her eyes from laughing so hard. Subaru, the chief culprit, toyed with Puck in the middle of his hand.

"Huh. So when you say they're late, can I take it that you've been waiting here for my sake?"

"Uh, isn't it the other way around? It's true that I should thank you, and if I moved without thinking, we might miss each other and I don't want that, but it's just coincidence that I stayed here with you."

"Right, it's just coincidence, Subaru. She makes me drag out my grooming for one reason after another and speaks to the lesser spirits about the same things over and over… She says it's all just coincidence."

As usual, just as Emilia was in the middle of completely self-destructing, Puck added fuel to the fire.

"Sheesh, Puck!"

"She should just be honest with herself. That's a cute thing about Lia, though…don't you think, Subaru?"

"Oh, definitely! Everything about Emilia-tan is the brightest star in my sky!"

"Now Subaru's teasing me… And what is that 'tan'? Where did that come from?"

She was finally voicing some doubts about the way he was speaking to her.

Up until last time, it was a subject Emilia had managed to let slide. Subaru put a hand to his chin and made what sounded like some kind of diabolical chuckle.

"It's a sign of my affection. It's like how Puck calls you Lia... A way for two people to show how close they are to each other."

"...Not that I remember being quite that close to you?"

"Wow, that statement kind of hurts, you know. I was kind of making a down payment. I'm totally planning to have a relationship with Emilia-tan that goes hand in hand with the pet names. Okay?"

At the very least, he hoped to get close enough to her by a few nights from then that she'd forgive him for it.

Emilia's face expressed surprise at Subaru's strong approach, then her cheeks reddened a bit.

"F-fine. I'll accept that. Hey, don't look at me like that!"

"Er? I thought I was getting brushed off? What's that positive reaction? Explain this, Mr. Puck."

As Emilia turned her face aside, Puck sat on her shoulder and twirled his mustache.

"My daughter doesn't have many friends, so being called by an intimate nickname makes her happy. Put simply, she's easy."

Subaru exclaimed in surprise, "My leading lady's easy!"

He thought he'd merely climbed a treacherous wall, but he felt the sudden realization that it was more. He continued, "But we're still a long way apart... I need to learn a little more about this whole nobility thing."

"Ugh...could you not mention something I *really* don't want to talk about?"

"I just want to reach an agreement on E M P (Emilia-tan's Majorly Pretty). Oh?"

Subaru pressed silliness onto Emilia when he abruptly looked back at the mansion and narrowed his eyes. Emilia followed Subaru's gaze, tilting her head as she watched the twins come out of the mansion.

"Ram and Rem, huh... It's a bit too soon to be breakfast time, though..."

The image of the sunlight reflecting off her silver hair seemed to burn into Subaru's eyes as he confirmed that events were proceeding.

It was the time of Roswaal's return. The twins simultaneously bowed their heads before them.

They spoke with the same stereo effect he'd now heard many times over.

"Master Roswaal, lord of the manor, has returned. Please come with us."

Subaru watched Emilia nod to them as he turned toward the twins with a hand casually pressed to his rear.

"Sister, Sister. Since last we saw him, he has become a muddy drowned rat."

"Rem, Rem. Since last we saw him, our guest has become a stained, filthy rag."

Subaru made a pained smile at their sharp comments as he looked up at the sight of the mansion.

He would change clothes, tidy himself up, and head to meet Roswaal for a fresh start.

—Because this time, he intended to take a completely different approach than before.

4

—And so, his first week at Roswaal Manor began in earnest for the third time.

For this third loop, Subaru wanted to emphasize gathering information.

"My keywords are *magic* and *chain*…but that doesn't tell me anything yet."

The only thing he knew for sure was that someone would attack in the dead of night on the fourth day.

Under the present circumstances, if he told Roswaal and the others, they'd no doubt ignore him. Subaru simply couldn't explain where he got his information. Subaru could even get himself suspected as one of the assassins arrayed against them. If he at least had a physical description of the attacker, things might be different, but…

"That's why I've gotta spend this time gathering intel. If the Return by Death conditions are the same as before…"

On the royal capital loop, he'd died three times and had a breakthrough on the fourth. If things were as before, he'd be able to return one more time. So this time he'd gather the intel he needed for a breakthrough the fourth time around.

"To be honest, I don't like picking a plan that's giving up from the start…"

However, his options being very limited, he had to resign himself to some sacrifices. At any rate, he had no intention of throwing away his opportunity. It was the difference between resolving to redo everything and aiming from the start to overcome the challenge. This time, he'd focus entirely on getting out of the loop.

"For that, I had to tell Puck under the table to keep Emilia safe."

In the middle of playing around with Puck in the garden, Subaru had whispered to Puck to pay attention to Emilia's surroundings. The little kitty could read minds; Subaru figured he'd know Subaru's earnestness was no lie.

"I made things pretty vague, but he seems genuinely protective of Lia."

After all, he'd given Subaru's pushy suggestion a warm reception. He could now assume that Emilia would be relatively safe.

It wasn't much, but it did relieve a bit of the burden on his shoulders.

"After that, there's Roswaal and the loli… But after that, what?"

Subaru scratched his head all over, plucked out a hair, pinched his feather pen under his nose, and stretched his back.

His head hurt from the difficult dilemmas. That being said, he had to do whatever he could. If possible, he wanted Ram and Rem, and of course Roswaal and Beatrice as well, to get through those four days safely. He had his reasons for not running no matter how formidable the challenge.

"My concentration just ain't cutting it. What to do… Huh?"

As he leaned back against his chair, it made a creaking sound when he heard a voice from outside.

"Pardon me, Dear Guest."

Faster than Subaru could reply, the door opened and he saw a pink-haired maid—Ram.

Subaru raised an eyebrow as Ram came in with a steaming cup sitting on a tray in her hands.

"Oh my, Dear Guest, you really are studying."

"That's super rude, you know. I am kind of an actual guest at the moment?"

"Dear Guest, you are the manner of houseguest known as a freeloader."

Looking calm and composed, Ram let herself into the room and began serving tea.

Watching from the side as she worked, Subaru could not conceal his bitter smile at her words.

A houseguest and freeloader—he thought the terms fit all too well.

"Here you go, Dear Guest."

"Oh, thanks. Hot-hot-hot…"

When he took the cup and looked down into it, he saw steam rising from the surface of the hot amber liquid. The tea of this world was nearest to black tea in appearance and taste. The rich aroma was just as easy to enjoy.

Ram's attitude was very blunt, but it was odd that she'd come in to serve tea like this. As he watched Ram's polished movements, Subaru slowly tasted the tea he'd been offered, nodding.

"Mm…really does taste awful."

"This manor serves tea using leaves of the highest quality, so that is quite a statement."

"If it tastes bad, it tastes bad. I just can't think of it as anything but black tea. Tastes like…plant."

Ram coldly watched Subaru's scowling face as she served herself tea that she had brought like it was the most normal thing in the world, sitting down on the bed and stretching her legs without a care.

"I don't have words for the guts you have, slacking off in front of a guest."

"I believe you were the one who said to take it easier, Dear Guest? I am doing this only to respond to your request. You should be thanking me."

"This is, like, even pushier than you were before, though?"

Subaru voiced his complaints as he sank back in his chair and made a loud sound. Ram listened to that sound as she wet her tongue with black tea, finally giving Subaru a sideways glance.

"And, Dear Guest leaving in two days, have you made any progress?"

Subaru broke out in a small, bitter smile as he listened to her exceptionally dry delivery.

—It was already the second night since he had begun the third loop.

For this third time around, Subaru had been treated at the mansion like a guest, a sharp difference from before. That was because Subaru had requested as much at that first breakfast.

Now that he was being treated as a guest, Subaru had his own room and Rem and Ram took turns serving him as he continued the language study he'd begun the last time.

—All of it was to justify his leaving the mansion temporarily without creating a stir.

He was forming plans in his head while his fingers continued copying I-script almost automatically. His movements were robotic enough to make one's stomach twist, but nothing was really getting into his head.

"Are you always this bad, or is your foolish head unable to concentrate?"

"Got some nerve saying that to a literary enthusiast like me. Aren't you inspired from watching me give this desk my all back there?"

"An uncouth statement to match such sloppy writing—I am aghast you call yourself a literary enthusiast, Dear Guest."

"This is the first time I've seen a maid talk to her guests like you do."

Ram politely ignored Subaru's resentful statement and browsed with apparent interest the pages filled with characters. Even with the distance so close, he glared as he watched the side of her face, unable to stop the feeling that his insides were being wrung.

Unlike the previous occasions when Subaru had been treated as a servant, he'd had little contact with Ram this time around. Beyond his time spent in pursuit of Emilia, he'd mainly stayed in his room writing characters like this. Though once in a while he spared some time to go tease Beatrice a little...

So the distance between Ram and Rem and himself felt far greater than when he was treated as a servant.

In spite of that, here was Ram visiting Subaru in his room, spending time with him and speaking to him like a very blunt friend. He couldn't help but find it strange.

"If you do not stop staring at me like that, I shall slap you, Dear Guest."

"Hey, the only one making the inside of my head go pink is Emilia... Oh, that's right."

Trying to deflect his unease as he averted his eyes, he set aside the tea and picked up a book with its back cover facing up. This was the picture book he was using as learning material; he was finally able to understand the characters in it.

"In other words, I want to make all this studying feel like it got me somewhere."

"It contains only common stories you should be ashamed not to know. You need to master basic I-script before calling yourself a 'literary enthusiast.'"

"Does calling myself that tick you off *that* much?"

Ram made no reply to Subaru's question as she poured the remaining contents of her cup down her throat. She then reached for Subaru's cup.

"Wait, you're gonna drink all the tea you brought here?!"

"You do not need it if you are making a face like that when you drink it. At least it shall be enjoyed by someone with a properly functioning tongue."

"I told you, I just can't get that plant taste out of my h... Oh, never mind. I'm gonna focus on this book, so you can kill time or head off, whatever you want."

Subaru made a brusque wave before leaning forward in his chair and opening the picture book.

First came the author's preface and the table of contents; after that came the body, written in the characters he'd now grown accustomed to.

"Err, let's see…a long, long time ago…"

So fairy tales start the same way in every world, huh, he accepted with strange ease as he continued reading the story. The fact that it was in a picture book meant the story was exceptionally concise with a clearly defined introduction, body, and conclusion. Child-level comprehension was prioritized, with pictures used precisely where there was room for imagination.

Incidentally, if one asked Subaru which fairy tale he liked best, he would reply, "The Crying Red Demon." If one asked Subaru which fairy tale he hated most, he would reply, "The Crying Red Demon."

"It's, like, a happy ending and a bitter ending slamming into you at once. Why can't it all be happily ever after?"

"Sorry to intrude on your deep thoughts, but are you finished reading?"

"I'm finished reading. The things that went against common sense were fun, so it was more interesting than I expected. Guess that's another world's culture for you. Maybe I should bring in fairy tales from my own homeland, too, like 'The Crying Red Demon'?"

" 'The Crying Red Demon'…?"

Subaru was mumbling about the copyright issues in another world's jurisdiction when Ram's eyebrows trembled in response. *Huh*, went Subaru, getting a rare rise out of Ram.

"It's the title of a fairy tale from where I come from. How about I tell it to you?"

Ram did not reply as Subaru made the suggestion with a thumbs-up. However, the way she sat on the bed with her hands on her knees, shifting her gaze to Subaru, clearly conveyed that he should get on with it.

"All right, attention, please. 'The Crying Red Demon.' A long, long time ago, in a certain land, there was…"

The fairy tale began with a bitter argument. "The Crying Red Demon" was a tale of friendship between the Red Demon, which wanted to become friends with humans, and his best friend, the Blue Demon—and what came between them.

It went something like this: The two demons living on the mountain tried various things to get the Red Demon in the good graces of the villagers, culminating in the Blue Demon committing wicked deeds upon the village, only to be driven off by the Red Demon, who thus befriended the human beings. The tale ended with the Blue Demon leaving; the Red Demon, dispirited at the Blue Demon's display of friendship, cried for the Blue Demon's sake.

"And so, the Red Demon read over and over the letter left at the Blue Demon's house and cried… The end."

Subaru finished conveying to Ram a somewhat abridged version of the fairy tale. It was a fairy tale Subaru himself had read many times over. He thought he was as faithful with his words as possible, keeping his own opinions out of it.

Ram lowered her eyes as she listened to the tale. Subaru stayed in the same position as when he'd finished the story, waiting for her to speak. Finally, Ram let out a small sigh.

"…A rather sad tale."

"I suppose so. But I think it's a happy story, too."

"I think the cast of characters was full of idiots… The Red Demon, the Blue Demon, and the villagers, too."

"Well, that's being a tough critic. Not that you'll get any argument from me…"

He agreed that none of the three sides had enough introspection. The villagers were pure suckers, and if the two demons had spoken more to each other, they might have found proper common ground. At the very least, surely they could have avoided the need for one to put distance between him and the other for the rest of their lives.

"That's why I love this story and hate this story. The Blue Demon's self-sacrifice was super cool, but he was an idiot beyond saving, too. I like to think I can save myself through putting in the effort..."

"So you think that about the Blue Demon...I think it is the Red Demon who is beyond saving."

Ram's reply made Subaru lift his head. Ram was looking at Subaru as she bit her tongue.

"He wrapped the Blue Demon in his own desires, losing nothing when the Blue Demon lost everything. I think that is a rather horrible result."

"What do you think the two demons should've done, then?"

"...If the Red Demon truly wanted to be friends with the humans, he should have gone to live in the village, even if it meant cutting off his horn. He should have done that long before the Blue Demon left."

"Man, that's a pretty extreme position, there!"

Subaru raised his voice at the radical view she'd provided, but Ram simply stroked her own short hair like she was saying, *Is it now?* She proceeded to toy with the ribbon holding her hair in place.

"Making the Blue Demon pay for something he wants is unforgivable. If the Red Demon wants it, the Red Demon should pay the price. The Blue Demon robbing him of that chance is a problem, too."

"That's a really strict view of it. Do you have something against demons...?"

"—Dear Guest, which of the two demons would you rather befriend?"

Subaru blinked at Ram's question. He hadn't really thought about it.

"...Which of the two?"

Ram nodded and stretched out both hands toward Subaru, raising one finger from each.

"On the one hand, the Red Demon who asks and asks and leaves others to pay the consequences, or the Blue Demon, the idiot drowning in his own martyrdom. Which?"

"Geez, you make both of those choices feel bad… So what, I'm a villager who just arrived here?"

It was rather rare for the point of view of the villagers to come up in a discussion about "The Crying Red Demon." Either way, Subaru was a little lost as he stared at the two hands Ram presented before him when she said, "…What an uninteresting reply."

"Don't say that! Since I've read 'The Crying Red Demon,' I sympathize with the two of them, so I want to help out both, okay?"

Subaru gently pressed both his hands onto both of Ram's hands. Subaru's reply drew a long sigh out of Ram; she glared at Subaru, who of course was close enough to touch.

"So you're the type who understands neither his position nor that of others… When distance grows, your type gets left behind by both."

"Distance, huh. Why not just tell people how you feel while they're still close? The Red Demon's not a bad guy for wanting to get along, and the Blue Demon's not a bad guy for wanting to help him, either. I'm the type who likes demons, not the type to just drive 'em off the island at the drop of a hat."

Ram sighed at the grinning Subaru and looked at her own two hands as he grasped her raised fingers. As she brushed him off, Subaru shrugged and sat back in his seat, readjusting himself to face Ram again.

"You know, Ram, you seem to like 'The Crying Red Demon' quite a bit."

"Dear Guest, you will someday regret fickle, indecisive thoughts such as wanting to be friends with both."

"I don't remember that being what we were talking about here?! I thought we were talking about demons?"

As Subaru shouted and shook his head, Ram made a small clap of her hands to indicate the subject was closed. Her quick-tempered behavior tugged at him, but Ram pointed to the book on the desk before he could say a word.

"Setting aside the tales from our Dear Guest's homeland… What did you think of the stories of this land?"

"Let's see... I suppose the one that stood out was the dragon one in the middle of the book and the witch one at the end. No matter how I slice it, those two are different somehow."

Subaru gave a wandering reply as he browsed the book. Those were the two tales that had left the deepest impression upon him. The former definitely got special treatment. As for the latter...

"The witch story was like...they felt they had to put it in but they went halfway. It completely ignored story structure...like a bunch of highlights."

"...That cannot be helped. We are in Lugunica... Of course the dragon story gets special treatment."

Subaru nodded as he flipped the pages of the picture book on the desk.

"Right, 'Dragonfriend Kingdom of Lugunica,' right? Now I get why it's called that."

Apparently the large kingdom Subaru was staying in was called the "Dragonfriend Kingdom of Lugunica." On world maps, it looked like the easternmost nation in the world, but apparently it had good reason to be called the "Dragonfriend Kingdom."

It was a simple tale, really. Long ago, the kingdom had come under the protection of a dragon, forming a pact.

"The dragon is said to have lent its power to Lugunica, protecting it in times of famine, plague, war with other nations, and other various predicaments."

"So that's why they call it 'Dragonfriend,' huh. It did say in the picture book that the royal family made a pact with the dragon. This is less of a fairy tale than ancient history, right?"

"I suppose so. It's a true story, after all. Even now, the dragon protects the peace of this land from under a great waterfall far away until the day its promise to the royal family comes to an end."

Subaru cleared his throat as he listened to the oh-so-strict Ram speak such words.

A promise made with a dragon in ancient times... The picture book had not drawn the details, but it was a big enough deal that the kingdom had been saved from crisis many times over.

Thinking of that, Subaru suddenly realized something about the royal family that'd made the pact with the dragon.

"Hey, the family that made the promise with the dragon…didn't it just die out?"

"It did, and suddenly at that."

"Isn't that, like, bad? Er, not that I'd know what bad means here."

No doubt the dragon had been promised something considerable in return for protecting its promise all that time. Yet with the royal family that would be granting it dying off on him like that, who would honor that obligation?

Ram began.

"No one knows what the dragon seeks, so it was not put in the picture book. Only gods know what the dragon will do in this situation…"

At that point, Ram paused for a moment.

"Rather, Dear Guest—only the dragon knows."

Subaru's breath caught. He wasn't warm, but he felt sweat on his brow regardless. He chewed over Ram's words, swallowed them, and breathed in and out hard enough to make his stomach churn.

Negotiating with the mighty dragon was the responsibility of the ruler of the kingdom. In other words…

"That has to be a mountain of pressure on Emilia, then…"

"Yes. The dragon can protect the kingdom or destroy it on a whim… Thus, the kingdom and its destiny rest upon Emilia's shoulders. Just thinking about it makes it seem like a story from that picture book."

There'd been a conflicted look on Emilia's face when she saw the picture book on the last night of the previous loop. Now Subaru understood why Emilia's hand had stopped when she was flipping the pages.

The size and weight of Emilia's burden had far surpassed Subaru's expectations. His mind wanted to cry out just from thinking about the heavy responsibility borne by those delicate shoulders.

"It cannot be helped."

"—Ah?"

"Everyone was born with a role to play and the responsibility to live up to it. This is what Lady Emilia was born to do. It is a path she must walk, no matter how treacherous it may be."

Subaru's voice was shaking with anger from a source he couldn't place.

"One girl's supposed to shoulder the whole burden like that?"

For her part, Ram's voice was cold and logical.

"I believe it is best if others can carry it with her. However, sooner or later, Lady Emilia must be seen to climb that summit herself."

Subaru slumped his shoulders when he realized Ram was holding back to not fuel his anger further.

He could vent at Ram all he wanted, but he'd be mistaken. Ram wasn't responsible for the weight of Emilia's burden; at any rate, Subaru had no right to be angry. That part really burned him.

"Oh, right. Ram, about that other story…"

Wanting to do something other than apologize, Subaru changed the subject and pointed at the picture book.

Contrary to how the story of the dragon in the center of the book had received special treatment, the story of the witch had only a few pages drawn for it at the very back of the book.

The story was titled, "The Witch of Jealousy."

"So this witch story…"

"I do not wish to speak of it."

Just like that, she seemed to verbally cut things off after the story of the dragon.

Subaru opened his eyes wide without thinking as Ram briskly got up, tray and cups in hand.

"I have been here too long. I do not wish to cause Rem too much trouble. Dear Guest, I shall call you again for dinnertime."

"R-right…"

Ram, turning her back like she would brook no argument, immediately headed out of the room.

But just before her hand reached the door, Ram stopped and looked back at Subaru, left in her dust.

"About the demon story from earlier…"

"Mm, right. 'The Crying Red Demon.' What of it?"

"Don't tell Rem that story. She would probably find it distasteful."

Surely no one would have that kind of reaction over a simple fairy tale. Regardless, Subaru, feeling overwhelming pressure from Ram's words, could only nod meekly in response.

Seeing this, Ram finally left. Subaru, feeling drained, flopped onto the bed.

It felt like there was something more to Ram's last action than just banning him from telling Rem a fairy tale.

"What the heck's up with all that…?"

Venting at the ceiling, Subaru picked up the picture book and flipped through the pages.

The final chapter, "The Witch of Jealousy," was a short tale only four pages long.

"A scary witch, a frightening witch, it is terrifying to just speak her name. That was why everyone called her 'The Jealous Witch'—"

There was no story structure, just contents conveying the raw terror of the witch. It was straight-up eerie, doubly so when written in characters meant for small children.

"And after all the trouble of studying to read this thing…"

His feelings of success, satisfaction, and the glow of having just read a book seemed to fall by the wayside.

Subaru turned in bed and switched his head to a different subject: thinking of what he could do for the remaining two days of that loop.

He'd put his preparations for the last day in order and shifted to what he'd do two mornings hence.

Subaru squished his countless worries one by one until he finally fell asleep.

5

"Err, my time here's been brief, but thanks for taking care of me."

In the mansion's entry hall, all the human beings in the mansion (meaning only four people, with Beatrice not included) were seeing Subaru off as he made his good-byes.

Subaru had asked that he be allowed to stay for three days. That time had passed; that morning, he would journey onward.

Subaru wore his tracksuit and carried the convenience store bag containing his starting equipment, but he also carried a knapsack over his back that Roswaal had generously provided. The knapsack was fairly heavy from a decent sum of coinage, Roswaal explained simply.

"My thanks for taking care of Lady Emilia."

Among those seeing Subaru off, Emilia called out to him, a look of deep concern on her face even then. Subaru, grateful for Emilia's feelings, vividly thumped his chest.

"I'll be fine. I'm just gonna take it easy. When I become a strong, wise, and rich man suitable for you, I'll come riding back on a white horse."

"You have your handkerchief? And drinking water, lagmite ore, and, and..."

"She's totally acting like she's my mom?!"

Emilia fussed about this and that. The way she asked last, "Can you sleep all by yourself?" made Subaru wonder just how much she longed for the company of others. Or perhaps she was acting on instinct, voicing the unease Subaru was desperately shoving down inside him.

Roswaal came to shake his hand.

"Weeell then, be in good health, Subaru. It has beeeen a short time, but it was quite enjoyable. Do not be concerned about my parting gift. Consider it a smaaall reward for the memories you created these last three days."

Roswaal added a wink to the last part. Subaru could guess what he meant; the knapsack over his back was jingling just from their shaking hands.

"I get it; you're paying me to keep my mouth shut. I won't say anything. I swear on the dragon."

"It will keep others from approaching you as part of some wicked scheme. Besides, in this nation, to swear upon the dragon is to make the highest of oaths. It is not that I doubt you, but strive not to forrrget that."

Subaru raised a hand in response to Roswaal's reminder; he then turned to the twins, standing behind the clown-faced nobleman. The two stood silently as Subaru reached and patted them both on the shoulder.

"You two were a huge help, especially Rem with those really delicious meals. Ram… Mm, well, she cleans toilets really well?"

"Sister, Sister, the Dear Guest's flattery is despairingly awkward."

"Rem, Rem, the Dear Guest's flattery is a complete disaster."

"Well, excuse me, I really couldn't think of anything else! But thanks."

Having said his good-byes to everyone, he pushed open the front doors before he got cold feet.

From the entrance of the manor, he cut through the garden, passed through the metal gate, and continued on to the forest path that was a straight shot to Auram Village. Subaru's stated plan was to head from there to the nearest highway, hire a passing carriage, and head to the capital—but that plan was a feint.

"Subaru, thanks for everything. If anything happens, come back anytime, okay?"

With Emilia's statement of farewell, her words gentle until the bitter end, Subaru departed, walking the path toward Auram Village. The silver-haired girl waved until she could no longer see Subaru from the mansion. Her oh-so-adorable behavior dulled his worries and made his sense of duty burn once more.

—After heading down the path to the village for a while, Subaru stopped and cautiously looked around the area. When he was sure no one was around to watch him, he left the path and dove into the woods. He did so regardless of Ram's and the others' admonitions that this was dangerous due to the many wild animals within.

Ignoring their warnings, Subaru pushed his way through the foliage as he headed deeper into the forest. At some point, he ascended a slope, not slowing his pace when branches and briar patches scratched him.

He proceeded up the mountain like that for about fifteen minutes.

"Okay, I'll do it here."

Subaru left the greenery, the soaring sky greeting his vision. Subaru had cleared the forested slopes, arriving at a foothill nestled among the mountains. He could watch the mansion below from the cliff right in front of him.

From there, he could observe the familiar, luxurious sights of Roswaal Manor. He'd circled around from the forest path and cut through forest and mountain to arrive at the perfect observation point.

"It has an especially good view of Emilia's room. I'll see anything weird happening right away."

He could make out the window to Emilia's room even at a distance. He couldn't see inside, but it was a good spot for watching for any signs of trouble. And on the night of the fourth day, trouble would surely come.

"In other words, tonight. All that's left is to wait for something to happen."

From that morning, Subaru had about sixteen hours to kill—surely he could hold his concentration that long.

This way, he could figure out what would happen at Roswaal Manor beforehand and rush back to the manor immediately. This time Subaru would have the element of surprise on his side.

If he'd remained at the mansion, Subaru would be one more victim of the attacker's curse. With limited means of counterattack and low overall combat ability, Subaru couldn't take on the attacker straight up. He desperately needed any shred of information he could get on the assassin.

So, what to do? Subaru had come up with a simple answer.

"This time, my goal is to identify the attacker and nail down the details of the attack…even if it kills me."

Having died twice so far, Subaru had determined that the attack was an assassination having to do with the royal succession. He didn't know if he'd been collateral damage with Emilia as the main target or if he'd been killed as some kind of message to her. But having been murdered twice already, Subaru considered it highly likely everyone close to her was being slaughtered.

"Putting aside if countermeasures will work...seems like Roswaal has his guard up anyway..."

Subaru based that on the premise that Roswaal, the nobleman with a scheming mind behind his clown face, was not such a fool as to leave his king piece, bearing the name of Emilia, defenseless on the chessboard. The existence of Ram and Rem, the two servants he'd left behind at the mansion, was further evidence.

"To be honest, at first I thought it was nuts to have just two maids taking care of a huge mansion like that, but..."

They were lord and vassal, their mutual trust rock solid, bonds of loyalty formed through long service. Seeing Ram's slavish devotion and Rem's adoration of her had told him that much.

Roswaal had surely surrounded Emilia with people who would never betray him. The fact that one maid had retired several months before, yet, according to Ram, no replacement would be hired, assured him Emilia would be protected.

"The problem is, I don't know if they're on guard *enough*, given that I died from the attack already. If I'm the only one who died, well, good... Wait, that's not good."

If Roswaal's defense plans simply didn't account for Subaru, a wild card, then all was well and good. If it wasn't so, that meant Emilia would come to harm as well.

And Subaru, having died three times at the capital and two at the manor, was accustomed by now to reality foiling the best of plans.

You needed to expect the worst case...and then expect worse than that.

"Here, the worst case is that Roswaal's guard is down and Emilia gets assassinated. Of course, that'd mean Roswaal, Ram, Rem, and then Beatrice get slaughtered, too... Ugh, damn it."

Just picturing the worst-case scenario filled him with disgust.

Though it was to stop all that, he wanted to vent at his entirely logical decision to watch events unfold from the outside.

Of course Subaru, who wore his heart on his sleeve, planned to stay on guard the whole time, ready to instantly rush back to the manor if anything happened, running around and warning of the enemy attack, but...

"Well, it'd be nice if the guy's super cautious and runs off just from my yelling at him, right?"

Subaru voiced the optimistic view as he pulled a rope out of his knapsack. It was a rather long rope he'd borrowed from the manor's warehouse. Subaru firmly tied one end around the trunk of a nearby tree and the other around his own waist. He used complex knots along the way as if his life depended on it, which it kind of did.

"And last, the knife to cut the rope... She'd probably be ticked off if she knew I was using it like this."

As he spoke, he took out the knife that he'd lovingly dubbed Shooting Star. In the present loop, he'd been in a position to lay his hands on it for the first time only that day.

"I used it a whole bunch during the four days of the other loops, though."

During his time doing odd jobs as a servant, Subaru's kitchen duties mainly involved peeling vegetables and washing tableware. Shooting Star was the beloved blade that Subaru had used to cut potato-like veggies, apples, and, from time to time, his own hand. When, this time, he'd come up with a plan that required a knife, he grabbed that one without a second thought.

"Hopefully just for cutting the rope, but if worse comes to worst..."

The knife was not only to facilitate his escape but to wound himself if the time came, for surely stimulation from the pain of self-harm would make him able to resist the gnawing sleepiness of the curse.

If worse came to worst, he might have to turn that blade upon the enemy. And if it was worse than that—

"For suicide, huh? Geez...can I do that? Something that scary..."

Subaru looked at himself reflected in the blade's edge as a laugh at his own expense came over him.

As he looked at the blade in his hand, memories of Ram and Rem rose in the back of his mind. Ram had insulted Subaru for his clumsy knife work; Rem had shot him shocked sideways glances when he'd cut his own hand with the knife. They angrily shouted things like, *Do not cut what you are not supposed to.*

"...They'd be angry with me for misusing it like this, too, wouldn't they?"

He could totally picture in his mind both girls angry with him, with Ram glaring down at him and Rem looking aghast.

Ahh, that scene was just—

"They'd be totally pissed, huh... I hope they would be..."

The longing words leaked out from his lips. One way or another, he truly wanted to bury himself in that day-to-day life again.

"I don't wanna die— I don't wanna let them die..."

Subaru said it for his own benefit as he remembered the faces of the people he'd only just said good-bye to.

Subaru had cast away Emilia and the others to prepare for the next loop. Yet this time, just like the last times, he'd formed definite bonds with the girls.

He suppressed his throbbing chest. This was his punishment, the natural price to pay for what he had done.

It was a cross to bear that Subaru, having formed a plan premised on losing something, could not shirk. He had to carry both the sweet and the bitter thoughts with him.

Subaru had spent those thrown-away four days prying open that raw wound, enduring pain like that of having his flesh gouged and his bones broken, all so that he would remember it.

"You said it yourself, Subaru Natsuki. Even if everyone else forgets...you'll remember."

That was why he couldn't think of this time as something he could forget.

Subaru had to continue to crave a happy ending until the last possible moment. No one had the right to decide that Emilia and the others were no more than bubbles on the edge of the time stream.

Subaru kept hidden among the trees as he observed Roswaal Manor. The resolve permeating his presumably stressed body quieted his breathing and lowered his heart rate.

He felt like his body was acting in accordance to his will in a way it never had before.

Trusting his body to that hard-earned feeling, Subaru stayed put and waited for time to pass.

6

As evening drew near, the setting sun bathed the hill Subaru was on in an orange light. Squinting from the sun's rays, Subaru moved his tense body around, shaking out the cobwebs.

He'd already been watching the manor for something like eight hours. During that time, there had been no sign of anything unusual; the mansion remained entirely peaceful. So things really were fine there until night fell.

"Come to think of it, Rem didn't go shopping this time…"

There had been no sign of the Day Four event of Rem going shopping. Perhaps she simply didn't need to because Subaru's departure meant one less mouth to feed. It was an odd discrepancy.

When Subaru realized he was smiling at the memories, his sense of tension lifting, he pinched his own cheek. This wasn't the place or time to let up on his concentration.

"Like I can do something stupid like that with eight hours to go. Concentrate, concentra—"

He stopped mid-word. For better or worse, it was at the very moment Subaru switched gears that the attack came.

"—!"

The instant his eardrums detected a faint sound, Subaru dove to the side without hesitation.

He'd devoted his five senses to determining when to do the evasive maneuver he'd settled on beforehand.

The next moment, he heard something exceptionally heavy make a smashing sound, snapping trees in two. The trees all around him, plus their leaves and branches, came down with a wild cacophony of snapping sounds.

Amid all that, Subaru rushed straight for the cliff and leapt straight down.

"—Aa!"

Even clenching his teeth, he couldn't stop himself from letting out a faint cry, his insides turning over from the weightless feeling of falling. But his lifeline cut that short after two long seconds. He let out an anguished cry from the pain of the ropes biting in.

"Emergency escape…!"

Cutting the rope with his knife, he resumed his descent, the bottoms of his shoes digging into a slanted rock face. Sliding and hitting his shoulder, Subaru landed on the ground roughly, somehow keeping his footing, and ran without pausing for breath.

He tossed away the knapsack to lighten the load, breathing raggedly as he ran without a care for proper form.

"I saw it! Yeaaaah…I totally saw it!"

The object that had attacked Subaru by surprise and mowed down various trees was a spiked iron ball as large as a man's skull. It was basically a killer bowling ball on a really, really long chain—the weapon known as a "morning star."

Subaru had hit the dirt when his eardrums picked up the faint metallic sound of that horrible weapon's chain.

Having witnessed its fiendish power for himself, Subaru still wasn't biting with his teeth lined up right.

The way that thing had flown at him, his body probably would have been splattered if it had connected. Now Subaru could understand how half his body had been sent flying.

"But…he came here, huh?!"

He stomped on branches, leapt across a gulch, and raced across areas with poor footing.

Subaru had anticipated that he might be attacked. Having distanced himself from the manor, he determined that an attack on him was just as possible as a raid on the mansion itself. If the objective was to kill anyone involved, Subaru was still on that list.

"But that's based on knowing I was at the mansion since days ago!"

That would mean the assailant had been observing the mansion for several days, drawing up plans in secret.

"—!"

Out of breath, he'd lost his way, focusing on not tripping as he headed down a game trail.

Subaru, breathing roughly, clicked his tongue at the scene unfolding before him.

"So I've been totally dancing on the other guy's palm?"

Dismayed, Subaru stood before a cliff that hemmed him in.

Looking at the hard, jagged rock wall, it was like a natural fortress for resisting all attempts to climb. Naturally, Subaru had no way at the moment to overcome that obstacle.

Subaru turned around and girded himself, taking deep, ragged breaths.

The forest before him had grown darker at some point, with the trees filtering out the setting sun, making him feel cut off from the world and very, very alone.

"If you're coming, bring it on…!"

Subaru shoved away his misgivings, opening his track jacket in front and stripping it off. He spread out the track jacket with both hands, quietly waiting for his assailant to arrive.

He was being pursued. He'd been backed into a corner. That moment, Subaru felt as helpless as prey caught in a predator's trap. But he wasn't so cute and helpless that he'd let himself get eaten without a fight.

He'd make the other guy earn it.

"Damn it…you coming or not?!?"

Subaru's body demonstrated uncanny reflexes toward the lethal attack before his eyes.

He raised the track jacket aloft with both hands, catching the flying iron ball from below, enveloping it as he barely evaded by the skin of his teeth a ferocious strike to his body.

But the top was ripped from his hands as his body smacked against the wall with an undiluted impact.

But the moment Subaru lifted his eyes and saw that the iron ball, having missed its target, was stuck in the face of the cliff just as he'd hoped, he got a firm grip on the elongated chain.

Then he glared down the chain he gripped—in the direction of the assailant holding the other end.

"Now, show yourself, bastard! I've gone through a lot of trouble to see your face!!"

He raised an angry shout and talked trash to lift his own spirits.

Gripping the chain in one hand, he used the other to re-grip the knife he'd cut the rope with earlier. He resolved to swing it in the assailant's face if worse came to worst. If it came to that, Subaru wouldn't hesitate.

His eyes hardened. He wouldn't run no matter who or what came out.

His life was in grave peril, but somehow, he was still alive. Maybe he didn't have to throw away this time; maybe it was still possible to drive off the assailant.

Having already given up once, Subaru desperately reached out for any glimmer of hope.

Perhaps that glimmer was Emilia. Perhaps it was the maid twins. Perhaps it was that cheeky little girl or maybe Roswaal. Without intending to, Subaru forgot his situation, remembering the collection of memories he thought he'd shoved aside.

He'd made promises. Promises he had to keep.

But then…

"—You leave me no choice," she said.

The chain made a sound. He felt slack in the chain as its wielder drew closer.

But Subaru didn't pick up those subtleties as his eyes opened wide.

He couldn't speak. His lips quivered as a whimper came out of his throat. Unintentionally, his fingers grasping the chain let go as he made a small, listless shake of his head, as if rejecting the reality before him.

Walking on the grass, stepping over branches, a young girl emerged from the darkness.

She was wearing a black, rather short apron dress. She wore a white lace hairpiece. She gripped a handle chained to the iron ball thoroughly unsuited to her small stature.

Her blue hair rustled in the wind as she made a familiar tilt of her head, a neutral look on her face.

"...You're kidding, right, Rem?"

One of the girls Subaru had meant to protect was wielding the fiendish iron ball before him.

7

Instantly, the back of Subaru's mind was completely filled with white noise.

He desperately wanted to deny the sight before his eyes, but he could think of nothing that would let him.

—Subaru's thoughts were white, pure white, with nothing in them whatsoever.

His breathing stopped. His heart seemed to stand still, like it had forgotten to keep beating.

What freed Subaru from that state was the cold feel of the drop of sweat rolling down the skin of his forehead.

—*This is bad. Bad bad bad bad bad bad.*

His empty thoughts became filled over and over with violent unease and panic. No rational thoughts came. Was this truly Rem before his eyes?

Was this truly the Rem Subaru knew, her polite words sliding in like daggers, punctual to the point of obsession, doting on her impudent sister, harboring a serious inferiority complex?

With Subaru having lost his earlier will to fight, Rem looked at him as she ran her free hand through her hair.

"If you do not resist, I can grant you a quick end?"

"—You really think I'm gonna say yes? That's like telling me to eat shit."

"How very rude. Yes, I suppose that is in your nature, Dear Guest?"

Rem was behaving just like she had at the mansion, her curtsy and polite speech so thoroughly out of place that he felt like he really was seeing things.

But that could not make him dismiss the brutal foreign object in Rem's hand.

"I'll grant you that a girl with a blunt weapon is kind of hot, but…"

A spiked iron ball on a chain. A blunt weapon that could turn an opponent into mincemeat with one blow. Rem had to be quite a sadist to pick a weapon like that. Subaru, having tasted its might and losing his life to it once already, knew only too well that Rem's control of the iron ball was absolute.

Little by little, Subaru ground the reality down between his teeth, his mouth forming the words he was reaching for.

"It's kinda cliché to ask, but…why are you doing this?"

"It is nothing complicated. You are suspicious, so I will render judgment as a maid should."

"Haven't you ever heard of 'love thy neighbor'…?"

"I am fully committed to this, so…"

Rem looked at Subaru like she expected a prompt response, apparently having no intention of letting him play for time. If he moved now, she'd kill him for sure.

It was less of a stalemate than staring down the barrel of a gun. Subaru's brain spun as he desperately tried to wring a little info out of this without his anguish lowering his guard.

"—Does Ram know about this?"

Abruptly, he invoked the name of the sister sharing Rem's face.

Ram wore three crowns: she was arrogant, rude, and overbearing. As a maid, she was inferior to her little sister in every respect, but Subaru had spent more time with Ram than anyone else at Roswaal Manor. If even Ram had become his enemy—what did those days they spent together mean?

That was why Rem's reply was the one Subaru had sought without knowing it.

"I intend to finish this before Sister is aware of it."

Subaru took a deep breath and looked back straight into Rem's eyes. Rem raised her brows as she watched Subaru lick his lips as if he'd come back to life.

"So you decided this on your own? Roswaal didn't order you?"

"I will eliminate all who oppose Master Roswaal's wishes. You are merely one."

"Man, can't he train his lapdogs not to bite at people just passing thro— Ugh?!"

Subaru taunted Rem a little to probe Rem's true feelings, only to have the chain leap in from the side.

"You shall not insult Master Roswaal."

The blunt impact made his vision waver; a sharp pain conveyed the vertical cut in his left cheek.

With the iron ball still stuck in the rock face, she'd smacked Subaru by using the chain as a whip.

So that was the price he paid for his flippant taunt. But he'd gotten something for it.

At the very least, he could now confirm that Rem's loyalty to Roswaal was the real thing. She no doubt really believed silencing Subaru was for Roswaal's benefit. She'd decided that Subaru's leaving Roswaal Manor was disadvantageous for Roswaal, who was supporting Emilia's candidacy.

In other words, this was—

"Ah, that's what it is— That's how little you trust me, huh?"

"Yes."

Her grudging nod made Subaru feel pain equal to a sharp blade being thrust deep into his chest.

Subaru had dreaded that answer, for accepting it meant looking at his days at the manor in an entirely different light. So Subaru didn't say it. He locked that horrid feeling deep in his chest. But he couldn't help himself from laughing at his own obliviousness.

"Damn, just look at me. I thought I'd done all right, but I was so wrong..."

"...My sister—"

"I don't wanna hear it—! Take *this*!"

Rem hesitated slightly for one instant as Subaru shouted and drew his cell phone from his pocket, thrusting it before him.

—The next moment, a white light cut through the darkness of the forest, freezing Rem momentarily.

"—Raaah!"

Subaru screamed as he leapt in and tackled her small body, knocking her away.

Rem was able to wield that violent device with unbelievable force, but in a straight-up collision, Subaru's greater height and weight won out. His charge held nothing back, sending her small body flying; she lost her balance and stumbled to the ground. Subaru didn't spend even a moment to look at her as he rushed past.

He wheezed as he shoved air into his lungs and thought as he ran.

If this was Rem's decision alone, Subaru had two options for survival. One surely was to return to the manor and speak directly to her master. But if Roswaal thought the same way Rem did, he'd simply be going from the frying pan into the fire.

"But even so…there's Emilia…!"

His memory of her shone brighter than that of any other. If he could trust anyone, it was her.

—But would she, a royal candidate, trust Subaru's words when she had the most to lose from doing so?

"—?!"

Instantly, the voice from the back of Subaru's head struck him with the force of a thunderbolt.

Without any doubt, it had been his voice that doubted Emilia's heart. It was Subaru himself who had doubted her, knowing how she was forthright, earnest, and unhesitant to put herself in harm's way for others.

"Why…am I doing…!"

His standpoint had changed, and so had his thoughts. But to doubt Emilia?

If Subaru couldn't even trust the person he'd resolved to protect, who could he believe in?

He was pathetically fleeing through the mountains because of the big plan he'd formed to protect the life of someone whose heart he doubted. How sane was that?

—He'd gather intel this time? Yeah, right.

Why was he here, under threat from a completely unexpected direction, running for his life like this? He'd been too proud. He'd been naive. He hadn't thought it through.

His breath ragged, half running and half falling down a slope, Subaru was awash in regrets.

He whined as tears clouded his vision. His steps grew clumsy. Suddenly, the trees opened wide into a clearing; Subaru saw that night was creeping across the sky. Then—

"—Ah?"

A blade of extremely concentrated wind lashed out, slicing off Subaru's right leg at the knee, sending it flying away.

Subaru watched his right foot leap and bounce with great force as he lost his balance, slamming into the ground. The impact made the cut on his cheek bleed again; his shoulder bone sounded like it'd exploded as it rammed into the rock. Subaru screamed, the cut across his whole body jabbing into his brain like an electric shock.

"Aaaaaaagh! M-my leeeeeg?!"

It didn't hurt, and that felt scarier.

Pieces of his lost lower leg were blown off, sailing into the thickets ahead. A delayed gush of fresh blood dyed the ground reddish-black; only then did the pain invade his nervous system in earnest.

"—!"

He clawed at the ground as unspeakable pain rippled through him.

He pressed down on the wound, thrashed his body, pounded his free right hand against the ground, smacked a tree, and clawed at the bark as his consciousness boiled from the heat. It hurt, it hurt, it *really* hurt.

He felt the pain shaving away his nerves as if a carpenter's plane were whittling him from the inside out. Having lost so much blood so quickly, it gradually dawned on him that he was dying.

"Mana of Water, grant thy healing."

A soft palm abruptly pressed down on Subaru's thrashing body. Unable to move, Subaru shifted his bloodshot eyes and noticed the girl in the maid outfit at his side.

It was the blue-haired Rem. Rem, who had tried to kill Subaru just now, enveloped her palm in a pale light, pouring warm magical energy onto Subaru's amputated right leg. He felt the itch of healing magic.

The pain didn't vanish completely, but shock seized Subaru at the surreal scene. Subaru didn't know why Rem was healing him at a time like this. Sensing Subaru's gaze, she gave him a soft, casual smile. What seemed like a tiny ray of hope died with the words that followed.

"I will not be able to ask you anything if I let you die so easily."

It truly sank in what an optimistic idiot he was.

Rem stood up as she finished her first aid, making a sound with her chain as she pulled along the iron ball.

Subaru was lying faceup with the iron ball gouging the earth as it neared him. The closer he saw it, the clearer it looked like the crude, unrefined, specialized tool for violence that it was, existing only to take life.

Rem had deliberately brought it where he could see. Her intentions were crystal clear.

It was the easiest way for her to demonstrate that his life was in her hands.

"—I am confiscating this."

Rem spoke as she crouched and opened up Subaru's firmly closed hand. His hand had been locked around the knife since his encounter with Rem, unable to let go.

Rem roughly pried open his fingers and took the knife, turning it around in her hand.

"Had you stabbed me with this earlier, you would have been able to flee a little farther."

Rem knitted her brows, speaking like she couldn't comprehend Subaru's illogical act. But Subaru, suppressing his breathing amid the throbbing pain, shook his head.

—There was no way he could have stabbed Rem with that knife.

That knife had been the implement in his hands when he'd spent such busy and gentle times with Rem's back to him as Ram taught him how to peel vegetables. He couldn't stab Rem with that.

—Subaru's heart lacked the strength for that.

As Subaru continued shaking his head without a word, Rem sighed and discarded the knife into the forest thicket.

She seemed to refocus her attention as she made the chain clank and coldly looked down at Subaru.

"I ask you, are you working with one of Lady Emilia's rival claimants to the throne?"

"...My heart belongs to Emilia."

The moment he spoke, the chain ferociously lashed Subaru's upper body. His shirt, scratched all over during his flight, easily tore open, as did the skin underneath.

Subaru's scream echoed through the forest.

"Who hired you and on what terms?"

"E-Emilia-tan's smiling face is...priceless."

She moved her wrist the other way and did the same thing again. Feeling like she'd lashed him in precisely the same place, he knew his anguished cry served as praise for her skill.

She asked more questions like that. He made more replies like that.

Several times more, the chain rang out. Several times more, Subaru's painful cries matched it.

When his consciousness faded, Rem treated him with healing magic. Trapped in a hell of repeated healing and violence, Subaru's spirit frayed; he lost consciousness several times like that.

Yet, his heart did not submit to Rem's lashings.

Rem must have felt tired of Subaru's obstinate attitude when she wiped the blood spatter off her face and looked up at the sky.

"If I do not get back soon, I will be late preparing the meal..."

"...Dinner, huh. What's on the menu today, huh..."

"Let's see. How about mincemeat pie?"

"S-sorry, I think I'll have to skip it..."

Rem finally showed some sign of emotion as she sighed at Subaru's behavior, flippant to the bitter end. After that, she fell silent for a while before looking down at Subaru, her eyes colder than ever before as she interrogated him.

"—Are you a member of the Witch Cult?"

Subaru knit his brow, perplexed at having vocabulary he'd never heard before thrown at him.

He didn't know what those words meant in regards to the place, the circumstances, or Rem's real thoughts.

"Answer, please. You are one of the Bewitched, yes?"

"...Be what?"

"Do not play games with me!"

Agitated, Rem's pale blue eyes shot daggers through Subaru in a rage. It was literally the first time Subaru had seen Rem worked up like this since they'd met.

Rem's pale face glowered as she looked down at Subaru with pure hostility.

"I don't know them... My whole family's atheist to begin with..."

"Still denying it? It is plain you are involved with the witch. Her stench is all over you!"

Hatred. Rem's eyes seethed with dark hatred as they glared at Subaru. Subaru's eyes widened, feeling like this part of Rem, this vortex of emotion, put every single thing she'd done in a completely new light.

"Even if Sister or no one else notices, I can smell it on you! The leftover stench of that monster makes me want to spit in disgust!"

Subaru fell silent. Rem, standing before him, bit her lip so hard that she seemed to be grinding her teeth.

"I was anxious and angry when I saw you speaking with Sister. You, someone involved with the one who put Sister through so much...weaseling into our precious home—!"

Her words of undiluted malice mercilessly bathed Subaru in bitterness.

"I have been watching you since Master Roswaal welcomed you... but the entire time, it hurt to watch you. I could not bear it."

Subaru had been unable to say a word. Then, Rem drove the dagger home.

"Even if I knew that the whole time Sister was taking care of you, she was just pretending to be friendly!"

"—"

Rem seemed to be making up for her seemingly inadequate emotions by slamming all her bottled-up resentment at Subaru in one go. Rem stopped speaking as her shoulders shook, her eyes filled with rage as they glared at Subaru. Then, her anger abruptly wavered from surprise.

"—What the hell...?"

For, as Rem spoke words filled with hatred, Subaru had been crying quietly.

"I knew it was...something like that."

Sobs came up his throat, hot tears slipping out of his eyes and falling upon his cheeks.

The flood of seemingly ceaseless tears continued as Subaru said in a sorrowful, halting voice, "So that's what it was... I knew there was some reason behind all the kindness. But...I was too afraid to ask..."

It was the two of them who had drilled the basics of work into good-for-nothing Subaru.

Ram had scoffed at him for not knowing how to put on a butler outfit. Rem had re-tailored the ill-fitting suit and taught him how to put it on. Ram had patiently stuck with Subaru when he'd been painstakingly learning characters. After the promise to have Rem cut his hair, she'd often been staring at him; he'd been happy to have people paying attention to him and urging him on.

They were all kind memories he could never forget.

"I finally learned how to peel veggies without cutting my hand. I learned how to do laundry right. Didn't finish learning how to clean the place, but..."

He couldn't have hoped for more in four days. But he'd thought that, if he could get past those four days, there was much more to learn in the days to come.

"Reading… It's just the simple stuff, but I can do that now. I studied like I promised. I read the picture book. It's all thanks to you two…"

"What are you…talking about?"

The tone of Rem's voice fell, like she was creeped out by Subaru's rambling words. Subaru looked straight up into Rem's eyes.

"I'm talking about what you two have done for me…"

"I recall no such thing."

"—Why don't you remember?!"

The sudden burst of rage made Rem take a step back without thinking.

Subaru forced his lying body to rise, glaring at Rem with his teeth bared as he shouted.

"Why'd everyone leave me behind…! What did I do to you…! Tell me what I did to you…!"

He couldn't control his emotions. He knew full well he'd be ripped to pieces, but Subaru's heart, his very soul, could not stop shouting.

He'd been summoned to another world, subjected to senseless things, and in spite of it all, he'd gritted his teeth and pushed forward.

But he'd reached his limit.

"What'd I do wrong? What's wrong with me? Why do you girls hate me that much…? Even…that promise… I've always…"

"—I—"

"I've always lo—"

—The impact did not permit him to say any more.

The sudden force bent back Subaru's body; it gently hit the tree trunk behind him.

Subaru heard nearby sounds like faint breathing and frothing water. When he shifted his gaze, he immediately discovered the cause.

"—"

His throat.

Half of Subaru's throat had been ripped out. He was gurgling air and bubbles of blood from the middle of his windpipe.

Dumbfounded, he looked at Rem's face as she stared at the wound.

Having seen that much, Subaru's eyes lost their spark, going dizzy and white.

He couldn't speak. His mind felt like someone had turned off the switch.

Everything grew distant. There was no pain, no sadness; he left behind all his emotions.

But in the end, he had the faint sense he could hear someone's sad voice.

"—Sister is too kind."

CHAPTER 5
THE MORNING HE YEARNED FOR

1

"—!!"

He wasn't aware of the exact moment he returned to consciousness. The sound of heavy rain kept ringing in his ears. His vision flickered between red and white.

The world was bent and warped.

Unable to feel his arms or legs, he made a thick, anguished scream as if someone were wringing his intestines like wet laundry.

He twisted his body and leapt, every movable part of his entire body unleashing fierce incomprehension.

—He didn't know what was going on.

The burning pain of his leg being severed and the scars of his body being lashed all over by the chain were…gone.

He'd lost his blood. He'd lost his life. He'd died.

He hadn't wanted to die. He hated the pain, the suffering, the sadness, the fear, all of it.

He wanted to push it all away. Everything he could see, everything he could touch, everything he could feel.

"—!"

He heard something. He heard someone's voice.

He heard a voice, like someone was desperately trying to calm a wild beast.

The meaning didn't get through. He didn't understand the meaning. He didn't want to understand the meaning.

It was useless to listen. Listening would only get him hurt. Listening wouldn't change a thing.

Yet as he rejected all, color returned to the world, as did sound, as did shape.

The senses of his entire disheveled body told him, correctly, that blood was reaching his limbs.

His flailing hand hit something, breaking fingernails and ripping the back of his hand, making it bleed. The sharp pain jabbed into his brain, somewhat lessening the force of his scream.

Then he realized it. Someone had grabbed and wrapped up his hurting arms.

He felt something similar on his legs. Something was covering him, making him unable to move either leg.

Right above him, his returning vision saw the familiar white ceiling he'd seen several times over now.

He realized he was lying faceup on the soft bed.

He finally breathed out, strength draining from his stiffened body, when…

"Dear Guest, Dear Guest. Have you finally calmed down?"

"Dear Guest, Dear Guest. Have you finally stopped flailing?"

The instant his ears heard the two familiar voices, Subaru remembered to scream.

2

Subaru's fourth first day at Roswaal Manor had begun in the worst way possible.

Subaru lived with the shame of having already died six times since arriving in that world.

They were most certainly not peaceful deaths. Each death came with its own commensurate sense of loss.

You didn't get used to the pain and suffering of it. Though he picked himself up each time, no one could understand the loneliness, the desolation, the anguish he felt.

He'd resolve that no matter what pickle he might find himself in, his heart, at least, would not falter.

But that resolve had been shattered by his latest Return by Death.

His sense of loss, of despair, of loneliness, gouged Subaru just as deeply as the bonds formed over the days before.

There was no way he could recover. He didn't have the strength *to* recover.

Emilia, sitting on the bed beside Subaru, smiled at him as she patted his injured right hand.

"—All right, done. I think it's nicely patched up, but you mustn't thrash around like that, okay?"

—At that moment, Subaru and Emilia were the only two people in the room.

The two maids who had been present when Subaru awoke retreated in the face of Subaru's disgraceful behavior right after waking, leaving things to Emilia.

"Ram and Rem were really so worried about you."

Subaru reflexively raised his face at the mention of two names he didn't want to hear.

Subaru's reaction put a bit of surprise on Emilia's face, but she instantly brushed it off with a small shake of her head.

"They're feeling unusually down, thinking they may have offended you somehow. How about you say something to them next time you see them?"

"Offended, huh? No, they didn't do anything... There's nothing between those people and me."

Emilia's feminine eyebrows softly grimaced at the insensitive tone of his voice. Her reaction was in the corner of Subaru's vision, but no apology or excuse came from his lips.

Instead, what came out was a question without the slightest hint of sarcasm.

"Hey, Emilia, do you...think I'm a bother?"

Emilia raised a finger and seemed to speak rapid-fire to hold Subaru in check.

"How could I think you're a bother? You saved my life, Subaru. What are you supposed to do if someone you owe a debt to just gets up and leaves? It'd really put me in a bind."

Subaru listened in silence, belatedly realizing that he was staring intently at every detail of Emilia's face and actions.

"Whoa, I was seriously..."

He was disheartened that it was he who'd given Emilia such a look of distrust.

Emilia had unexpectedly hit the nail on the head, had she not?

To stop thinking of your benefactor as your benefactor was the lowest thing you could do.

Emilia was the only oasis Subaru had in an uncertain world. Subaru, having lost everything else he'd set his heart upon, had nowhere else to turn.

"—"

He suddenly had a small thought.

Perhaps it was to Emilia that he should reveal the truth of the Return by Death?

"That's right..."

Now that he thought about it, Subaru had tried to change his dead-end reality completely on his own so far. But all he'd achieved was a dead-end fate, with both the future and the past blocked off.

Breaking through that stalemate required fundamental change.

Maybe the answer was to form a bond of trust with a third party, someone he could rely on?

"—Emilia, there's something I want to tell you."

The clouds seemed to lift as Subaru's feelings of hesitation and unease parted inside him.

Hearing the tone of Subaru's voice fall like that, Emilia sat back down in a chair, looking at Subaru with a face tense with concern.

Watching himself reflected in her violet eyes, Subaru thought of how he should begin this.

How should he talk about Return by Death? Perhaps Subaru ought to first find out if it was something that happened to other people of that world, too?

It was a pretty funny story, really. The chances were high she'd think it was a big joke.

But Emilia would listen to Subaru tell it, wouldn't she?

Then and there, that was the hope that kept Subaru going.

—He'd talk to her about Return by Death. And that he hoped she would lend him her strength.

Subaru, well aware that here he was, already receiving her gratitude and yet making another request, opened his mouth.

They'd change this extremely confusing situation. They'd fight against Fate and win...*together*.

—Or so he thought.

"Emilia. I c—"

He began his confession. The moment the thought formed, *it* came.

"—"

Discomfort. *Something's wrong*, Subaru's mind told him.

What's wrong, he wondered back, but he immediately noticed why.

Sound. Sound was gone. There was no sound anywhere.

His own heartbeat. Emilia's breaths. The sounds of morning filtering through the window. All had completely vanished from the world.

And that was but the prelude for what was to come.

—Next, movement followed sound, vanishing from the world as well.

The passing of time lengthened. A single moment extended to eternity. The next second simply never arrived.

Emilia's serious expression remained before his eyes, unmoving. She was like an ice statue, her next motion an eternity away.

Subaru was the same. He couldn't move. His mouth, his eyes, nothing for eternity.

Sound had vanished, time had stopped, and Subaru's hand could not even reach out to beg.

For some reason, only Subaru's mind continued on during the phenomenon beyond his understanding.

—And then, suddenly, *it* came.

A black cloud. Subaru, unable to blink, suddenly saw it fill his vision.

In a world where nothing could move, only the cloud was still in motion. The cloud wriggled and changed shape. Its mass was such that it could be held in the palms of one's hands. Bit by bit, the contours of the cloud took form, and it finished changing shape.

—Subaru saw something like a black palm.

It had five fingers. It didn't reach to an elbow, but he could definitely make out a forearm.

The black fingers shifted. The gentle movements of what clearly had the shape of a hand swam through the air. Subaru's mind gasped when he saw where it was headed.

The black fingers slowly reached to Subaru's chest…and seemed to go right in.

Subaru felt the feeling straight to his soul. The feeling of the fingers brushing against his internal organs, stroking his rib cage…

Discomfort and unease gripped Subaru. The black cloud wouldn't stop moving.

It was as if it hadn't found what it was looking for and had to look deeper, deeper into Subaru's chest.

—Hey, hold on here.

His voice wouldn't come out. His body couldn't resist. Subaru's mind let out a terrified yelp.

—This isn't funny.

Subaru was shaken beyond what he could call his innards, to the very core of his being.

Could anyone put into words why having your internal organs damaged hurt?

The question is pointless.

No one needs to think about it.

In that instant, Subaru felt no need to put into words what that excruciating pain felt like.

It was really simple. Having his heart mercilessly squeezed felt like his very soul was being crushed.

He couldn't scream. He couldn't writhe from the pain.

There was only suffering. And along with suffering came something that made Subaru wish he *could* scream.

The pain was pulling apart the person called "Subaru." His mind was frayed, twisting, falling apart. Subaru was being cut into pieces, unable to remember what a logical thought felt like—

"—baru,"

"—?"

"Subaru, what's wrong? Don't go all quiet like that. It worries me."

Her hands were on his thighs as the silver-haired beauty gazed into Subaru's eyes with concern.

Subaru seemed to stop holding his breath when he was sure his fingers were moving as he intended. He gingerly touched his own chest, confirming from the outside that his heart was making quiet beats.

His body moved. His voice came out. He couldn't feel any pain from his heart.

—But the fear remained.

Subaru fell into despair, for *it* had ripped his one hope to shreds.

Just thinking about defying *it* a second time made him see the swaying black cloud in his mind.

Subaru had no choice but to face facts.

Unable to hold back her emotions, Emilia put her palm against Subaru's face, at a loss as she asked an uncertain question.

"—Wh-what's wrong? You've been acting weird since earlier. If something's wrong…"

"—I want to ask you a favor."

Subaru cut off Emilia's worried voice midway, lying down and turning away his head.

He couldn't face her. His features probably looked horrible.

If he looked at Emilia in his current emotional state, there was no telling what he might say to her.

Working all out to keep his mind steady, Subaru could manage to say only one thing.

He threw away the words he wanted to say. He threw away the feelings that wanted her to hear.

He threw away everything.

"Don't have anything to do with me."

Listlessly, that was all he said as he curled into the bed. He didn't even look at Emilia's shocked reaction.

Unconsciously, Subaru had firmly grasped a single fact the moment the palm touched his chest.

—He would not be permitted to break free.

Subaru was alone. And he would remain alone.

3

Having brushed off Emilia, Subaru gloomily began his fourth loop.

Roswaal went to Subaru's room after he'd hurt Emilia with his heartless statement.

Subaru largely didn't remember what they'd talked about. But he felt like he'd been appraised like an expensive vase. He didn't know if that was just this time or if it had happened before and he just hadn't noticed.

"I shall treat you as a guest for as looong as you prefer."

Subaru felt like he'd said something convenient like that.

He also felt like the details didn't matter anymore.

If he left the mansion, they'd shut him up for good. That was certain. But even if he was dead weight in the mansion, he couldn't avoid getting ground into mincemeat in the near future.

He felt like his saved game guaranteed a BAD END. The fact that it was autosave made it extra brutal.

"—"

Subaru was on top of the bed and not moving much, but his breaths were quick and ragged.

Fearful of falling asleep, Subaru had used the feathered pen in his hand to cut the back of his other hand several times. Every time his eyelids seemed to droop, he forced his consciousness awake through pain. If he slept, he didn't know what he'd wake up to.

He'd already died three times.

In the royal capital loop, he hadn't experienced more than three deaths. To Subaru, plunged into that first day for the fourth time around, dying a fourth death was unknown territory.

—Maybe, if he died here, he'd never come back.

He couldn't find a way to avoid death. But still, he didn't want to die.

He distrusted all and struggled against all in his desperate fight to live. He forgot the passage of time, the churning of his empty stomach; Subaru became eager to simply exist.

The pain of his wound felt like affirmation of his existence. The spaces between the holes in his hand vanished.

Pain. Joy. Pain. Joy. Pain. Pain. Pain—

Suddenly, his face shot up when he abruptly heard a little girl's voice.

"—You certainly have a cowardly look about you."

A girl was standing at the entrance, leaning against it, shooting Subaru a look like she was gazing at a beast.

Beatrice, whom he had yet to meet even once during this loop, had come to visit.

Subaru's vigilance ratcheted up at the unprecedented change of circumstances.

"—So it's you this time?"

He belatedly realized that his voice was low and scratchy. It surprised him. His voice held more hostility in it than he'd imagined. Maybe he was voicing his feeling that the world was cursed.

"What an incorrigible fool, to waste away like this in the span of a day or two."

"No one asked you— What'd you come for?"

Beatrice, having mocked Subaru's disgraceful sight and received his sullen retort in turn, narrowed her eyes slightly.

"...Puckie and that little girl asked me to pay you a visit."

"Puck and...Emilia?"

"You were acting oddly since you awoke, I suppose, so they suspected that I had done something to you when you first woke up. A rather rude suggestion, if I may say so."

It was true, and Beatrice was innocent, but those things didn't register with Subaru.

Surely Subaru's heartless words had hurt Emilia, yet she was concerned for Subaru all the same, enough to speak directly to Beatrice, even if her suspicions were misplaced?

As a result, Beatrice, with a weakness for Puck to begin with, had Puck begging her to help them, so here she was, reluctantly showing herself in Subaru's room.

Emilia's concern for him brought just a tiny bit of warmth to Subaru's heart.

Even if it was meaningless as far as breaking the stalemate was concerned...

"Got it. I'm all right now. You came to apologize, and that's enough."

Beatrice's lips twisted as Subaru tried to brush her away.

"Why must I apologize to you, I wonder? Before anything else, I will not be leaving until that misunderstanding is cleared up."

Instead of leaving the room, she marched over to the bed. Subaru was about to pile on more complaints when...

"—Hm?"

Subaru watched as she crinkled her nose and tilted her head. If she just stayed quiet she'd look pretty adorable, but...

Beatrice looked displeased at being stared at and covered her face, glaring at Subaru.

"'Tis not just your dull face, I suppose, that is rotten. It is quite thick all around you."

"—Huh?"

"Perhaps I speak of the scent tickling my nose? It would be wise to avoid meeting the twins for a while."

Beatrice pinched her nose and waved with her free hand as if driving off an unpleasant scent.

"—"

But Subaru's mind couldn't let go of the keyword *scent*.

Scent. Certainly someone had used that word around the end of the third loo—

"A smell coming from me...?"

"—The scent of the witch. Perhaps your nose is broken?"

He remembered that word. He'd come across that piece of vocabulary only recently. So that meant—

"The jealous witch?"

"In today's day and age, there is none other who would be called witch, I suppose."

Her statement, belittling him as a petty idiot, aroused only more questions in Subaru.

"Why is that scent coming from me?"

"Who is to say? Perhaps the witch took a liking to you, or perhaps she hates the very sight of you. Either way, the witch giving you special treatment makes you attract trouble."

Beatrice slumped her shoulders, her gloomy behavior indicating any further talk about it was unwelcome.

Witch—a being shunned throughout the world to the point that the fairy tale "The Witch of Jealousy" would not record her name.

But Subaru had no connection to the witch or the story; he'd read about it only in a book.

Naturally, without any memory of having met the witch, he had no memory of how he might carry a lingering scent from her touch.

—Rem had also said he stank of the witch, hadn't she?

He felt that the overwhelming hostility was related in part to the scent of the witch. If that was so, he'd earned her hatred through something he had no memory of; with one slander piled on another, she felt she had no choice but to silence him.

Subaru, having grasped something that was wholly outside his control, sighed at length. As Subaru remained silent, Beatrice looked at him as she reached toward the doorknob.

"If nothing's wrong with you, I'm leaving. I should tell Puckie that we had a chat and what we talked about, I suppose."

She seemed ready to vanish into the Passage when he called out to stop her.

"Wait a sec."

Beatrice looked distinctly displeased as she looked back at him.

Subaru stubbornly arrived at the words and tossed them out.

"You feel bad about what you did to me, don't you?"

He didn't know if it meant anything or not—but he thought it was worth a shot.

Beatrice shot Subaru a sour look as Subaru knocked against the bed and asked again.

"Do you feel bad about it? Yes or no?"

"I think no such thing."

"I'll tell Puck on you."

Beatrice repositioned herself to face Subaru, crossing her arms and raising her nose with a haughty air.

"Ugh…perhaps I think it a teeeeeny bit."

"I'll forgive you if you'll do one *little* favor for me."

"…Would you speak it, I wonder?"

"Could you protect me until sunrise on the fifth da— The morning after tomorrow?"

It was a thoroughly shameless request to make of a girl who looked younger than he did.

Beatrice was silent for a while in the face of Subaru's heartfelt request.

"That is a rather vague statement. Perhaps there is a reason someone is after you?"

The question Beatrice countered with was quite natural and sensible.

Beatrice kept Subaru in her sights as she paced around the room.

"In the first place, I do not want to bring discord to this manor. This manor is a place that, to me, I must not lose, I suppose."

"…I don't want to cause any trouble. I just wanna put out any sparks that fly."

"That is quite a sentiment coming from someone trying to make it another's problem?"

"For once, I don't have a comeback."

Beatrice sighed as Subaru bowed down before her.

Subaru was still bowed as he thought he heard a sound like the door being closed from the inside.

The sound of Subaru's request being denied and Beatrice returning to her archive.

The moment he heard that sound, Subaru's threadbare hope snapped.

"Could you put out your hand, I wonder?"

With Subaru filled with resignation, Beatrice walked to the side of the bed and offered her tiny hand.

Beatrice's irritation sent Subaru, in complete shock, rushing to take her hand. As he did, Beatrice scowled as she looked at the damaged back of his hand.

"Disgusting. Perhaps you are an unsalvageable deviant who delights in self-harm?"

"Roswaal's got the deviant market locked up. I was just trying to give myself a tattoo and messed it up."

"Your artistic sense, skill, and talent for lies are completely lacking... There is no saving you from that."

Exhaling, Beatrice put her tiny palm on top of Subaru's hand, as if trying to cover the wounds. Her smooth fingers invited his in until their hands intertwined.

"—I shall grant thy wish. By the name of Beatrice, the pact is formed."

Beatrice's solemn statement left Subaru completely at a loss for words.

Suddenly, the girl before his eyes looked completely different than before. As her fingers gripped his, the warmth they conveyed made his mind see the aura of mystique surrounding her.

"Makeshift or not, a pact is a pact— Perhaps I have been moved by your irrational request."

Beatrice released his fingers and crossed her arms once again. Subaru bowed before her, suppressing the wave of emotion that hit him.

He didn't put the emotions into words, but they gushed from a bottomless well deep in his heart.

He didn't know how to react to being offered salvation from the least expected source.

"Seriously...a little girl's gonna make me cry..."

"Could you not say *little girl*, I wonder? Also, I will *never* forgive you if you say *one word* to Puckie about this."

"So that's the important part?! Desperation gets you demon-possessed, I tell you."

Subaru made a bitter smile in response to Beatrice's look of genuine hostility.

His fourth loop had begun with despair. It was a small smile, the only of this loop, but it was there.

4

By forming a temporary pact with Beatrice, Subaru gained a tiny but tangible piece of security. However, the circumstances pressing down on Subaru had not fundamentally improved at all.

As was his wont, Subaru continued life as a hermit in the room he had been granted; Beatrice was not hovering around Subaru, protecting him twenty-four hours a day.

The problem was from the night of the fourth day to the morning of the fifth—to reduce the effort needed to protect him during that time, he'd be leaving the room, not showing his face again until the appointed hour.

In return, the one who visited Subaru time and again, and currently nodding while sitting on the side of the bed with a charming smile on her face, was Emilia.

"I see, so Beatrice came to properly apologize. I'm glad. A job well done."

For Emilia to approach him like this after Subaru had treated her so poorly, which weighed heavily on his conscience, it was no exaggeration to say he thought of her like a goddess, his one light in a dark world.

When Emilia visited again and he tried to apologize for his initial rude statement, she simply brushed off Subaru's horrible words.

"You were just overwhelmed, right? It can happen to anyone. It can't be helped. Ram and Rem will be pleased to hear you say that, though."

Subaru gave no proper reply to the gentle request she'd slipped in at the end.

Their loyalty was so great that they'd kill someone merely for knowing an inconvenient truth. Subaru had experienced that firsthand, but he couldn't hate them for it even so.

He closed his eyes and thought back on his days at the manor. Back then, during those memories, were there not moments when Subaru and the sisters drew closer together?

—Maybe he just wanted to believe it was so.

Emilia looked at the tray left on the side of the bed and the untouched meal, slowly going cold, resting upon it as she murmured in a sullen tone.

"So you really didn't eat breakfast, did you?"

"...Sorry."

After snapping at Emilia, Subaru had become more quiet and withdrawn. Though Subaru acted like that, Ram and Rem diligently went about their duties as servants.

Even when they knew he would never touch the food nor thank them for it.

One was rude, while the other was polite only on the surface, but both were very formal and professional at heart.

Subaru knew that. Despite knowing that, he could not accept the food.

—For all he knew, it might be poisoned.

That was the thought that passed through his mind when he looked at it.

He hated himself for doubting the two of them. However, Subaru knew a future existed where the sisters waved around horrid weapons to kill him.

He knew they had many virtues, but they'd try to kill him anyway.

It was when Subaru had accepted that fact that his despair had truly begun.

"Maybe it's tough, but it's bad for you if you don't eat at least a little bit."

"My stomach won't take it... Well, maybe if Emilia-tan went 'Say aah' for me I could eat, but..."

Subaru cursed what an incurable joker he was, sending such a flippant remark Emilia's way when she was genuinely worried about him.

However...

"Here, then. Say aah."

"—Eh?"

"I said, say aah—"

Emilia had set the food tray on her lap, lifting a spoon and looking at Subaru.

She used the spoon to scoop up some soup, which was still somewhat warm, and gently brought it toward Subaru's mouth.

Subaru immediately shook his head, unable to understand what Emilia was trying to do.

"No, nonono, wait, hold up, Emilia-tan, what are you doing?"

"What do you mean, what? You said you'd eat if I did this, didn't you? So eat. I'm saying 'say ahh' and everything."

"Err, this is like a ritual that girls don't actually do; their faces just go bright red and that's as far as it goes, I thought?"

"If you're going to speak like a child, you can't be embarrassed at being fed like one. That would be silly."

As Subaru dragged his feet, Emilia went "Say aah" again with a powerful, compelling stare. Subaru finally buckled under the pressure, feeling like he'd gone red to the tips of his ears as he opened his mouth.

"A-aah…"

"There, swallow. Here's the next one. Here, here, here, here, here."

"That's too fast!! Was that aah just to get my guard down?!"

The way Emilia carried soup to his lips, automatically with no wasted motion whatsoever, made him wonder if she'd been in a fast-feeding competition or something. Subaru tried to keep up with one spoonful after another before roughly waving his hand midway.

"T-time-out, time-out! Can we stop? It's going down my th-throat the wrong way…!"

"Goodness, and it was going so well, too… Subaru?"

"*Cough, cough*, r-really, my throat feels…all weird…"

Subaru averted his face from Emilia, faking coughs to try to make the action seem more natural. He didn't want Emilia to see his face just then.

Something hot was welling from deep in Subaru's eyes. He opened his eyes to give his tears somewhere to run and desperately tried to stop them from flowing.

She continued to be kind to him in a world where he could see no hope.

He wondered if he was truly worthy of such treatment...

...for Subaru Natsuki was in despair precisely because he rejected that he was.

"Hey, Subaru."

As she called out to him in concern, Subaru lightly cleared his throat and tested his voice as he got back in order.

"...Mm, ahh, ahh. Okay. Yeah. I'm all right now. I think. I'm all right."

He made the richest expression as he turned toward Emilia...

...and met her extremely gentle eyes, looking right at him.

"Let's continue."

"...The way you put that makes this feel really naughty somehow..."

"—?"

Emilia, tilting her head, apparently hadn't noticed the risqué, bewitching nature of her statement.

Or maybe it'd all been in his head to begin with.

And so he finished eating, with Emilia offering a 'Say aah' and him opening his mouth, cheeks red from shyness and complicated sentiments. With the meal finished, Emilia clapped once in satisfaction.

"Good. Now, what do we say when we're done eating?"

"That was great."

"That's bad manners. Once more, and say it right."

"Thank you for the food."

"You're very welcome."

Faced with Emilia's broad smile, Subaru patted his belly, which strangely felt nice and full.

His stomach felt no discomfort at having been stuffed after two days of going empty.

"Ram said, 'He hasn't eaten properly in a while so we must be gentle on his stomach,' and that's how Rem made it. They're such good girls, aren't they?"

Emilia's words, as if boasting on behalf of the sisters, stabbed Subaru's doubts like a dagger.

If that was the truth, he'd be happy enough to cry at such a show of concern. But Subaru knew better. The very pain of the delusion made him want to cry.

If only their gentleness and kind treatment didn't have *that* lurking behind it.

"Well, now that you've eaten, too, you must be tired, so I'll head back and let you rest."

"You could always sleep here beside me?"

"Good, good, seems you're already your usual self. Now, I do have things I need to be doing, too. Don't tell anyone I was slacking off, okay?"

Emilia winked and stuck out her tongue.

Subaru, remembering what Emilia would normally be doing at a time like this, felt deeply ashamed.

Emilia had a kingdom resting on her shoulders; she didn't have one second to waste as she spent each day striving for a better future. She shouldn't have been wasting a single second of that precious time on someone worthless like Subaru.

"—Emilia. Keep your door locked at night and don't let anyone in, okay?"

Perhaps he said it because Emilia's kindness had rekindled the tiniest spark of the will to defy Fate.

Emilia brushed back her silver hair and inclined her head ever so slightly at Subaru's sudden admonition.

"Or you'll sneak in?"

"Right, exa... *No!!* Hey, that was Puck not Emilia just now, wasn't it?!"

"Wow, got it in one."

Puck popped his head out of Emilia's hair and grinned at her and Subaru. He swished his tail as Subaru glared at him, no doubt having been listening in that hiding place from the very beginning.

"I didn't want to intrude on such a lovely scene, but your emotions suddenly turned serious, huh? That got my attention."

"...I just have a bad feeling, okay? You take good care of Emilia, now."

With the black cloud lurking, Subaru had to be evasive when speaking about the future. Even so, Puck, able to read emotions, accepted his words without question.

"I'll have you know I *really* don't like feeling left behind in this conversation," Emilia complained.

"It's just saying a cute girl like you should always be careful about night visits, and to watch out for cars and men. Right, Dad?"

"That's right, Lia. Daddy forbids you from seeing men…bad-looking, dark-haired men in particular."

"Brutus?!"

Puck laughed out loud as Subaru invoked the name of the famous betrayer. Emilia pinched the laughing Puck and shoved him back into her hair, this time rising to her feet.

Subaru saw both of them off and, now alone in the room, flopped onto the bed.

He'd gotten them to watch out more, but it was a small comfort. To begin with, the current crisis had little to do with either of them, so he figured they'd be all right.

"Aw, no…"

The instant Subaru's mind felt a smidgen of relief, his consciousness dove into a deep sleep.

The pangs of sleep that he'd kept at bay with pain for so long suddenly rushed back, robbing Subaru of his will.

And his stomach was full, too. His consciousness felt like it was sinking downward, unable to resist.

5

Subaru's consciousness felt like a floating cloud, trapped between dream and reality.

He'd heard somewhere that dreams had the side effect of organizing the waking brain's information. That would explain why Subaru, having delayed his sleep so long, beheld a string of such clear and vivid memories, as if they meant to haunt his dreams.

Subaru's vivid, "dead" memories replayed over and over, etching themselves deeper into his mind.

He moaned, tossed, turned; he made anguished sounds as sweat drenched his entire body. Immersed in tears and faint sounds, his soul was whittled down, down, down, and when the final thread was cut, surely nothing would remain.

That was how far he had been worn down, both mentally and physically.

"—"

Abruptly, the tension in Subaru's body vanished.

It was as if the cold and terror that made his body shake had been swept aside.

—It was his hands.

Someone was holding Subaru's hands.

Someone's touch from the real world pulled back Subaru, drifting in unconsciousness in the bed. It was a warm sensation, a gentle sensation, one that conveyed compassion.

He felt like he'd been saved. He felt like a gentle breeze blew into his tattered mind. His ragged breathing eased; he forgot his suffering and returned to peaceful sleep.

Who did it? What was it? Was it real or just a convenient trick of the dream?

He continued to feel warmth lingering between the palms of his hands—

6

"—Just how long are you going to sleep, I wonder?"

"Whoaaaa!"

Subaru cried out in pain, having been violently kicked, followed by a hard landing on the floor.

When Subaru shook his head and rose up, Beatrice was there, scowling, one leg raised in an unladylike manner. Beatrice snorted, once again unable to hide her displeasure.

"You were sleeping quite comfortably while I bothered to come at the appointed hour."

"It's like, you've got to put people down even when you don't have to?"

As Subaru talked back, he broke out in a cold sweat at having unintentionally slept. He'd gone as far as to hurt himself to stay awake and to keep his guard up.

"Sleeping on the all-important fourth day. Maybe I really do have a death wish."

"Would you cease your muttering, I wonder? There are more appropriate places for it."

Beatrice, looking down and watching as Subaru lightly poked himself, sat on her stool as she spoke. Seeing her in her usual position like that, Subaru realized something was off and looked all around.

—He was already in the archive when he awoke.

"Well, this is a surprise. Did you carry me in my sleep?"

"I would not like to spend time in a room filled with that scent of yours, I suppose. This archive is my place and none other's. Could you behave yourself while here, I wonder?"

Subaru decided that Beatrice's actions, taken without asking him, had improved his situation.

Beatrice's Passage would keep an assailant from narrowing down Subaru's location. Surely Rem had no sure means of breaching the Passage herself.

"You actually thought this out, huh?"

"Do not just sit on the floor mumbling. Would you like to be swatted like an insect, I wonder?"

Oh, so that's what you're reading, said Subaru, looking at the pages open before Beatrice as he stuck out his tongue.

Apparently, thinking of this as *consideration* would be overstating the case. Subaru rose from the floor, abruptly staring at his own two hands.

An odd sensation remained. Someone had held his hand as he slept, hadn't—

"Hey Beatrice, don't tell me *you* held my hand while I was asleep?"

"I won't be telling you such a thing, I suppose. I would not, even if Puckie asked me to."

"What a thing to say... But hey, at least we can die together!"

"No. Absolutely not."

Beatrice, rather sour, tapered her lips as Subaru looked around the room once more.

The archive, filled with books as usual, lacked any convenient place to sit.

"How am I supposed to kill time in here...?"

With the time limit so close, his anxiety and stress were heightened; it was an open question as to how long he could keep his cool. If he could just immerse his head into something and forget the passage of time—

"Oh, right. Are there any books here written just in I-script?"

"—To think that you cannot read but the simplest things. How many humans do you think would cry with joy at just the *thought* of entering the Mathers family's archive of forbidden books?"

"Well, I do feel bad for them... So what, you're here full time?"

Subaru had never seen Beatrice walking about except at mealtimes. Aside from the exception of her having visited his room the day before, Beatrice was always in the archive on her stool.

Beatrice lowered her head a little at Subaru's question.

"Such is the pact I have made."

"Another pact, huh? Maybe I shouldn't say this when you're helping me, but isn't it rough?"

Beatrice closed her eyes and spoke as if to cut off all further inquiry.

"All the pacts, they are things I desire, I suppose."

He'd heard the term *pact* several times since arriving in that world, always with heavy overtones.

Beatrice spoke the word with the same weight as Emilia and Puck did for the spiritual pact they had. Subaru appreciated as much, having formed one temporarily with Beatrice himself.

Beatrice looked so young, yet here she was, in and upholding a pact—for some reason, Subaru felt something like an unendurable ache deep in his chest when he looked at her.

"Hey, are you really fine with all— Whoa!"

"Your questions are becoming annoying. You can read something and be quiet, I suppose."

She underscored her statement by tossing a book at him. When Subaru caught it, he realized that the book he'd caught was written in I-script, down to the title.

When Subaru lifted his face, Beatrice had already lost interest in him, lowering her eyes to the book in her own hands, making a show of declining conversation.

She seemed to be strenuously insisting that he leave his half-asked question unfinished.

While her demeanor left no room for words of thanks, Subaru was grateful and happy.

7

Time in the archive of forbidden books passed gently and quietly.

With neither exchanging words, only the sounds of the pages being softly turned echoed within the archive.

That said, Subaru's heart wasn't into reading at the time; all he was doing was turning the same page over and back again, making the same page sound like a prank.

—Shut in the archive of forbidden books, he had no way to know what was going on outside.

Beyond the room not having windows, the very nature of the archive was to be in a separate space, locked off from the outside world.

He had no way to tell the time of day or feel the passage of time. He wondered what time it was by then.

By simple logic, being in the room for half a day would get him through the problematic night. But he had only a vague sense of just how much time had passed while he'd been in the archive.

He couldn't trust his own senses, but he also hesitated to ask Beatrice.

It wasn't for any reason as simple as not wanting to stop Beatrice while she focused on her reading. Subaru was afraid that any action he initiated might stir up something.

His fingers turning the pages of the book were numb. The tip of his tongue begged for water.

His heart was beating like an alarm bell. He was out of breath.

How long could he remain strong against such tension, he wondered?

If the start had been so brutal, the end might be without any warning whatsoever.

A murmur abruptly echoed through the silent archive.

"—Calling."

Subaru's face seemed to leap up as Beatrice put down her book and slid her legs onto the floor.

Rather than speaking to Subaru, it felt like she was murmuring to herself.

"A call for me, I suppose?"

Beatrice waved a finger as she spoke. The next moment, Subaru's whole body felt ill as space bent.

Subaru made a small moan as his entire body shuddered from the sensation that most resembled floating. Hearing this, Beatrice looked at Subaru as if only just remembering he was there.

"Ah, you were there, weren't you? I forgot, I suppose?"

"That's a bad joke, forgetting about a guy right in front of your face…"

"—Puckie is calling. It would seem this is an urgent matter."

With that as Subaru's only warning, Beatrice strode past him to the door like it was the natural and obvious thing to do. Subaru's voice shook as he called out to stop her.

"W-wait, hold on! If you go out now…"

"You can stay shut in here if you like. Perhaps you will be safe here?"

Beatrice left behind her words of obvious sarcasm as she passed through the door. Subaru, blood rushing to his head from her attitude, seemed to kick away his chair as he leapt up and reached toward the door. He'd hesitated for only a few seconds, but…

"Aw, to hell with it. What's the big deal, right?!"

Spurring himself on with the foul-mouthed statement, he roughly opened the door and stepped outside.

The next moment, it hit him.

"Ah—"

Without thinking, Subaru's voice leaked out of his lips like a complete idiot.

His hand shielded his eyes from the piercing sunlight of the morn that greeted him.

Deeply moved, he waved his hand in the air as if to confirm it. Subaru's body wobbled forward toward the window just on the opposite side of the corridor that peeked out over the inner garden—beyond which the sun had just begun its rise.

It was the morning of the fifth day that he'd yearned for but had never reached.

"You mean...I made it? Past the fourth night...?!"

Unable to believe the result before his eyes, he pushed open the window, almost pounding it.

Holding down his hair as a cool breeze blew in, Subaru took a breath of the fresh morning air.

He stumbled, bumped his back against the wall, and slid down, having lost the will to stand.

He could do nothing but stare in shock.

He'd given up. He'd surrendered to despair. He'd been worn to the bone.

And yet, Subaru had passed beyond the fourth day and arrived at the fifth.

"Ha-ha-ha..."

Without realizing it, a dry laugh came over him.

Once it began, he knew no way to stop it.

"Heh-heh, ha-ha-ha. What is this? Hey, what is this? This is just... Ha-ha..."

He couldn't think of any rational way to show how he felt at that moment.

Hugging his knees, Subaru remained squatting in the hallway, laughing like a madman.

He thought it was a far-off place that his hand would never reach.

He couldn't speak. He couldn't find the words. Finally, Subaru had—

Suddenly, a voice like a bell interrupted Subaru's hollow joy.

"—Subaru?"

Lifting his gaze in annoyance, he saw a silver-haired girl standing deeper in the hall—Emilia. He was able to find her safe and sound, here on the morn of the fifth day.

Both of them had gotten past the fourth night. That fact made Subaru tremble.

He'd hoped for this chance. If the morning of the fifth day greeted both of them, they could rekindle that promise and have it granted.

He'd introduce Emilia to the kids in the village, they'd both walk around the blooming flower garden together, they'd form the same memories together—and yet...

"Emilia...?"

Subaru began feeling a sense of accomplishment that barely seemed real while Emilia watched him in silence. Then, as if Emilia had remembered something, she rushed over to Subaru.

"Subaru, where did you go?"

"Er, I..."

"I mean... No, that's fine. It's fine, just...come with me."

Emilia pulled up Subaru with surprising insistence and ran off with him. She looked like she wasn't going to take no for an answer as a smirk came over his face.

"Where are we going... Hey, Emilia, listen to me. I've worked really hard to get to this point..."

Subaru stared at the side of Emilia's face as he tried to find the words to convey his success.

"Why are you making a face like that? I mean, it all turned out all right...didn't it? I'm safe and sound, and you're... Yeah. Let's go to the village...together, and then..."

"—"

"There's lots I want to do with you and talk about with you. A lot's happened. I wanted you to know th—"

"—Subaru."

With one brief call of his name, she interrupted him. That was when he noticed the momentary wavering in her eyes, the irritation she could no longer conceal.

The look she had was like when they'd been fighting for their lives at the fence's shop.

"What in the world h—"

Happened, he tried to ask but couldn't. For before he could put the word on his lips, a different sound slammed into his eardrums.

—He thought it was a yell. Perhaps it was a wail instead.

It was a long, high-pitched sound filled with sadness that scarred the very soul.

The morning air of the manor was rent by the unending cry of pain, as if someone were being torn asunder.

They passed through the corridor and headed up the stairs. The east wing of the second floor of the manor was for the servants' bedrooms, where Subaru's room on previous loops had been.

Emilia led him by hand to the innermost room. And there stood…

"Roswaal and…"

…The man with long indigo hair narrowed his eyes as he saw both rushing over. Beside Roswaal stood Beatrice, leaning her back against the wall as a gray cat curled up on her shoulder.

With the three of them having arrived, Subaru was about to ask about the circumstances when Roswaal spoke simply.

"Inside."

Roswaal motioned to the open door of a bedroom beside him.

When Subaru turned toward Emilia, she nodded to him as well. Emilia's clear violet eyes settled things for him.

Holding his breath, Subaru walked in.

Here, too, the yell continued unceasingly, filling the whole of the room. Subaru entered, his eyes wide open, frozen from tension—and then he saw.

It was an immaculately preserved room. It looked like a girl's room with minimal furnishings employed to maximum effect, a reflection of a steadfast maid's personality.

Though Subaru had received an identical room, it felt different.

For a moment, such feelings let Subaru forget the sight before his eyes. But the moment passed as the horrible truth crashed upon him, a truth from which he found nowhere to run.

"AaaaaaAAAAAaaaaaaaAAAAaaaaA—!"

It was Ram yelling, tears pouring out, her deep sadness threatening to rip her throat asunder.

—And there lay Rem, still clinging to her older sister when she had breathed her final breath.

8

How many times had his mind gone blank from what he'd experienced?

How many times had he come face-to-face with tragedy beaten into him?

Wasn't it time someone saved him from this?

"—"

The blue-haired girl lay upon the bed, no longer breathing. Her skin was pale; her eyes would never open again. She was dressed in a delicate negligee that somehow seemed perfect on her.

Subaru abruptly realized that he hadn't seen Rem out of a maid uniform once.

"Why did…Rem…"

As Subaru murmured, brushing his short hair back with his hand, he fell to his knees.

His head hurt. His brain came up with the wonderful suggestion that the sight before him was all in his sleep-deprived imagination.

This was his fourth loop at the manor. To Subaru, who'd already died and gone back three times, Rem was the person he was most wary of.

"Then why…why was Rem killed…?"

Surely it was Rem who killed Subaru, not the other way around.

Suddenly, a little devil on Subaru's shoulder whispered—maybe she wasn't really dead?

Maybe it was all a trick, a trick to make Subaru drop his guard? A

joke in exceptionally poor taste was incomparably better than the nightmare before him being real.

He approached Rem to check her pulse, but…

"—Don't touch her!"

As he reached out to touch Rem, his hand was slapped away, hard.

When Subaru yelped and looked up, Ram was glaring angrily at him. The tear-filled rage on her face easily drowned out any words of retort Subaru might have used.

"Don't…touch my little sister!"

She refused to let anyone come between them.

With a tearful voice, Ram repeated herself as she clung to Rem's body, tears flowing quietly down her face.

There was no sign that the devoted, pain-filled older sister expected her little sister to ever awaken.

That made the truth clear.

—Rem really was dead.

As Subaru wobbled out of the room, Roswaal stood by the doorway and voiced his deductions.

"Appaaarently, death by debilitation. Her vigor was stolen as she slept, her heartbeat gennntly slowed, and the fire of her life puttered out, likely the work of a curse rather than magic per se."

Subaru's eyes snapped open at the word *curse*, the word for what the clown believed to be the cause of death.

Death by debilitation via a curse: that was the direct cause of Subaru's deaths during the first and second loop. In other words, Rem had died from the same curse that had previously killed Subaru.

"But I thought the curse came from Rem…"

The second loop, Subaru had died from debilitation via curse as well as having his head smashed by an iron ball.

Subaru had deduced from that night's circumstances that the witchcraft and the iron ball were linked. But Rem herself being killed by a curse had ripped his hypothesis to shreds.

"Then the shaman and Rem are separate…?"

Subaru's mind was in chaos as the thought of a new, separate shaman arose.

Rem had slain Subaru out of loyalty to Roswaal. At the very least, that was the only answer if Rem's words during the third loop were true.

He wondered if Rem, who'd killed him by her own hand, and the shaman were connected somehow. But if that was the case, Rem being killed this time around made no sense whatsoever from the shaman's point of view.

So maybe Rem and the shaman weren't connected to begin with...?

The first time, the magic of a shaman had slain Subaru; the second time, the shaman's spell had debilitated Subaru when Rem murdered him for whatever reason. The third loop, Rem had eliminated him with no connection to the shaman whatsoever.

"The fourth time...I didn't do anything, so Rem was the target instead...?"

It was baseless supposition, but based on the circumstantial evidence, it was the only reasonable conclusion.

If Subaru had been the target for reasons related to the royal succession, he could understand it as an indiscriminate preemptive strike against Emilia's side. The victim, be it Subaru or Rem, was random.

"You appear to be in raaather deep, serious thought?"

The mismatched blue and yellow eyes looked down, reflecting Subaru in them. Subaru's eyes rose as he felt like Roswaal's scrutinizing gaze was seeing into his very soul.

"It pains me to ask such a thing...but do you have aaany idea about what happened, good guest?"

"Wh-why would you think...I..."

"Myyy, forgive my rudeness. I am simply somewhat...displeased at the moment, that one of my pretty retainers has suffered such a fate, you see?"

Roswaal abruptly shifted his gaze from Subaru to the painful sight inside the room.

Looking at the side of his face, it truly sank in to Subaru just how precarious his situation had become.

Subaru had no way to prove his innocence. This time, Subaru had done nothing to earn the slightest smidgen of trust from the others.

Emilia tugged on his sleeve, speaking with an anxious voice.

"…Subaru."

When he looked, the shimmer in her violet eyes seemed to be pleading with him: *If you know anything, please say it.*

Her eyes and her calling his name told him that much.

The implication of answering Emilia's earnest request hit Subaru hard.

He'd have loved to tell everyone what he knew. He wanted to shout it at the very top of his lungs.

When Subaru made no reply, Emilia's small fingers trembled a little as they held his sleeve.

He'd thought that repeating the past would lead to a better future, yet here he was, every silver lining having a dark cloud, with the outcomes worse than he ever imagined possible.

"Subaru…"

Confusion clawed at the inside of his head. He'd thought that it would all be swept aside and things would be better someday.

No, he thought they'd become better already.

—And the moment he thought it, *this* happened.

"—"

The moment he pictured the black cloud and the world stopping, ceaseless pain gripped his head.

His breath caught. The sensation of Emilia touching his sleeve made Subaru's stomach twist in pain.

If Emilia kept her pleading look trained on him, Subaru's heart would falter. Even if he didn't, Puck, able to read emotions, could easily expose the fact that Subaru was hiding something. But still, Subaru couldn't explain anything about Return by Death.

And that meant the torture would continue, pain without end, over and over.

He felt his tongue quickly dry. Unable to resist his urge to flee, he took a small step back.

"—If you know anything, you'll never escape me."

To the girl crying her eyes out inside the room, Subaru's small action looked like nothing more than an attempt to flee for his own convenience.

Instantly, a raging gust of wind made the door violently shake, its passage blowing Subaru's hair down flat. The moment after the sudden gust made him close his eyes, a sharp pain heralded a vertical cut on his cheek.

"Ow…!"

He immediately touched his cheek, moistening his palm with blood. Wind. The wind had wounded him.

From within the room, Ram was shooting Subaru a hate-filled look as she trained her palm toward him.

"If you know something, spill it!"

"Wait, Ram! I…!"

Can't, Subaru was about to say, but the word died instantly on his lips, since he knew what would befall him.

But he was coming up empty for any way to kick that can down the road.

With Subaru holding his tongue, Ram shot him another gust of wind as a warning of what would follow.

Had he been able to calmly assess the matter, he would have called it a Blade of Wind.

Wind magic—magic that inflicted cuts like the whirlwind monsters of lore. The sharp slice had enough power to leave a cut on the floor between Subaru and Rem, slice the door in half, and stop right at Subaru's cheek; such was the power she threatened him with.

If *that* hit him full force—faced with the phenomenon before his eyes, Subaru forgot to breathe. But Beatrice extended her cream-colored palm in front of Subaru and countered the Blade of Wind.

"—I am one who keeps her promises."

She gave her raised palm a small shake, as if that were no great feat, as she looked back at Ram.

"I have made a promise to protect this man from harm while he stays at the manor."

"Lady Beatrice…!"

Whereas Beatrice's demeanor was elegant, Ram bit her tongue with indignant anger.

As Ram raged to the side, Beatrice looked up at Roswaal, still standing right beside them.

"Roswaal. Your maid is being quite rude to your guest."

"Certainly. I find that sinceeerely unfortunate. If possible, I wooould like to welcome him anew as my guest, as soon as he breathes out what he is holding within, to feel all the lighter."

"How could he be involved in this matter, I wonder? He was in the archive of forbidden books all night."

"This is too grave a matter to simply drop. Surely you cooomprehend this?"

With negotiations having failed, Roswaal shrugged and raised his palms into the air. Subaru saw the multiple orbs of differing colors that floated from his palms.

They were red and blue, yellow and green—even Subaru, untrained in the ways of magic, understood that those four colors represented magical power. Their beautiful glows contained energy beyond his imagination.

"It is just like you to engage in petty tricks. Just because you have a little talent, a little more power than others, a pedigree just a little finer than others, you need to flaunt in others' faces... You are quite a child, I will have you know."

"How very haaarsh of you. Is the difference between we, who walk about normally, and you, passing time in a room where time has stopped, sooo great? Perhaaaps we should put it to the test."

He could feel the magical tension between them making the very air twist. Subaru was becoming a third wheel as hostility rose.

"Hooowever, to think that you would go through such trouble... are you truly sooo fond of him?"

"Your jokes are in as poor taste as your makeup, Roswaal. Puckie is my ideal partner. That human cannot match such lovely fur."

Beatrice looked defenseless as she stood before Roswaal's four glowing, floating balls.

However, the "simply standing" girl projected something around her so powerful that it made the air itself bend. Something invisible but frightening was about her.

As the situation became explosive, with both wielders of supernatural power glaring at each other, Ram's shrill voice wedged itself between them.

"Who cares about that? Who cares?!"

Everyone looked at her as she stormed over, hands holding the hem of her skirt.

"Let me through and do not interfere. If you know something, say it, all of it. Help…help me avenge her!"

It was a sad, painful plea. The words gripped Subaru's heart. He truly wanted to tell her what she wanted to know.

But Subaru had no words to offer her.

Ram shot Subaru a despondent, despairing glare. Emilia stood beside Beatrice, as if they were both shielding Subaru from her hostile gaze.

"I'm sorry, Ram. I still believe in Subaru."

Emilia put her palm toward Ram to hold her in check while looking back at Subaru from the corner of her eye. Her eyes wavered, trying to find the words, before dropping for but a moment.

"Subaru, please. If there's something you can do for Ram and Rem…please."

Her compassion made Subaru feel more ashamed.

Emilia had sided with Subaru, even in such extreme circumstances, even though Subaru had said such horrible things to her at the start of the week, even though he was still holding his tongue in silence…

"I'm sorry—!"

As if crushing Emilia's concerns under his heel, Subaru stepped not forward but back.

In that instant, Emilia's eyes went silent as her emotions raced. They spoke of shock, sorrow and, above all, unbearable disappointment that her trust was about to be betrayed.

What Subaru truly saw in Emilia's eyes was his own despair. He knew his actions had opened the door to a nightmare and could never be taken back.

That was when Subaru, no longer able to meet Emilia's eyes, turned his back on her.

Instantly, Emilia reached out toward his back. But this was to block the Blade of Wind before it reached Subaru.

The wind crashed against pure magical power; mana bounced off mana as Subaru ran.

"Subaru—!"

Shaking off the voice trying to stop him, Subaru rushed down the corridor in a daze. He felt the magical confrontation behind him increasing in severity, but Subaru lacked the courage to look back.

He was weak. He was fragile, unable to do anything.

That was why he'd run out on Emilia, who'd trusted him after all that, and Beatrice, who'd tried to save his life, spurning their goodwill and good intentions.

He didn't know what to do anymore. What he did know was that Ram shouted behind him like she was spitting blood—

"—I'LL KILL YOU!!"

Having lost her other half, the girl pursued him with a cry that threatened to tear her asunder.

Covering his ears, shaking his head, making wordless sounds, Subaru ran. He ran.

And he kept running.

9

With his attention devoted solely to running, he didn't know how much time had passed. Out of breath, his knees begging for mercy, sweat dripping down his chin, he kept running. If he didn't keep running, the incoherent emotions following behind him might catch up.

And when they caught up with him, this time everything would be finished.

Ram's sad, painful yell, and the malice and hatred it contained, still rang in his ears.

He couldn't go back.

Now that he'd run, Ram and Roswaal would not spare him; surely Emilia and Puck could no longer trust him for keeping his mouth shut. Beyond that, he'd abandoned Beatrice despite forming a pact with her. She would not be his ally any longer.

"I can't help it…! I want to…but I can't!"

He didn't know how it'd come to this. He didn't know what he'd done wrong.

Subaru didn't know what he might do so that the world would forgive him.

"After it was…so much fun…!"

Suddenly greeted by another world, he'd had no choice but to live within it. For Subaru, surrounded by a vast desert of anxiety, the manor that had welcomed Subaru had been his oasis.

Those beloved days, that beloved time, which didn't amount to a single week, seemed so far from Subaru in that moment.

He'd redone, he'd relived, and the world had sunk its fangs into him.

—*Can't do it anymore.*

Suddenly, that was the murmur that arose in the back of his mind.

—*There wasn't any point in trying anymore.*

Bewitched by his own voice pleading with him to give in, his pace relented.

If he did as the words said, it really would be easier, he thought. Subaru, after all, was the type of person who looked for the easiest solution to any situation.

It wasn't just Subaru. That's what people in general did. When faced with two unpalatable choices, they looked for a third way.

Who could blame him for feeling like there was a third, Heaven-sent option?

Blood suddenly drained from his head, making his heart, beating so powerfully, feel distant.

His limbs grew heavy; he found himself dragging his feet as if they were rejecting him.

"—"

It was right around when he stopped that he noticed the trees all around him. He was in the forest. Having rushed out of the mansion, he'd apparently gone off the road to the village, getting himself lost on a mountain path.

The gloom from the sky being blocked off and the briars all around him made Subaru think it resembled where he'd died the third time around.

The instant he recalled his own death, the third choice hit him in the face.

"If I die…"

—Would it save him?

"Yeah, that's right. If I die, this'll change."

When he said it with his own lips, they formed a smile as if there could be no finer idea.

He'd died three times. He'd arrived at the fourth world, where he failed at anything and everything.

This time he'd valued only his life. This time, his life was the only thing he had left.

What was the meaning of continuing to struggle and struggle if this was the result?

"If you're gonna do it, do it already. It doesn't matter what happens to me anymore…"

Biting his lip, he aired his bitter hatred of the situation he'd become wrapped in.

The blue sky unfolded before Subaru's eyes, reflecting his hate right back. And…

"…A cliff."

Surely this was made-to-order by God himself.

Answering that one prayer surely meant there was a Heaven he should be grateful for.

—So that the foolish and pathetic Subaru Natsuki could find peace.

The cliff seemed to invite him as he headed toward it, wobbling and dragging his feet.

The wind was strong. Using the sleeve of his jacket to shield himself from the strong headwind, Subaru stood at the cliff's edge, peering into the blue sky beyond. Below him was a precipice with a face lined with sharp rocks, a drop dozens of meters onto a rocky place below. If he fell from this height, nothing would greet him but death.

Subaru panted heavily as he looked down at the rocks below, able to acutely picture his own death.

He heard the loud heartbeat he had forgotten once more. His lungs let out the air they'd been holding. His entire body was drenched with sweat, making Subaru feel cold as he closed his eyes.

—If he kept his eyes closed and took one step forward, it'd all be over.

Subaru wondered what would happen if he died this time.

Would he return to the first day at the manor and begin the loop anew? He thought he wouldn't mind.

If he did actually return to the first day, Emilia would be there, and so would Ram, Rem, everyone. Subaru would work as a servant, see everyone's faces, and die peacefully in his sleep on the fourth day.

If he continued that over and over, at least Subaru would be immersed in a little day-to-day peace.

It seemed like a good plan. If he could not hope for greater salvation, death wasn't so bad, he thought.

"—"

And yet, Subaru's body, standing atop the cliff, did not move forward. Only his knees moved—to shake.

He reached down to stop his knees from trembling, collapsing the moment his hips bent. Falling to his knees, it was as if he were prostrating himself before the sky. Subaru bit his lip at how pathetic he was.

"Just one step... I can't even do...one simple thing..."

—Perhaps he simply lacked the courage.

Even under pursuit, he lost to his impulses, too indecisive to put it into action.

His resolve and determination were so frail it was funny; Subaru could only remain on his knees and cry.

He didn't know why he should live, yet he was too afraid of death to die.

Subaru wailed, clawing at the ground at how truly pathetic and unsightly he was.

He continued to weep and mourn his own wretchedness until his endurance finally gave out.

10

Subaru thought that the scene he saw while unconscious was a nightmare.

He was in a well-lit room, at a dining table with Emilia. Roswaal was in the seat of honor, with Beatrice there pouring black tea to Puck, his head diving into a plate right beside her.

Emilia chided Puck for kidding around at the dining table, and Rem wove in and out, performing her duties, while Ram attended to Roswaal, ignoring all else.

Subaru just laughed. The others laughed with him.

—And so, he saw a nightmare full of happiness and warmth.

It was a bitter dream, a dream that brought sadness and a sense of wrenching loss.

His soul whittled down to the point of pain, Subaru's agony made him forget to breathe.

"—"

Suddenly, his face eased.

He realized someone was holding his hand.

The warmth conveyed to his palm seemed to push aside his negative emotions.

Then, he saw a light.

A white light. A dazzling light. A light that seemed to guide his consciousness back to—

11

"—Are you finally awake?"

When Subaru opened his eyes, the orange sky of the setting sun was right in front of him.

He realized, too, that he'd passed out on the ground lying face up. He recalled, too, what he'd been thinking about just before, as if it had consumed his consciousness.

—Namely, that he'd chickened out from suicide, wept shame-lessly, and fell asleep from exhaustion.

It was too shameful to be funny or pitiable. He'd acted like a baby. No, Subaru was far lower than a baby, for they had no capacity to sin.

"Could you say something, I wonder?"

"…Something."

"What an old, rotten joke. You are quite something, joking with that glum face."

Beatrice spat out a bitter reply as she tossed aside the hand of Subaru's she was touching.

Beatrice was wearing the same dress as always, something that looked extremely out of place on top of the cliff. It was like a land-scape painting where a lone little girl stood out.

"…No sane person goes hiking dressed like that."

"I had no intention of hiking in rustic mountains to begin with. Perhaps you should not have fled to a place like this and cried your-self to sleep?"

Beatrice was waving the sleeve of her dress, making her annoyed statement, when Subaru realized just what Beatrice was doing out-side the manor, to the point of showing up all the way over here.

"Why…?"

"Why what, I wonder?"

"Why did you come? I…"

—While Beatrice had honored her pact to protect Subaru, he could tell her nothing.

Seeing Subaru's words catching, Beatrice made a sour, exasper-ated face and snorted.

"I made a pact to keep you safe. Having you toss yourself off a cliff to kill yourself would be an affront to my dignity."

"Weren't you supposed to be my bodyguard only till…this morning?"

"—I do not recall saying anything about a time limit. You assumed incorrectly that there was one, I suppose."

Subaru groped through his memories while Beatrice, looking at him out of one eye, glanced away. Beatrice was using that contradiction between their "assumptions" about the details to continue her pact with Subaru.

It suddenly struck Subaru how a girl with a viper's tongue and a foul-tempered horse's personality like Beatrice could show such deep compassion.

Beatrice had not forsaken him. If that was true, then just maybe—maybe he didn't have to give up?

"This is no time for vain hopes."

"—!"

Beatrice shook her head, pouring cold water on Subaru's easy way out.

"You cannot regain what you have lost. There is little more I can do for you. You can no longer explain things to the older sister. You threw away that chance."

"I—!"

I'd have told her if I could, he wanted to shout.

Subaru would have confessed all and pled for forgiveness if his heart wouldn't have been crushed in the process.

Not because it would help Ram—he knew it wouldn't. Simply for his own peace of mind.

"At a time like this. Am I an idiot?…Yeah, I'm an idiot."

Subaru had come this far by putting on a face, apologizing, pleading, protecting himself over and over. And now, he'd been driven to the top of a cliff, physically and mentally, with nowhere to run.

Run, run, run, and run some more was exactly how Subaru had arrived at this point.

"If you know I can't go back…what do you plan on doing for me?"

"At the very least, I will have you die where I cannot see, so as not to disturb my dreams, I suppose. If you wish to flee, I shall take you beyond this domain."

Beatrice's kindness, wrapped in severity, cut deeply into his heart.

Beatrice's expression was cold, her gaze acidic, as if beholding an annoyance. Even so, the kindness of the intent behind her words struck Subaru like none other.

No doubt Beatrice spoke the truth. If he desired to flee, she would agree and aid him. He didn't know what waited for him after fleeing. But it couldn't get any worse thàn this.

His own foolishness having wrecked his oasis, what was wrong with throwing away everything and running?

"—"

Blood trickled a little from the painful cut left on his cheek by the Blade of Wind.

Touching the wound, Subaru realized too late that he'd felt its kind before. Subaru's very soul remembered its sharpness.

When he had been fleeing from Rem in the mountains, a Blade of Wind had severed Subaru's right leg at the knee. As he touched the wound, Subaru's instincts told him it was the same magic.

"The magic that gouged out my neck at the end, too...? So they... double-teamed me..."

His late understanding of how he had died deepened the silent despair in his heart.

Even now, he could still hear Ram's hate-filled roar, her heart-rending wails from losing Rem.

That was the moment. That was the point of no return.

Subaru ought to have never fled the manor. Even if he didn't have the resolve to endure the pain, he should have faced Ram and spoken to her.

He'd missed his chance, and now their hearts were separated forever.

Having let it slip through his hands once, Subaru could never have it back.

—At least, in that world.

With a low, gloomy voice, Beatrice interrupted his silent contemplation.

"The older sister endured for the younger. The younger sister lived for the older. Neither could exist without the other."

Beatrice ran her fingers through her own ornate hair, not looking back at Subaru as she continued to speak.

"Now that one half is lost, the whole can never return. Roswaal is unlikely to forgive it, either."

"What do you mean by that? What do you know...?"

He felt like she was avoiding something. Something really important.

Subaru urged Beatrice to share her true thoughts. But she moved her fingers from her hair to Subaru's sleeve, tugging and gently pulling him to the ground as she extended her foot.

Subaru was in shock at how he seemed to flow right onto the ground. Beatrice tossed back her hair.

"Does it truly matter to you, I wonder? These last four days, you spent most of your time holed up in your room and had little contact with them. Would the older sister let you press her about these matters now? I think not. It has nothing to do with you."

"It's not like...!"

Like I don't know anything about them, he would have said, but Subaru's words died on his tongue.

His repeated loops had given him more than two weeks of time with them. Subaru could have responded that he'd forged memories with them during the time that this Beatrice knew nothing about, but he did not, for he suddenly realized something.

Subaru realized it was possible he knew nothing of Ram and Rem, not their true faces, their feelings, or the bond between them, just as Beatrice had stated.

Subaru wondered what he really had learned about them during those first three lives.

What was the point of Subaru feeling such loss and despair when he didn't truly know anything about them? Was it all really just a bad dream?

What was it that Subaru could draw on to refute Beatrice, who looked sternly down at Subaru at that very moment? Or did Subaru not know anything, not a single thing, about the two of them?

Even though he'd thought of them as precious people he wanted to protect...

"So in the end, I got worked up and pathetic all on my own, not knowing, not understanding anything…?"

—*It has nothing to do with you.*

Subaru knew nothing. He'd beaten away all his chances. He had nothing left but the skin on his back.

Within the darkness covering his eyes, the memories of the days he'd spent at the manor broke apart, one by one, into dust. Subaru's heart, too, shattered.

Lying on his back, Subaru put his palms to his face and wailed at his own powerlessness.

Had it all been a utopia beyond his reach from the beginning? Was everything Subaru had seen simply a dream, the time he'd spent there a mere illusion?

Subaru looked like he was about to break out in tears when Beatrice called to him.

"…How long are you going to stay like that, I wonder? Stand before she finds you."

Impatient from Subaru still not moving, she roughly grabbed the palms covering his face and yanked them up.

As his field of vision opened, the lightweight girl used her entire weight to haul Subaru to his feet.

"—"

The sensation conveyed by her palms took away his thoughts.

Ignoring Beatrice's intent in rousing Subaru so insistently, he felt her palms, weighing how they felt.

"H-hey. What do you think y— Why so interested in my palms, I wonder?"

"I've felt these hands before, just like this… Earlier, did you?"

"…I shall regret it for the rest of my days. Perhaps you were simply too wretched as you slept like that?"

Abruptly, Beatrice looked away, giving him only her cheek. Subaru flexed his hands several times, reflecting on the warm, peaceful sensation he'd felt from them while he slept.

—While Subaru had his nightmare. A dream with an agonizing sense of despair and loss, over and over again.

That hadn't been the only time he'd felt warmth when in pain. It'd happened before—

"Back then...someone held both my hands..."

Beatrice suspiciously raised an eyebrow. Subaru brought not only his right hand before him but his left as well.

It was difficult for one person to hold both hands of someone who was asleep. He doubted a single person could lie on a bed alongside another and hold both hands without difficulty.

"—"

So why did he feel like both his hands had been held? The reason was simple.

"Ram. Rem."

Both had held Subaru's hands while he slept.

It had been here on the fourth loop, before anything had happened at Roswaal Manor. Seeing Subaru suffer as he slept, both of them had taken pity on him and given him some small measure of compassion.

"—"

I will kill you, the hate-filled voice had cried out, her rage pounding into him like a curse.

The cruel words had scarred his heart. But more than that...

"—Can't you make the crying stop?"

It was Ram's sad cry of despair at having her other half ripped from her that never left his ears.

Some corner of Subaru's heart, which should have been shattered already, cried out.

—By nature, Subaru was the sort to pick the path of least resistance.

He didn't want to feel pain, suffering, despair. Just the thought of living with such burdens made him want to run.

"What...stupid things am I thinking here..."

For he thought he didn't want to run anymore. He wanted to do *something.*

"I lived this time and everything..."

His shameless plea to Beatrice had allowed him to reach the fifth day with ease. It was the thought of what had greeted him that very day that settled Subaru's decision.

"That's right. My life's mine. That's why—"

What was wrong with fighting for an easier, more enjoyable life?

"—I'll decide how to use it."

The moment Subaru said it, he crossed a line inside. There was no going back.

Beatrice furrowed her brows at Subaru's words. However, before he could ask her why she was doing that, her eyes looked toward the forest, full of caution.

"—You dithered too much."

Beatrice's regret-tinged words came as the rustle of the wind through the forest's trees deepened. Mixed with the sounds of the swaying leaves, the sound of footsteps reached Subaru's ears, too.

He turned around. A girl with pink hair stood before him.

12

Ram, the forest at her back, glared at Subaru.

"I've finally found you—you will go no farther."

Pain swept over Subaru's heart as he beheld the look on Ram's face, thick with hatred.

As she stood there, Ram had none of her usual meticulous look. Branches had torn and punctured her skirt; there was no sign of the headdress normally on her head. Her pink hair, buffered by the wind, had lost its usual beauty.

—The sisters dressed each other and did each other's hair.

Subaru knew this. He remembered that they'd told him at some point.

He knew several other secrets between the two sisters.

"Would you relent, I wonder? So long as the pact is active, I cannot hold back against anyone."

"Lady Beatrice, it is you who should stand aside. I cannot hold back against you, either."

"A joke, I suppose. Did I hear you say to hold back in regards to me?"

"Perhaps you have forgotten you are not in the mansion, Lady

Beatrice? Do you truly believe you can protect that man away from the archive, here in the forest?"

Subaru held his silence as the two girls continued to square off before him.

Beatrice's words of regret proved that Ram's words were no empty boast. Beatrice's strength came with limitations, and this situation was beyond them.

Even so, Beatrice stubbornly refused to move, upholding her pact in front of Subaru.

From behind, Subaru reached out toward Beatrice. Then...

"*Boing...*"

He grabbed hold of the girl's two ornate hair rolls and pulled on them, hard.

He let go. The large amount of hair bounced quite generously. Bouncy-bouncy—

"Mm, that felt pretty good."

"W-w-w-wh..."

Her eyes wide open, her tongue quivering, Beatrice turned around, all flustered.

Subaru inclined his head slightly as he looked at her.

"Mm?"

"What are you doing, I wonder?! You have a death wish, I suppose?!"

"Don't be silly. I don't wanna die one tiny bit. When you die, it should be one time, to end your life for good. I truly believe that."

As he spoke, he patted Beatrice on the shoulder and calmly walked past her.

Straight ahead, Ram glared at Subaru's face with astonishment. As Subaru walked before her, she heightened her guard, exhaling from pursed lips.

"Quite some nerve. Finally resigned to your fate?"

"Not exactly. More like...I decided to do something."

Not understanding Subaru's intent, Ram scowled.

"—What?"

"Sorry. Because I was sloppy, I brought you girls so much sadness."

"—! So you *did* do something to Rem...?!"

"No, sorry, but I honestly don't know. There's so much I don't know. But..."

Subaru's words trailed off as he took a moment to breathe.

"There's so much I don't know, but I think I know one thing now."

"—What's the point?!"

Ram shouted back, unable to accept Subaru's display of resolve as anything but childish games.

Ram swung down a foot, kicking the earth like she was stamping her feet.

"Rem's already dead! There's no taking that back! What good is it that you know something *now*?!"

"I'm not gonna say I can do anything. It's because I couldn't do anything that things ended up like this. I know more than anyone that's not gonna convince anyone."

He wasn't being defiant. Even now, regret deeply pierced his heart.

He hated himself for his own stupidity and weakness. If you could die from shame, he might have been dead already.

Still, his shameful behavior, his shameful living, his pathetic helplessness—these had brought him to this place.

And, thus, to his conclusion.

"And what is it you know about Rem and me?!"

"...You have a point. I don't know any of the important stuff between you. But..."

Subaru had spent almost twenty days together with them. They didn't know that, and he was unable to tell them.

But Subaru remembered.

Even if they had forgotten, Subaru's soul remembered. He'd seen them. Laughed with them. Spent time with them.

The worlds Subaru had walked with Ram and Rem—those worlds really had existed.

Which was why—

"There's no way you girls knew this, but..."

"What..."

"—I! Love! Both of you!"

The blunt, worrywart big sister.

The sarcastic, superficially polite little sister.

Subaru thought fondly of the days he had spent with both girls.

They were precious memories to him, even though they had killed him more than once.

Enough that, if he had the choice to spend time with them once more, that was a choice he would make.

Subaru's shout made Ram open her eyes wide, freezing in shock.

Of course it did.

From Ram's point of view, Subaru's declaration was meaningless, empty nonsense.

Furthermore, he'd already abandoned them in an instant.

Ram's thought process froze for only a moment. In the next instant, her body thawed and leapt into action.

But a momentary opening was an opening nonetheless.

"—!"

Subaru's sprint was just a moment faster than Ram's switch to anger-filled attacking.

Turning his back to Ram, Subaru rushed past Beatrice, his body moving like the wind—making a beeline toward the cliff.

"Wait—!"

Behind him, a girl's high-pitched wail reached out.

Subaru's mind never caught up to which girl's voice it was.

He'd meant to be determined, but now his thought process was in tatters, like someone had clawed it apart.

His heart beat hard, but his body creaked all over, as if to betray his mind. His limbs felt like leaden weights.

He was running with all his might, but the world seemed to move in slow motion. It was as if Subaru's mind were putting off the results of his change of heart as long as it possibly could.

—So stupid. He was conflicted even then.

He knew why. He'd tenaciously clung to living without shame to that point.

Even when he'd wanted to die, he'd chickened out in the end, able only to fall to his knees.

But Subaru could do it *now*.

"It's rude to Beatrice, huh…"

With those words, Subaru voiced his final regret and left everything behind.

He raced to the cliff. A few steps more. He was too scared to count them. Pathetic. Insane. He had the urge to laugh. But he didn't laugh. He couldn't laugh.

All that he was leaving behind was a life of living death. To Subaru, giving up on a future in that place meant he'd already died inside.

If he could live as a dead man walking, he could do "something" with that life.

And that decision, to do something instead of doing nothing, was one only Subaru could make.

"—I'm the only one who can do it."

His feet left the ground. He clawed at the air. He could touch nothing. He could reach nothing.

So fast. The wind was strong. His eyes hurt. His head hurt. The ringing in his ears was distant. He felt like he'd left behind his beating heart. He couldn't hear the ringing. The ringing inside his skull was like a broken record.

If it ended with his death, that was that.

But if, if only he could go back, then…

For she had cried out, "I'll kill you."

If he could go back—

"—I'll save you, I swear!"

The moment after he voiced his determination, his head smashed into the hard ground.

He heard the echo of something spectacularly breaking apart, and then nothing.

The hate-filled voice could not chase him any longer. Nothing could, not anymore—

13

—All that was there was "nothingness."

Absentmindedly, he looked around the nothingness of his mind.

Perhaps *looked around* was not the proper phrase.

Eyes did not exist within his mind. Nor did hands, nor feet, nor any pieces of his body. All that remained was his incorporeal, floating mind.

Knowing nothing, aware of nothing, he looked about.

Darkness. A room with nothing.

A room that was a world without a floor or a ceiling, covered in pitch-blackness so great that it defied thought.

Suddenly, in the world of everlasting darkness, there was *meaning*.

A silhouette abruptly emerged in "front" of his mind.

The contours of the silhouette were slender and as pitch-black as the rest, the upper body more of a fog, rejecting his mind's recognition.

With the emergence of the human shape, the mind gained its first strong desire.

He felt a breach in the cold as the shadow gently moved, as if to convey something to his mind.

He didn't understand. He was aware of nothing.

But for some reason, his mind could not avert itself from the shadow—

"—I cannot meet you. Not yet."

With that faint whisper, the dark world abruptly vanished, and in so doing, the shadow, and his mind, went with it.

AFTERWORD

Hello, Tappei Nagatsuki here; it's been a while. Say hi to the gray cat over there.

Thank you very much for picking up this volume after the first. I do not think anyone out there is brave enough to pick up Volume 2 first, but to any such daredevils, look at the shelf; Volume 1 should be right beside where you found this one. And if it's not, just say to the sales staff, "There's a first volume for this, right?" and order it. That's one more sale for me!

There you go, direct stealth marketing to get Volume 2 buyers to pick up the whole series. You know how these things are—we always have to write cliff-hanger volumes and resolution volumes so we can go, "Continued in the next volume!" and all that.

This series will continue to have long stages where we go over things again and again. I think having fun with the changes that happen each time while bringing a resolution closer and closer is a good way to go.

Hey, don't worry, this time the resolution volume, Volume 3, comes out just next month, yay!

Volume 2 brings an all-new cast of characters. I'm sure all the readers of the web-novel version were really looking forward to seeing them.

In particular, the maid sisters and the loli librarian are especially popular, and Otsuka-sensei really made them shine. Thanks to him, our heroines are marvelously lovely, and Ros comes off miraculously shady. Really, I can't thank Otsuka-sensei enough.

Now, then, continuing from the games for Volume 1 and concerning the background behind the creation of this volume...

Personally, I'm very fond of stories with low-status, low-power males going through thick and thin, all for the sake of a girl. That's why I started with a main character lacking in power: also knowledge, talent, caution, sensitivity, and good sense, with nothing special about him at all. As he lacks great power or even wealth, any reader can identify with him.

And so, the powerless main character who returns upon death is born. Our story is framed as our main character being flung around by a silver-haired heroine: a lovely, unattainable flower.

I worked out the background with input from a friend I'd known for ten years, hammering it out over the bar at a certain family restaurant, and expanded upon it until it became what you see today.

In other words, this series was created in late-night sessions at a restaurant, trading wild ideas with my buddy.

Since I've used up more than half my afterword on silly stuff, I'll use the rest to give people proper thanks.

Mr. Ikemoto, the editor, thank you for staying on after Volume 1. Volumes 2 and 3 whittled down my soul so much I thought I was a goner, but we got them done somehow. I owe you one.

Otsuka-sensei, how you drew up those illustrations even faster than last time just isn't sane. How you whipped out those designs just like that and drew them up makes me feel like time flows differently for you. When I saw your work, I was so happy, I was in another dimension.

Of course, there's Mr. Kusano for the binding design. After how Emilia looked surreal for Volume 1, here we have the maid sisters looking so fleeting, setting protective instincts on fire. Thank you very much.

Many thanks to the proofreaders, executives, and bookstore sales-people: You're why I get to keep publishing. Thank you very much.

More than anyone else, my greatest thanks goes to all you readers who picked up Volumes 1 and 2. Truly, thank you very much.

I hope to see you again in a couple of months when Volume 3 comes out to resolve the cliff-hanger.

Tappei Nagatsuki, January 2014
(who looked ready to die from stress right
before Volume 1 came out)

HOW EVERYONE'S BELOVED REMRIN AND RAMCHI CAME INTO BEING

ARTIST: SHINICHIRO OTSUKA

8☆'s

THIS IS WHERE IT ALL BEGAN...
(JUST KIDDING.)

DESIGNED TO BE EXPRESSIONLESS
AFTER READING BACKGROUND INFO.
BUT, THE AUTHOR AND EDITOR SAID,
"THEY'RE POPULAR, SO MAKE THEM CUTE!"
SO I RE-DID THEM.

CLASSIC STYLE
FOR RAM AND REM
ACCORDING TO THE
WEB NOVEL. THE
OUTFITS LOOKED TOO
PLAIN SO I TOSSED THEM.

EXPANDING ON THE
~~CUTE~~ DESIGN TO MAKE
THEM LOOK MORE
JAPANESE, BUT THEY
DIDN'T LOOK LIKE MAID
OUTFITS, SO...

MAROON
DOLL?

I LEFT THE HAIR
JAPANESE-STYLE AND MADE THE
SKIRTS INTO MINI-SKIRTS AND...

Voilà!

パック

Puck

"Puckie! Puckie! Have you come to steal away the preview for *Re:ZERO*, Volume 3, I wonder?"

"Whoa, what a naughty girl you are, Betty. Well, the third volume finishes the Mansion Story arc."

"Yes, it is finally being resolved. In the one week since being summoned, Subaru's been beaten and killed so easily so many times even though he's the main character. Just watching him keeps me on tenterhooks, I suppose."

"Heh-heh, you're actually worried about him, aren't you, Betty? Such a good girl. The third volume gives a few glimpses into your kindness. I wonder when it goes on sale?"

"Puckie, you are such a tease… It goes on sale on March 21. Also, did you forget that *Re:ZERO* is being serialized in *Monthly Comic Alive*, I wonder?"

"Lia looks so cute on her cover. Lia on the cover in February, the mansion maid twins in March…that has to be keeping Subaru pretty happy."

"Such a lout cannot help but be pleased, I suppose? I am much happier doing this two-page short with Puckie, anyway."

Beatrice

ベアトリス

"I can only conclude that they put cute girls on the covers because the readers demand it."

"That is both pragmatic and calculated—another wonderful thing about Puckie, I suppose…?"

"There's also extra *Re:ZERO* visual complete-illustration collections for covers and character illustrations by Shinichirou Otsuka-sensei. They have pretty detailed character intros that are worth a look."

"Extra background on characters to fill in things not in the novels… That is so unfair!"

"That's the executives working hard. If they don't do their jobs, all our hard work in the novel will be for nothing. Subaru sure had a tough time in this volume, too. I wonder if he'll find the future he's after?"

"Will we find out when Volume 3 of *Re:ZERO -Starting Life in Another World-* goes on sale on March 21, I wonder?"

"He swore he'd save her, but will he really? We can only hope!"

"How you raised your paw at the end… Ahh, Puckie, your fur is the bestest fur ever…"

Re:ZERO

—Starting Life in Another World—

THE Asterisk war